meet me in my mind

lily christie

Advance Praise

From the minds of early readers

"Once in a while, you come across a book that so gracefully captures the essence of what it means to be human. As a young adult, this book does just that—and more. Every page invites introspection, and it leaves a mark."

Ben, Journalist

"A celebration of self-discovery and the courage it takes to embrace who you truly are."

Debra, Manager

"This is a love story to growth in your twenties. It feels like a coffee with a blanket on a cold morning. This is not the work of a debut, this is the kind of work that is produced by a seasoned author."

Ally, Case Manager

"Grabbed my attention and refused to let go. A testament to the power of great storytelling, creating a connection with readers that lingers long after the final page is turned."

Dana, Psychologist

"The storyline had me crying and feeling so seen. The writing captures deep moments with a sparkle of humour that has you feeling like you're glowing. Remarkable."

Margaret, Librarian

Printed in Australia by IngramSpark

ISBN (paperback): 978-1-7638058-1-1
IBSN (ebook): 978-1-7638058-6-6

A catalogue record for this book is available from the National Library of Australia.

Text Design by: Busybird Publishing
Cover Design by: Lily Christie
Title Page Illustration by: Abbey Gebethner
Editing support: Alex Munroe

Environmental Impact
The purpose of print-on-demand book manufacturing is to reduce environmental impact. Often, any books that go unsold are destroyed – meaning wasted paper, wasted energy, added greenhouse emissions, pulping, and landfill overflows.

The print-on-demand model of book manufacturing reduces supply chain waste, greenhouse emissions, and conserves valuable natural resources.

We're co-writers in the story of planet Earth.
Help write a happy ending.

Or, rather, no ending at all.

Busybird Publishing
2/118 Para Road
Montmorency, Victoria
Australia 3094

www.busybird.com.au

Acknowledgement of Country

I was proudly born and raised on Awabakal Country
where I still live and write.

I want to pay homage to traditions of story – in particular, its
role in healing when we share and create space for storytelling.
I acknowledge the Awabakal people as the traditional owners of
the land on which this book was written and extend my respects
to all Aboriginal and Torres Strait Islander peoples.

**I acknowledge this land always was and always
will be Aboriginal land.**

Playlist

If you like a bit of music magic while you read, or if you'd just like to listen for the vibes – there's a playlist for this novel.

These 15 tracks from the playlist are by Australian artists.
Give them a follow online and support them where you can.

We love Aussie music!

"Bugs" by Patrick James
"Collide" by Odette
"Fly Away" by Tones And I
"FMU" by Last Dinosaurs
"Happy You're Here" by Sycco
"It's Been A Long Day" by Spacey Jane
"L.S.D" by Skeggs
"Memories & Dust" by Josh Pyke
"Over Again" by Hein Cooper
"Resolution" by Matt Corby
"Rush" by Troye Sivan
"Stockholm" by DICE
"Therapy" by Budjerah
"Today Could Be The Day" by JANEY
"What's Not To Like" by Lime Cordiale, IDRIS

For the full playlist of 70+ tracks, find me on Spotify – Lily Christie.
Playlist: meet me in my mind (book beats)

Visuals

For character mood boards, visual inspo, and project aesthetics –
Find me on Pinterest and Instagram

@writtenbylilychristie

I encourage you to let your own mind play, first. Books send our minds express post into pure imagination. That place is yours. Honour it. Enjoy it.

Let yourself daydream into what this story is for you.

Meet Me In My Mind

Hello, you.

The words on these pages found me. *And now, this book has* found you.

Funny how life goes 'round and 'round, like that.

I hope you find a little piece of you, somewhere in here.

Breathe in, and out. Now, enjoy.

Lily xx

1

Sentimentality

I believe I've been here before. Lived a life, I mean. Maybe even lifetimes. I haven't always believed that, but my mum sure did. From the moment I was born, when she first held me in her arms, she had a strong sense of intuition.

When I was growing up, she'd often look at me and say, "Oh, Maggie, it's like you've been here before!"

As I got older, I started to realise ... *maybe she was right.*

Now, in my twenties, I feel like I just learn things. Hard and fast. Like in a past life, I'd been lost. I tripped and fell down, taking all the wrong turns, stumbling my way through. I'd been aimless, naïve, and a little reckless. Almost certain I could just glide my way along, unsinged by any parts of the world that caused burns.

It was as if the world had always happened *to me*, and I'd never really landed on my own two feet. I think I got so lost, the world just swallowed me whole before that could happen.

But that wasn't going to happen again. Not in this lifetime. Because this lifetime ... *I was* happening *to the world.*

"Mags, that cold brew?" *Oh, bugger.*

My boss, Roy, had a booming voice. It was kinda scary, especially when he was glaring at me from the other side of the coffee machine.

"Yeah, sorry. I stuffed up. One sec." I'd made an oat latte on autopilot.

I was working at Bronte's, a little hippy, earthy café in the heart of L.A. It was shithouse. Chipped, white paint covered the bricks on the outside and inside, and the coffee was crap. American coffee was crap. Period. The smoothies were ace though, and cheaper than Erewhon.

I was getting paid cash in hand, which was good because visas suck. I got tipped really well, mostly because I was Australian, I think. When I waited on tables and served coffees, I'd just say, "G'day", and people always tipped me well for it.

Sure, Bronte's was shithouse, but it was right across from the beach, like the ocean was close enough to touch. It reminded me of home on the east coast of Australia, so I loved that part.

Although, I'm not really the sentimental type, and I never have been. I wasn't sure anything could ever change that ... so I didn't miss home all that much.

You could catch me in a daydream, any time of any day, but lost in nostalgia?

Never.

I'd learned to find a rhythm in the present. Even as a child, I held my head high and walked with a bold stride. Little Maggie was very sure of herself, and that confidence grew with me, stronger through every season. I felt like I knew the way, because I had answers to all the questions I'd already asked in a past life.

I navigated my way through my coming-of-age like I held a map to guide every step I made. I came out the other side as a mature young woman. Well, mature*ish*, but that was beside the point. The point was, that in this lifetime, I wasn't stumbling through reckless naivety. I could see myself clearly, I knew who I was, and I wasn't afraid.

... That didn't come without its challenges, though.

I was spacey and dreamy *all* the time, and I think that came from a place of feeling a little bored with life. I'd look around at people my age, and I just wouldn't light up about the same things they did, because those things already lit me up in the last life.

Honestly, sometimes life just felt grey. Or beige. Sometimes even pitch black. I didn't enjoy the feeling of simply existing in a mundane world, suffocated by the ordinary, constantly craving something a little ... *brighter.*

So, I did the only thing I was sure could bring me the experience of a life I'd never lived, with emotions I'd never felt, and places I'd never been.

I became an actor.

A character's life felt so much more exciting than my own! Every time I got to deep dive into a fictional world within the pages of a script, little electric sparks would buzz under the surface of my skin. I got to swim around in a character's mind, see the world through their eyes, and bring them to life!

I wanted to feel it *all* in this lifetime, and acting gave me endless opportunities to do that. It felt like magic, like an express ticket to a new, colourful, sparkly reality. I could fly away from the beige shades of the familiar, and land right in the centre of a chasm of colour. It would completely consume me, all at once, and I *loved* the way it felt.

Acting filled my mind with an illuminating glow, and I could see into spaces I didn't even know existed. Like my mind could create a world of infinite possibilities, well outside the bounds of anything that felt ordinary.

It really was pure magic to constantly feel the exhilaration of discovering something new. Something I'd never experienced, in any lifetime ... something *extraordinary*.

Inevitably, though, it would always come to an end. The electric buzz would fade into a gentle hum, and any glitter left over from an acting gig would stick to the edges of my daydreams.

That's why I built myself a rocket. Just for me, inside my mind. So I could blast off into my dreams again. It would take me to a place where every corner of my mind was coated in light. I'd end up high in the sky on cloud nine, wandering in a world of my own.

There were times I'd just live there, drifting around my daydreams for months at a time. Heck, it might have even been years. I could see it all, feel it all, and once I was wrapped inside that magic ... I never wanted to wake up from it.

But not *wanting* to wake up from it was very different from the reality of *needing* to wake up from it.

When I'd land again, back in my own body, all the thoughts, words, and feelings in my mind would scatter. I'd lose my breath, desperately scrambling to pick them up.

It wasn't that I couldn't pick them up again. I could, and I could carry them damn well, too. But it became so exhausting ... and I was tired. *So tired.* Years of scrambling through chaos and losing my breath had me starting to feel debilitated. And forgetful.

And I'd *panic.*

I knew if I didn't get help, I'd miss out on everything this lifetime had to show me, and I didn't want that. This lifetime, I was feeling it *all.* Properly.

I'd done my time tripping through past lives, and I was tired of chasing leftover fragments of a fictional extraordinary. This was my chance to really live; to be the human I was always meant to be. I just hadn't ever found her until now.

If I wanted to discover exactly how an extraordinary life would feel, in a world full of vibrant hues, sparkling and dancing the way they did in my mind ... I had to get some help.

A few months before I moved to L.A., I saw my doctor. I told her absolutely everything I felt and thought. I told her all about how I *wanted* to live my life, and how I didn't want to feel like I was missing out on any part of it.

She listened carefully, tilting her head. I remember speaking urgently, tapping my knees together furiously. I overcompensated the feeling that I was making no sense at all by throwing in dramatic hand gestures. Once I finished my string of dizzying rambles, she tilted her head to the other side.

Then, with a gentle surety in her tone, she said, "Has anyone ever told you that you may have *ADHD*?"

... I spent the next two months in therapy. Weekly.

Figuring out how to accept the brain I didn't know I had felt non-negotiable. The therapy helped, a lot. But the medication? Not so much.

When my psychiatrist prescribed it to me, he explained how it should settle my brain down and keep me steady. It would keep me centred, in the rhythm of the present. The rhythm that I thought I already had.

There were two key takeaways from that appointment. One, the medication was meant to work fast. Like, from day one, fast. And two, I'd very likely lose weight. He warned me of a key side effect: *zero appetite*. He said he'd see me again in three months, and I smiled politely, but I knew.

I wouldn't even be in the country.

I boarded my flight to L.A., having only eaten two slices of Vegemite toast in two whole days. But I had no choice but to accept my newfound brain. I'd just signed with an international agency, based right here in the heart of Hollywood.

I caught their attention after landing a couple of supporting roles in Australia, and I didn't want to be overly *woo-woo* about it, but I'd seen a lot of angel numbers that week. They kinda felt like cosmic cues! It was my time, and that plane was like a real-life rocket into my dreams!

With a mind that sprinted so fast I was sure it could beat the plane to L.A., I had to call upon the most Aussie coping mechanism I knew …

Laughing about it.

I joked about it in my head; how losing weight would probably help me get parts, how my chaotic brain would probably freak people out, how the timing was so bad, that it was silly.

She'll be right. Right?

Before I landed, I giggled to myself, felt like my own best friend, and gave myself a little hug in my mind.

As the plane touched down, I peered out the window from my seat by the wing, and I whispered to myself,

"You're happening to the world, Mags."

I stepped off that plane feeling the most *me* I'd ever felt. Unafraid, accepted, and ready to see all the colours.

2

Ready, Set, Rizz

Maggie

When I was nine years old, I auditioned for the school musical. It was *Seussical the Musical,* and even though I'd only had one voice lesson, they gave me the lead. You'd think that meant I was Cat in the Hat, but I wasn't. I was Horton the Elephant.

From the first rehearsal, I was obsessed with all of it. Obsessed with acting, singing, dancing, and above all, I was obsessed with my character, Horton. It got me so excited to become him and see the world how he did. Life was instantly glittering in colour, and I never wanted to see it any other way.

I'm not sure I was entirely convincing as an elephant, performing in a costume with hula hoops sewn underneath to make me look like one. But even at nine years old, I just ... *got it.*

We did four performances, and I didn't know at the time, but there was a casting agent at the closing show. Turns out, they thought I *got it,* too.

I picked up jobs in advertising growing up, mostly kid's toys, never anything pulling me out of school for more than a day. By the time I graduated high school, with below-average grades that

I'd largely attribute to undiagnosed ADHD, the only job I wanted was to act.

I bounced between hospo jobs, failing the majority of auditions for years, only landing one-off supporting roles on TV. But eventually, I got a movie! Well, technically, it was an indie short. It was kinda low budget … but on my IMDb, it was listed as a feature film!

It was called *Shattered Glass*, and I was cast as the teenaged, trainwreck best friend to the lead. It got buzz in the U.S., mostly because the lead actress got caught up in a cheating scandal … with a Hollywood A-lister twice her age. But I didn't care. I was happy to piggyback on the attention.

That's how my agent in Sydney connected me to the big, wide world of L.A. More importantly, to a kick-ass Hollywood agent, Cherie Everly.

The timeline after that feels a little dizzying, to say the least. But L.A. is a dizzying place, and it moves super-fast. Like a blink-and-you'll-miss-it kind of fast.

I landed in L.A., and Cherie and her partner Jill picked me up from the airport. I'd only met Cherie over Zoom, and meeting her in person was everything I'd hoped it would be. I loved them both, instantly, like I'd gained two cool aunties. The kind you tell your secrets to when you don't want your mum to judge you.

Plus, Cherie is pretty much the poster woman for modern *badass*. She has this sleek caramel bob; it frames her face and makes her cheekbones look snatched. With that, came a certain aura of intellect about her. You could sense it before she even opened her mouth. The thick, tortoiseshell glasses she wore might've been a tell, too.

I lived in their house for two months, going to auditions and acting my little heart out. But after twenty-three "not this one" calls, I started to feel friggin' guilty for living in their spare room.

So, I bought myself a shitty van with a huge dent on the left-hand side, and I lived in that instead. It felt a bit like my life had become the plotline of a Disney movie, but honestly, I'm glad I did it. Laying in it at night, I'd think about how ridiculous it was and laugh myself to sleep. It helped me remember *me*, every day.

You could get away with living in a van here if you were strategic. I'd park it in sneaky spots, or sometimes on Cherie's street. She hated it 'cause her street was fancy. She'd always ask me to stay with her instead, but I was too polite to say yes. I felt too guilty. It wasn't her fault I couldn't land a role.

Running low on cash, I took the job at Bronte's, spending most of my shifts behind the coffee machine. The café was wrapped around the corner of a bustling street, and Roy, my boss and the owner of Bronte's, was *brilliant*. Funny, sharp, and witty in the driest of ways.

Tall and broad with deep brown skin and a beer belly, he had a hard, unreadable exterior. But underneath that, he had a big heart, and he'd show it by sharing little gold nuggets of wisdom. He could be scary sometimes, the way his voice could boom, but he'd always play along with my goofiness. I loved him instantly, too.

By the time I settled in at Bronte's, we were in the sweltering summer apex of July. Every day was a scorcher. Roy kept the sea-facing windows open, and I'd exhale in relief whenever I felt the breeze against my cheeks. I'd daydream a lot, watching all kinds of people weave between towering palm trees lining the footpath.

L.A. was a melting pot of culture, creativity, and contrasts. The Hollywood business allure collided with the laid-back essence of the Californian coast. It was chaos and calm, all mixed in together. Admittedly, it kinda made me feel a sense of belonging.

I never told Roy I was there to become an actor. Why? Well, try saying it out loud without sounding like a wanker. *Impossible.*

After working at Bronte's for two months, I asked for a day off because my "parents were visiting".

They weren't. It was for an audition.

It was a first-round audition for an Amazon show, based on a young adult romance novel titled *More of You*, by Nic Fenway. The script was adapted as a limited series, with two seasons of five episodes each. The book itself was wildly successful, and the show was lined up to be big.

You could strike up a conversation by asking any 16-to-30-year-old woman if they'd read *More of You*, and you'd have yourself a new friend. I'd read all Nic Fenway's books. She was a romance writing wizard! Bonus points for her ability to write spicy chapters without using the word *throbbing*. I just hated that word; it gave me the ick.

I was auditioning for the female lead, Sarah. She was funny, but also incredibly sexy, and I thought that was beautiful. That was part of the reason why I wanted the role so badly. Women can be so many things all at once, which wasn't often seen on screen. It was usually one or the other.

Sarah's love interest was Liam, and Cherie told me he'd already been cast. It was Chris Rowan. I asked Cherie how I even got an audition when she told me his name. Chris was *in demand* and all that. She said it was my *look*, and she also told me Chris worked with one of the producers on his last show.

It made me giggle when she told me that, 'cause you know what they say ... *it's not what you know ...*

One week after the first audition, I was asked in for a callback. I'd been to eighteen callbacks out of the twenty-three "not this one" calls, so it wasn't anything to get excited about. It was a Sunday, so Bronte's had closed early, thank goodness. I couldn't lose that job, or I wouldn't eat. My tips had also been scrappy 'cause I was speaking in an American accent all the time to practice.

Surprisingly, that callback was more like a screen test, almost as if I'd skipped a step entirely. The dizzying pace of L.A. had kicked into a new gear! The acceleration was exhilarating, but I'd be lying if I said I wasn't masking anxiety in that audition. I'd only made it to one other screen test since being in L.A., and when I didn't get it, I cried myself to sleep for three nights.

I was styled like Sarah, which was essentially just me. They told me to leave my dress on, they just added a cardigan. I relied solely on my rizz to prove myself, and luckily for me ... *it worked.*

Next, I had a chemistry read with Chris. I'd never got that far; I was shitting my pants. I spent hours trawling through Reddit, reading about people's experiences, most women saying how traumatising it was. I also watched an obscene amount of Chris Rowan content.

Chris was very ... *heart-throbby.* His eyes were big, round, and blue, like sapphire orbs. He had dark, espresso-coloured hair that flopped over his forehead, and a smile that was disarmingly flawless. A dimple creased his left cheek when he flashed it.

I wanted to work out how I could make him laugh. I knew they'd want us to banter; it was a Sarah and Liam thing. He talked about watching *Step Brothers* over a hundred times on *Late Night,* and how much he loved music on *Kelly Clarkson.*

He'd always have a band T-shirt on, in nearly every paparazzi shot. A lot of them were Australian bands, too. Once I noticed that, I felt like I had enough to work with.

I wore the same dress I had on at the screen test, with green loafers, frilly white socks, and a lilac cardigan. Very Sarah, but also, it was straight from the tiny wardrobe of clothes I brought from home.

Three other girls were waiting. I was third. We had similar looks, but one girl was blonde. I figured they'd dye her hair. I wondered how many they started with in the first round and let myself be proud for a millisecond. Then I felt anxious again.

Mid-pondering what the girl with blonde hair would look like as a brunette ... a tall, red-haired man called my name as he headed out of the audition room. I think it might have been Chris's agent.

As I walked into that audition, I'm pretty sure I left my body entirely. But it went ... *well?*

Oddly, my auditions were stronger each round because there was more pressure and less time to prepare. I work best under pressure. It's how I've always been. It's an ADHD thing, but I'd made friends with it and could use it to my advantage.

Chris was easily twenty centimetres taller than me. He was broad, lean, and muscular, but not in a gym junkie way. In a grilled chicken and broccoli for lunch, kind of way.

I tried to be charming, but we'd gone so far off script that I think it just landed as goofy every time. I had Chris in stitches at one point. He even had to wipe his eyes! The lovey-dovey parts felt easy; he was, well, *Chris*. Pretty sure he dated his last few co-stars, and I understood why.

And of course, when we wrapped up ... I tripped on the way out.

It knocked me right off my high horse and back to my living-in-a-van, wannabe-actor reality. I made some sort of basic joke that it was "part of my audition", or something like that. I didn't wait for their reaction; I just beelined it outta there.

As soon as I closed the door, the last girl waiting to audition perked up, searching every line on my face for clues on how mine had gone. I smiled, let out a deep breath, and walked straight past her without making eye contact. I wasn't giving anything away.

3

Define Chemistry

Chris

Chemistry reads were kind of like a co-op job interview. You're thrown into a scene, staring into the eyes of someone you've known no longer than a few minutes. A handful of execs watch you like hawks, basically trying to decide if they want to see you bang on screen. Producers, writers, casting agents … they come up with the best pairings, and they want to see you connect.

My acting coach had always taught me, *book the room, then book the role*. It was solid advice. The setup of a chem read was stark. Green screen, a few cameras, no set or anything other than the script to support a genuine vibe. If the energy's off, it's painfully obvious, and the whole scene falls flat. No amount of talent can save it if the connection isn't there.

Also, *define chemistry*.

You can't, right?

Not between people, anyway.

So, a chem read could be weird. Very weird. Especially when they aren't going too well.

I'd met two women so far. They *both* fell flat. As each one walked out the door, I felt a stab of guilt for them. I knew how it felt, the "not this one" call. I felt awkward about being the one who'd already booked the job. I always wondered if the women thought I was the biggest douchebag.

I didn't want them to think I was basking in the glory of knowing the whole thing was already stacked in my favour. I tried not to be too intense, to be polite, to respect their craft. I really cared what they thought of me. I wasn't the type to just brush that off.

These women are auditioning like their careers depends on it, in an environment that, I imagined, wasn't far off from feeling like a fantasy suite. They walk in, audition with a bunch of mostly white dudes eyeing them up and down, and then walk out.

Hollywood was shit. But I wasn't above it.

I met my last girlfriend at a chem read … and my current one.

Sitting in front of the execs, I was beginning to feel a little on edge. They'd pretty much held poker faces the entire time. I didn't really have a measure of what anyone in the room thought of the other two reads; I just hoped it was the same as me. That they were bad.

I glanced at the doorway, mentally preparing, hoping the next person to walk in would be different. And that a tall cold brew with my name on it would magically appear before my eyes. When the door swung open …

I exhaled in relief. *Brilliant.*

It was Dom, my manager. He took the seat next to me, passing me one of the two large coffees in his hands.

Leaning in, he lowered his voice. "How's it been?"

"Not … great," I muttered. I held the coffee cup over my face to hide the *look* I was giving him from the execs.

Dom had been my manager for ten years; by my side since my first "you got it" call. We were so close that a quick side glance is all it took to communicate. In the environments of this industry, it was a practical method of operation. One that Dom and I had mastered.

I was only sixteen when I met him; he was twenty-four. He was a man of few words, but he didn't need to say much to fill a room. His presence alone did that. The orange-red hair and matching beard were probably loud enough, anyway. And the guy was huge. A six-foot fitness beast. I went to a CrossFit class with him once. I threw up; he casually knocked out a set of handstand push-ups. I never went back.

To the version of me that was a business, Dom was the CEO. He had the whole game figured out. The sharpness in his eyes made it clear that he didn't miss a beat. He'd do it all through an effortless calm, but you were an idiot if you thought you could catch him off guard.

I love acting, and I'll keep myself in tune with all the details surrounding that, but having Dom meant I didn't have to let those details pull me from what I was there to do—to act.

And to the version of me that was just ... me?

Dom was my brother. The high expectations I had on myself could be backbreaking. But he'd break his own back trying to protect mine.

Dom huffed, shaking my shoulder. "Right," he said. Then his knowing smile said, *sucks to be you.*

I just shrugged, raising my eyebrows through a slow, quiet sigh.

It really didn't "suck to be me", though. This role as Liam in More of You was the first time I'd been asked to consider a script. They gave it to me. You don't get that shit easily. I guess I'd earned it, in a way. I'd been through hundreds of auditions, hundreds of "not this one" calls. I was grateful they came to me, this time. It felt like recognition, almost like a *we're sorry for all the nos.*

Honestly, I was hoping my performance as Liam could be a game changer. I'd played leading men before, but this role was deeper, more layered. If I delivered, it could shift me away from being typecast as the stereotypical, coming-of-age, Byronic hero. Liam was emotionally charged in a way that demanded more than just charm and a make-out scene capable of landing an MTV Best Kiss Award.

The love story with Sarah was complicated and addictive, slightly toxic, but I was captivated when I read the script. The basic plot unfolded like this:

In season one, the underappreciated, unfulfilled, and married-too-young *Sarah* meets a more exciting guy—*Liam.* They have a hot and heavy, passionate affair. But Liam has a certain ... sly charm about him. Kinda like Jimmy Steve from the Netflix show *Shameless.*

If you know, you know.

In season two, Liam, obsessed with being in love and the rush that comes with it, becomes possessive. He also gets caught up in an underground boxing scene, and develops a new habit— ingesting a lot of cocaine. Inevitably, the affair crashes and burns. Meanwhile, Sarah gets divorced, explores who she is, and ultimately finds herself.

Nic Fenway, the author, told me *More of You* was loosely based on her life. The *real* Liam's name was John, and she said I reminded her of him. I wasn't really sure how to feel about that ... like if it was a compliment, or some kind of warning.

I did connect to Liam like I'd met him before, though. Or like I'd stared him down in the mirror every damn day for the last twenty-six years. It freaked me out, but it came with a thrill. I didn't have a cocaine habit, but I understood his other craving because I had the same one.

I *loved* being in love.

When I was in love, it was almost like some sort of ignited awakening. Like my heart would rise to its feet, strike a match, and catch on blazing fire. The feeling was so intense, so visceral, and *so* addictive.

When I wasn't in love, my heart would still beat, obviously. I knew I was alive; I wasn't moping around like the guys I played on TV shows. But it was a steady, predictable rhythm ... not the wild, erratic pulse that came with being in love.

In love, I'd do everything I could to keep that fire in my chest alight, even if it meant the self-sacrifice of being consumed by the flames. Which is exactly what I'd done for the last two months.

I was burning myself alive trying to keep my current relationship together. I didn't know how that was going to end up, but I did know that I wanted to feel in love again.

Slipping into Liam was going to give me that.

"Okay!" Nic piped up. "It's the Aussie girl now. I don't want to jinx it, but she's our girl. She's Sarah, I can feel it." She looked at me, nodding and smiling. I picked up that the nod was more of a silent prayer.

Dom jumped up. "I'll call her on my way out. What's her name?"

"Maggie Marshall," Nic replied, throwing me a wink.

I flicked my eyes back on the doorway, waiting, joining Nic in silent prayer.

Then, in she walked. *Maggie Marshall.*

"Hey everyone! I'm Maggie." Her voice was sweet, bubbly like she was speaking through a giggle. The other two women I'd read with didn't say more than a soft "hi" as they walked in.

She walked towards me and held out her hand. "Maggie," she repeated, just to me. "Or just Mags, if you want. Most people call me Mags."

I stood up and smiled. "Mags it is, then. I'm Chris." We shook hands, and as our eyes met, it was a flicker, but it was definitely there. *Chemistry.*

Her eyes were pale green, shaped like almonds. Her hand was sweaty, her cheeks a little pink ... nerves, I guessed.

I sat down again, and Maggie dropped her bag to the floor, chatting with Nic while the cameraman reset.

She was small ... tiny, actually. Surely five foot two, at most. Her hair was chocolate brown. I hadn't noticed when she walked in, but watching her talk to Nic, I could see it fell well past her waist. The ends were grazing her hips.

Looking at Maggie was like seeing the real-life image I'd formed of Sarah in my mind when I read the book. What she was wearing matched the description of Sarah in one of the scenes perfectly. A white sundress with a black lace trim, purple cardigan, green loafers, and white socks with frilly bits at her ankles. It was like she'd stepped right out of the pages and into the room.

Five minutes into the read ... I completely lost sight of the fact that we were in an audition.

Sarah and Liam had two sides: the friends who only speak through in–jokes and the turbulent, romantic dynamic. Maggie's American accent was spot-on, and we were bouncing off each other, improvising banter and drifting far off script. At one point, I was laughing so hard that real tears streamed down my face.

I could barely keep it together when Nic asked to see the romantic scene, but Maggie held that space like she owned it. She took her time, and it was obvious that no one wanted her to hurry up.

Especially me. I didn't want it to end.

Someone in the room said, "Cut," and I was a little disoriented.

Within seconds, Maggie turned to me and tapped my chest. She asked, "So you like Skegss?"

It was jarring how quickly she could drop the American accent. And that she tapped my chest. I forgot I was wearing a band shirt; I'd forgotten where I was entirely.

I managed to say, "Yeah, yeah. They're great."

She leaned in towards me, narrowing her eyes, and in that moment, I could see how fast her brain was ticking. If I could look inside her head, it'd be a tangled maze of thoughts; I wouldn't be able to find one quickly.

Smirking, she said, "Favourite Skegss song on three. One, two, three—"

"*L.S.D.*"

I jolted back. We were perfectly in sync.

She looked at me like a bright light had switched on behind her eyes. Her jaw dropped into a big smile, and she looked amazed. I was sure I mirrored it, because again ... I was disoriented.

She grabbed my arms with both hands and asked, "Did we just become best friends?"

When she let go, she had this cheeky grin. Butter wouldn't melt. I knew exactly what she was doing.

I flashed a grin back at her. "Yep!" Pointing over my shoulder, I asked, "Do you wanna go play karate in the garage?"

She threw her head back and laughed. "Yep!"

Watching her pick up her bag, I so badly didn't want her to walk out. Breathing in her laugh gave my lungs something I didn't know they needed ... *fresh air.*

She shook my hand again. "It was so great meeting you, thank you."

"Yeah, you too." I nodded and smiled.

Turning to the room, she said, "Thank you so much for your time and just ... everything, really. That was fun. And Nic, you've written an incredible story." On her way out, she tripped on a cord and her cheeks flushed rosy again. She called out, "That was part of my audition, just so you know!"

Then she made a kind of awkward, half wave, half peace sign ... and shut the door behind her.

I turned to face Nic, and my mouth hung open.

Stammering, I said, "I don't know what the hell that was, or what just happened ..." I ran a hand through my hair, glancing back at the door. My voice dropped, more intense. "But she's surely got to be Sarah."

"I know what it was," Nic said, smirking. "It was chemistry."

I laughed, but it was more of a breathy sound. I was still a little disoriented.

Dropping back into my chair, I knew Nic was right. You could feel it, and the way she said it made it seem like a logical fact.

There was no real definition of chemistry between people, but I did have my own version. And if I ever needed an example ...

Meeting Maggie Marshall was definitely going to be it.

chem·is·try / *noun* / (**Chris's version**)

A quick flicker of a spark. A reaction, waiting. When all the right elements collide, it explodes into invisible energy that scatters and lights up every micro molecule in the air. It doesn't always create something new. But it does linger.

4

That Call

It was fifteen minutes 'til Bronte's closed for the day, and I was a million miles away in my head. It had been two days since the chem read. If I didn't hear today, I was sure it was over. My phone was on silent in my back pocket, but you better believe it was on the harshest vibrate setting I could find.

"Is this a skinny cap?" a high-pitched voice barked at me.

I looked up from the espresso machine and into my own reflection in the oversized Prada sunglasses perched on the woman's face. She was snarling at me like she'd asked a trick question.

I wanted to say, *Yes, lady. Laced with Ozempic, just for you!*

But instead, I said, "Yep, that's your skinny cap." I plastered on my sweetest smile and slid the cup across the counter.

I didn't like how common it was to wear sunglasses inside in L.A. Talking to people indoors while they wore sunglasses felt the same as speaking to someone with AirPods in.

As I watched the barking woman walk out, I felt the buzz of my phone against my arse. I whipped it out of my back pocket and gasped. It was Cherie.

I called out to Roy, "Give me two minutes!"

"Mags, I am right here," he grumbled, rubbing his ear. I didn't realise he was standing so close; I might have burst his eardrum. "Go quick, we're packin' up."

I pulled my apron off so hard I felt it graze the back of my neck and bolted out the front of Bronte's, standing on the pathway facing the beach.

"Cherie?" I answered, puffed and panicked. "I've got two minutes; I've gotta close up."

"Maggie." Her voice was sharp, full of intensity. She usually called me Mags. I skipped a breath at the realisation.

My voice went high and squeaky. "… Yes?"

"You got it, Mags," she said. "You're Sarah."

Everything inside me stopped.

I couldn't take a breath. I didn't blink. I'm so sure I died for a moment. My legs felt wobbly, so I ducked into a crouch, thinking I'd faint if I didn't.

I heard Cherie chuckle. "I wouldn't worry so much about packing up today, sweetheart." At that, I jolted up to stand again and ran across the street.

Then, I let out the kind of squeal I would've made at a Jonas Brothers concert in 2010. "Ahhhhhhhh!!!" I squealed so hard I dropped my phone in the gutter.

I heard Cherie laugh again on the other end of the line while I scrambled to pick it back up. "I'm so proud of you, Mags," she said.

It was lovely to hear, but I could only stutter in response. "I can't even … I just, I …"

Gazing out at the beach, every single fibre of my little human body was screaming at me to run into that water. Like my soul knew my senses weren't caught up with my reality.

I blurted out, "I'll call you back." Then I hung up on Cherie and legged it for the waves, half-stripping to my undies on the way down.

Cherie kept trying to call me back, but I ditched my phone on the sand with my Bronte's uniform, and didn't stop until I hit the water.

I dove straight into a wave. It stung my skin. *Thank goodness.* I hadn't died, I was alive. The *most* alive. This was real. *Extraordinarily real.*

I was smiling so hard I started sobbing. *You did it, Mags.*

I'd blasted off into my dreams, but this time, I wasn't going to float around, high up in the sky. This time, I'd friggin' landed.

Headed back to Bronte's, I was copping stares left and right. I was completely drenched, barefoot, holding my sneakers in one hand. My hair dripped down my back. I hoped Roy would just fire me when he saw me. I was bracing myself for the guilt I'd feel telling him I was quitting.

My phone buzzed again. *Geez, Cherie.* Couldn't she just let me have this moment for five more minutes? I ignored it at first, but I was procrastinating talking to Roy, so I figured I'd better call her back.

I pulled it from my back pocket, wiped the water off the screen with my dry sock, and read a text from a random number.

> hey Sarah! Karate in the garage for the next three months yeah? (its Chris btw)

Holy shit! Chris texted me!

"Mags, what the hell, man!" Roy called out from across the street, standing in front of the café. He looked pissed.

I called back, "I'm sorry!"

Jogging towards Roy, I jammed my phone back into my pocket. He handed me the tea towel from his apron when he saw how wet I was.

"Don't you come in here making a mess," he warned. "I just cleaned this shit up."

I ran the tea towel over my wet hair, internally begging myself to just come right out and say it.

I took a quick breath. "Roy, I'm sorry. But …"

"Let me guess, Maggie Marshall." He cut me off with his booming voice.

He almost seemed dismissive, turning his back to me and heading inside. I tiptoed behind him, stopping just inside the door before I made a mess. When he got to the counter, he spun around, his face unreadable as ever.

He looked me sharp in the eye. "You got the part?"

Stupidly, I acted shocked and gasped. "What?"

Then I cycled through my best surprised facial expressions, gradually fading into a guilty one. Roy watched me like I was an idiot for trying.

He crossed his arms, leaning back. His tone was flat. "You think you're the first person to work here a few months for cash, and a year later, your agent is comin' in here buying coffee while you wait out front in a tinted Lexus?"

I blinked, completely thrown. I was trying to think of something to say, but any ounce of charm I could muster wasn't going to work with someone like Roy. I wasn't even sure if I was meant to respond.

Before I could decide, he scoffed. "Yeah, you're not. This is L.A., baby girl. And I've been here a hell of a lot longer than you."

I stood there like a stunned mullet. Eyes wide, dripping wet, staring at him. I felt so *seen*. I felt responsible, too. I didn't like the feeling of being the reason for the disappointment in Roy's narrowed eyes.

"Well," I said, swallowing hard. I tiptoed through the café, standing right in front of him. I had to wring out some charm from somewhere on my wet body. "I am not going to be sending my agent in to buy me coffee ..." I shot him a smirk. "She always gets my order wrong."

He rolled his eyes and huffed out a laugh. "My dear ... I'm happy for you." He put his hand on my shoulder. "This world will swallow you up and spit you out faster than you can say *Oscars*. This ain't no Australian talent quest. This is the big leagues, and they don't play nice, and they don't play fair."

Oof. Damn. I felt his words, deep in my gut.

He handed me my bag from behind the counter. "Don't assume that everyone else's heart beats like yours, Mags."

Second *oof.* I felt those words so deep; I instantly knew I'd never forget them.

"But ..." He perked up and smiled. "You've got a resilient soul. Maybe you'll be the one they don't break."

There was something in the way he said *don't break* that had me tearing up. So, whispering, I said, "Thank you."

He ushered me out the door, quickly changing his tune. "Don't come back here in a week for your job back, 'cause your arse is fired."

"I won't be, I promise," I said, stuttering while he half-pushed me out onto the street. "Thank you so, so much. For everything. I mean, it's been ..." He was shutting the door in my face. "A pleasure!"

He paused the moment before he clicked the door shut, speaking through the gap. "You can park your van out back if you need. Yeah, I know that, too." He locked it shut, smiling and waving at me through the glass. "Bye, Mags."

Then he shut off the lights.

Roy is an absolute, bloody legend.

5

Aunty Chez

Following Cherie's "you got it" call, I stayed with her and Jill at their house for a week. Jill was an entertainment lawyer, and their house definitely said so. It was real Spanish-style. Stucco walls with iron accents, red clay tiled roof, and a perfectly manicured yard with a pool that looked like a mermaid grotto. I'd unashamedly pretend I was a mermaid every time I went swimming.

Having time with Jill was pivotal for me. She taught me *so* much about the business. And on the surface, I knew I didn't *need* to know any of it, but deep down, it felt important. I'd feel the panic when she'd explain contracts to me because my mind would drift, but I'd feel the panic and sit across from her anyway. I needed to know that I was taking care of myself. Cherie and Jill were two extraordinary women. It was empowering to just be in their orbit.

Sitting on the back deck overlooking the grotto, Cherie and I were sipping hefty glasses of red wine. I was thinking about whether I felt the ADHD meds were working, trying to assess my own body and brain. I figured it was a no, because I was supposed to be listening to Cherie, and she caught me drifting.

"Maggie? Mags!" She clicked her finger in front of my face. "This is important."

I shook my head, refocusing. "Sorry, sorry. I'm here now," I assured her. "Please repeat."

"So," she said. She quickly checked she still had my attention before she continued, pleased that she did. "You'll check in next week on Tuesday, at the hotel, The Bennett. It's nice, across from the beach; you'll like it. You can leave your van here. Jill will move it to her garage. Then, you'll start on set Wednesday. And that will be same-same for five or so weeks."

She was reading straight from her planner, and I felt thankful she had one, because I certainly didn't.

She continued, "And then the third Friday in October, you and Chris will do a bit of press, because everything will be announced, out in the world, and people will want to meet you, Mags." She looked up, smiling at me, and I took a lengthy chug of my wine. She laughed. "Mags, trust me. You've got nothing to worry about, sweetheart."

I set down my glass. "What makes you say that, Chez?"

She winced, repeating it back to me. "*Chez?*"

If someone in Australia had the name Cherie, their name was Chez. It was obvious.

"Yeah!" I said. "You're Chez. *Aunty Chez*, actually." She looked disgusted; I wasn't convincing her. I threw my hands up in the air. "Come on, as if you're not Aunty Chez? Admit it." I leaned across the table and put my hand on her arm. Lowering my voice, I said, "It's who you are."

She brushed me off. "Cherie will do."

"No, no. It's Aunty Chez." I nodded, smiling, hoping she'd accept it. Her frown deepened, so I gave up. I mumbled, "You're Aunty Chez to *me*, anyway."

She rolled her eyes and huffed. "Fine. To *you*, Maggie."

"So, what do I need to do at 'press' stuff?" I asked.

"Just answer questions about the show. They'll definitely ask you questions about Australia, but I'd expect it to be stereotypical."

I took a deep breath, imagining it all in my mind. I wasn't worried, but I'd be lying if I said there wasn't a flutter of uncertainty.

As a follow up, I asked, "What if I, like, don't hear the question?"

I caught a flicker of confusion in her frown. "Well, Mags, they will be sitting or standing right in front of you. You'll hear the question."

I leaned across the table again. "No, Chez, I'm serious. What if I don't hear the question? Like ... if I *drift*?"

She pulled her glasses to the bridge of her nose, blinking fast. "You just ask them to repeat the question."

"Yeah, but Cherie ..." I slumped back in my chair. "What if I still don't hear it? I can barely hear *you* right now. There's, like, birds chirping, and you're flicking through your planner, and it takes *a lot* for me to concentrate. It's just ... my brain."

She tilted her head. "What do you mean by that?"

Ugh. I rolled my eyes and picked up my wine glass, taking another lengthy chug.

"I can't focus sometimes," I said, slightly hesitating. "Because I have ADHD. And I don't know ... it's just debilitating sometimes."

Cherie looked purely confused now, so I sat up straight to reassure her I was a capable, professional adult. I continued, "I mean, don't get me wrong. It can be very unserious, funny, even, at times."

I slumped back again, remembering that most of the time, I had to fight hard for the feeling of capable and professional. With a small, earnest shrug, I added, "But it also kind of sucks, too."

Cherie took her wine, relaxing into her chair. "What parts of it suck, Mags?"

By the look on her face, and how she'd settled in her chair, she was letting me know I could take as long as I wanted to answer. Chez was the best.

I thought about it for a moment, then replied, "It can just be frustrating because I get so distracted by random thoughts. They dart into my mind, like … like butterflies fluttering around in my brain. I try to catch the thoughts and refocus, but Cherie, have you ever tried to catch a butterfly? It's hard!"

Cherie took a sip of her wine, her gaze steady on me. She didn't rush to speak, giving me a small nod, encouraging me to keep going without a word.

I continued, "It's funny because it's so … *me*. But it also kind of makes me feel like I'm losing control. And that feeling makes me panic. Sometimes, that panic … *attacks.*"

She seemed deep in thought, considering her words. "When that happens, Mags …" She leaned forward. "What do you need me to do?"

I was a little stunned that she asked that. It was a very kind thing to ask. Soft enough that it made me smile, but sure enough that it made me feel safe.

"Just remind me that I'm *here*," I said. "Like, in the room." I gestured around the deck. "And on the Earth." I gestured out to the sky, laughing because Cherie's face said she was highly amused by my theatrics.

"Easy," she huffed. "I can do that. Also, Chris will be with you for all of it. There won't be much with you alone. He's a pro, he'll be 'right."

My jaw hit the floor. "Chez, did you just say, 'he'll be 'right'? " I waved my finger at her. "I'm rubbing off on you. I *knew* you were a *Chez*. My best friend back home, Ben, is going to love you. He already calls you Aunty Chez."

She rolled her eyes, laughing and sipping her wine, and I knew she'd always be able to bring me back to Earth. She dismissed my joke, then immediately started talking through scheduling again, like she trusted that I'd keep up.

That confidence Cherie had in me ... I'd hang on to it. Tight.

"Oh," she said, clicking her finger again. "You have dinner with Nic Fenway and Chris tomorrow night. Have questions and whatever else ready for Nic, if you want. Did Dom call you?"

My ears pricked up. "Dom? As in, Chris's agent, Dom?"

She nodded. "I spoke to him this morning, and he said he was inviting you to some bar or something beforehand."

Technically, Dom and Cherie were indirect co-workers. They worked as managers under the same talent agency, *ZETA*, which stood for Zenith Entertainment Talent Agency. Cherie first met Dom when he signed Chris as a baby! Well, a teenaged baby, but still, they'd known each for a long time.

Cherie was set to become a business partner at ZETA, which I knew would happen because of her *BGBE*—Big Girl Boss Energy. The thought of Cherie being Dom's boss cracked me up. Sometimes they could butt heads ... just a collision of two fierce minds, I think. Dom wouldn't take very well to answering to Cherie.

I quickly picked up my phone from the table and checked the call list. "No," I said, "He hasn't called."

"Mags, check your messages."

Cherie really did know me already. I was a caller. One or two texts made me feel overwhelmed, so I'd just let them build up and pretend they weren't there. Weeks ago, Cherie had texted me about a last-minute audition, and I didn't go because I hadn't checked my messages. She'd learned now.

My heart skipped a few beats when I saw it. "Oh!" I gasped. "You're right, he did ask me!" I read the text out loud. "Hey

Maggie, it's Dom. You should come to The Alibi tomorrow at five p.m. with me and Chris and a few others. It'll be fun. Go to dinner from there? Hope to see you."

My mouth hung open. Then a big, cheeky smile flew across my face.

Chez huffed again. "Maggie, please. Don't hide your excitement, by all means." She sounded like Miranda Priestley from *The Devil Wears Prada* which was the cherry on top in that moment.

I replied to the text, reading that out loud, too. "Yes! For sure! See you there!" I hit send before I could question the overuse of exclamation points.

Cherie was giggling at me, so I leaned over, grabbed her hand, and shook it like I was trying to physically hand her some of my excitement.

"Chez," I whispered. My eyes were wide and excited. I shook her hand again. *"Friends!"*

She laughed, nodding, knowing I'd been itching to go for a drink or do something, *anything*, other than sling coffees and go to auditions.

6

Prove Me Right

Chris

From the kitchen, I called out, "Chelsea? I've gotta go!"

I had no idea where she was. My house had too many walls. I grabbed my sunglasses from the counter, sat them on my head, and shoved my keys, wallet, and phone into my pockets.

"Chelsea!" I called again.

I was so desperate for the exhale I would feel when I walked out, if Chelsea didn't appear before my eyes in the next five seconds, I was leaving without saying goodbye. And in this house, that was a *big* deal.

Standing by the front door, literally counting to five in my head, she put her hands on my waist from behind me. It startled the crap out of me.

"*Oh shit.*" I gasped and spun to face her.

"Yeah, I'm ready," she said. She smiled, batting her lashes. "Let's go."

She side-stepped me to open the door, but I stopped her, grabbing the handle before she could. She was dressed up; she looked hot. But she wasn't invited. I put my hand on her cheek, thinking it would soften the blow of my question.

"Chels." I took a breath, smiling and trying to soften my eyes. "What are you doing?"

Chelsea's gaze of innocence was Oscar-worthy. She batted her lashes again, tilting her head and locking her eyes on mine while she tried to melt me. Frustratingly, the dress she was wearing only supported that attempt.

Strapless, short, and fiery red, it cinched her already barely-there waistline and nearly doubled the size of her chest. She'd undoubtedly tug it down all night, but she knew how to draw eyes. That ranked supreme on Chelsea's hierarchy of importance.

In two seconds flat, I undressed her and dressed her again with my eyes. Then I kissed her cheek in a silent, desperate plea for this to stay calm, smooth, and easy.

When I met her gaze again, I said, "You look stunning, Chelsea. But ..."

She didn't let me say it. "I don't care," she snapped. "I invited myself."

Dropping my hand from her cheek, I snapped back. "Chelsea, I'm only going for like an hour! I've got the dinner with Nic ..."

I hesitated, forcing out a breath. I knew I needed to soften my voice, or this was going to blow up. *Again.*

Softly, I added, "And Maggie."

"I know, but I want to meet her," she said, her voice just shy of a whine. The innocence was hanging on by a thread.

I shook my head. "She's not even going to be at The Alibi."

"Uh, yeah. She is." She nodded. "Dom invited her."

The innocence was Oscar-worthy, but it was still acting. I knew that Chelsea would have asked Dom to invite Maggie. She wasn't interested in a bar of my pushback, so she blamed him. Poor guy. Easy scapegoat, really.

She looked so proud of herself. Like, *look at me, I get whatever I want, and I don't care how it makes anyone around me feel!* It pissed me off when she looked at me like that. Like I'd somehow fucked up by not wanting to give her whatever she wanted in the first place.

And the blazing fire in my heart? The one that started off as being madly in love?

That's when it's flames would start to burn me alive.

Heating up, I threw my hands in the air. "Why, Chelsea? Why would you do that?" I searched her eyes. I found nothing.

"I just want to meet her! She's Australian ... it's interesting."

I rolled my eyes so hard that my head went with them. Chels could act, but that sentence was *far* from believable.

"Please, Chelsea," I said. "Spare me."

Once more, she tried the fluttering lashes. "Dom said he told you Maggie was invited."

I stared blankly back at her. With a tight jaw, I didn't say it, but I thought, *No, Chelsea. Dom did not tell me that. You should have told me that. Actually, you should have fucking asked me first.*

Before I could speak, she rolled her eyes and swung the door open, dismissing me entirely. I didn't follow, I needed that exhale away from her too desperately. I wasn't ready to give up on that.

"Chels, wait." I reached out and caught her arm. "This is so unnecessary." She kept her back to me, so I held a careful, firm grip. To the back of her head, I said, "You can come to set. Whenever you want."

I dropped her arm, and she stood in the doorway. Perfectly still.

I tried to take a deep breath in, but the air was like smoke. Thick, and suffocating. I could feel that she was two seconds away from roaring up the intensity from a subtle burn ... to a full-blown *singe*. And given the likelihood that I was about to turn into a pile of soot and ash ...

Here are five critical things worth knowing about Chelsea:

One, she was drop-dead gorgeous. Long, golden-blonde hair, pale blue eyes, legs for days. She was taller than me in heels.

Two, she knew it. It was her superpower.

Three, the world thought *we* were hot, together. I met her at a chemistry read, and we starred in a coming-of-age romance movie that teenage girls around the world became *obsessed* with. When we hard-launched our relationship at the premiere in New York, the court of public opinion announced their verdict: Chelsea and Chris were endgame.

Four, she was spoilt. Like, really, a spoilt *brat*. When I started dating her, I thought it was cute and attractive in a *damn, she knows what she wants* kind of way. After a year, it was exhausting and made me feel weak.

Her dad was a filmmaker, and he'd moved to Paris with his girlfriend who was our age. She looked a lot like Chelsea; it gave me the ick. We'd only been dating for three months when he left, and I asked Chels to move in with me.

At the time, I thought it was right, and good, and grown up. But in the last few months, deep down in my gut, I was realising I only asked her because I felt sorry for her.

And finally, most critically ... *five*.

If Chelsea auditioned for a role and didn't get the part, she'd call her dad, and he'd fire her manager.

Most recently, she auditioned for the role of Sarah, as in, *Liam's* Sarah. In *More of You*.

Chelsea meets with her new manager next week.

"*Chris*," she spat. It was sharp; there was venom in it.

She snapped back to face me, and the gaze of innocence had disappeared. I sighed, hoping for the best, but expecting the worst.

Practically hissing, she said, "I will come to set. Whenever I want. And I'm also coming now." She paused, stepping closer and narrowing her eyes. "And that won't be a problem, because *Maggie* is just *Sarah*." Resting her face back into innocence, she put her hand on my chest. Softly, she said, "And *you* are just *Liam*."

I sighed again. This was a classic Chelsea challenge. A pattern I knew like a role I'd played too many times.

What she was really saying was, "Prove me right, Chris." And that's when, deep down in my gut, I'd feel weak. But on the surface, I could almost kind of ... *peacock*. Because I knew I could do it. I could prove her right.

I mean, she *was* right. Maggie was just Sarah, and I was just Liam. It was a job. But I was starting to feel like Chelsea was infecting every part of my life as if she owned it. Like I was just here to give her everything she wanted, existing under the pile of soot and ash she left behind her flaming stride.

I didn't know how to get out from underneath it. I wasn't even sure if I wanted to, either. I'd been trying to figure it out, but something was just ... changing. I wasn't sure if everything I had was everything I wanted to keep, but I also couldn't picture my life any differently.

You don't learn how to navigate these parts of adulthood. You just fall into your twenties, and the universe says, *good luck, buddy!*

I was becoming increasingly hyper-aware of all these shitty things about myself, and my life, and the people I chose to share it with ...

But what does having awareness do?

I heard Dr. Phil say on his show that awareness without action is worthless. So where's the frickin' manual for the action part, *Dr. Phil?* What about that, huh?

Are you there, God? It's me, Chris.

Not knowing what to do next meant I just ... stuck with what I'd always done. I'd prove Chelsea right. It was the only thing that made sense to me. When I did, she'd be happy, and I'd feel strong. Strong enough to stop the flames from burning me alive. Like I could contain them, keep them in my chest, and at the very least, I could convince myself.

And I'd continue to convince myself, every day ... that I was still in love.

Hanging my head, I resigned from the idea of fresh air. I held my arm out the door, ushering Chelsea out before me.

We got in the car, and I checked my phone. Sure enough, a text from Dom.

Hey dude, I invited Maggie hope that's cool.

No, Dom. It is anything but "cool".

7

Almost Dribbled

The Alibi was a rooftop cocktail bar overlooking Marc's Beach, and you had to be on the list to even think about getting in. I knew that because I used to work here. Now, I was that arsehole who'd "made it", ordering top-shelf whiskey from the same people I once pilfered top-shelf celebrity drugs with at the end of our shift.

I didn't really like that feeling, but living in the heart of L.A., when you'd "made it", meant the options for a night out were kind of limited. Unless you liked flashing lights in your face when you were already vision-impaired after a night of … mixing substances. In that case, go anywhere.

Everywhere you looked at The Alibi, it was off-white, clean lines, and … not much else. It had a real crisp, minimal aesthetic. The sunsets from the rooftop were impeccable, though. If you got here at the right hour, a golden glow would cast over the entire place. It softened the edges of the stark, concrete walls, the sharp corners of the marble bar … and whatever mental state you were in.

The cocktails were impeccable, too. They had this Spicy Sunset Sour; it was some kind of margarita variation. And *damn*, the chilli hit sweet in the sugar of that drink. It would hit you; you'd blink, and you'd be stumbling through your front door at four a.m., falling asleep with your shoes on.

That's why Dom and I called it the Triple S, for short. The S's in our version stood for shitfaced, saucy, and scattered.

I wasn't planning on getting shitfaced, saucy, or scattered, because of the dinner with Nic and Maggie. But Chelsea was next to me, I didn't want her to be, and I felt equal parts annoyed as I did painfully guilty about that.

So, I'd downed two of those bad boys anyway.

Walking back to our table from the bathroom, I could already feel the effects of the Triple S's. I tried to focus on Brooks and Jordan, two of my close friends. They were speaking with Liv and Ash, two of Chelsea's close friends. But they all looked a little ... blurry. Considering that Maggie was yet to arrive, I got myself a water from the bar on the way back.

Sitting down next to Dom, I said, "Is Maggie coming? It'd suck if she missed this sunset."

"Cherie said she's always late." He tapped his phone for the time; it was 5:43 p.m. He shook his head and chuckled. "She wasn't wrong."

Scooting in a little closer, I asked, "Do you think I should actually call her Mags? Or Maggie?"

He smirked, catching the nervous energy in my tone before I did.

Grabbing my shoulder, he said, "I don't think she cares, dude."

Chelsea scrambled beside me, likely having heard me say "Maggie". She gave me a kiss, which was ... weird.

"Oh!" Dom jumped up, using my shoulder as a brace. "There she is, I'll go get her."

My eyes darted through the bar, and Maggie wasn't hard to miss. She was just so *bright*. In the moment I saw her, it looked to me like she was casting light on the sunset, not the other way around.

She carried this honeyed glow, golden and glittering, while she followed Dom to our table. Instinctively, I reached up to my head for my sunglasses, forgetting I already had them on. Slightly embarrassed, I tried to play it off like I was running my hand through my hair.

Through a beaming smile, Maggie said, "Ripper sunset, right?" She glanced around at the group of us, and for a second, you could have heard a pin drop.

We were all just staring at her, frozen. We surely looked like arseholes. She didn't move, though. She didn't try to hide, or dim her light. She just ... held it.

Brooks, likely highly aroused, jumped up and unfroze us all. "Hey Maggie!" He stuck out his hand. "I'm Brooks."

Maggie went straight in for a hug. "So nice to meet you! Sorry, I'm a hugger."

She gave everyone a soft hug, introducing herself as she moved around the table. Brooks, then Jordan, Ash, Liv, even Chelsea. When she got to me, she stopped, tossed her bag onto the table, and sat down.

"And hey, you," she said, leaning in close. She raised her brows and added, "We meet again."

I felt Chelsea's leg twitch against mine, so I put my hand on her knee before I responded.

"Hey, Mags ..." I started, but I was awkwardly unsure of what to call her. I weirdly tried to fade it into her full name. "Maggie?" I gave her a quick, uncertain smile.

She giggled and nudged my shoulder. "I already told you, silly! You can call me Mags."

Maggie's giggle was infectious, and it didn't take long for the boys to flock around her, firing off questions about Australian slang. She was so witty, animated … overflowing with charisma, really. But it wasn't tinged with anything remotely close to flirting.

The air definitely felt fresher. It was light, and fun … until Chelsea decided to drop a kettlebell onto it.

"So, Maggie," Chels began, tossing her hair and leaning across me. "How long have you been here?"

Maggie replied, "Like, around four months now, I think." She pulled one leg up under her, sitting cross-legged in her chair.

Mags looked *chill*. Like she could be anywhere, talking to anyone, and still be comfortable. Her hair was down, loose curls hanging at the ends, with the pieces around her face pinned back.

She had a very pretty face. It was lovely to look at.

Chelsea continued, "Oh, fun! And this is your … first job?"

Chels, you're tiptoeing right on the edge of patronizing here.

Maggie shrugged. "Kind of, I guess! I did a few smaller jobs back home."

"Oh, that's right! You were in *Shattered Glass*."

Chelsea's pitch went up an octave. She was about to lie, for sure.

Maggie nodded. "Yeah!"

"We loved that movie." Chelsea shot me a look. "Didn't we, babe."

I smiled, gave a little nod, but I knew. I had never heard of that movie. And Chelsea sure as hell had never seen it. Chels had done a ton of Maggie Marshall sleuthing online, no doubt.

My knee started tapping … involuntarily.

Maggie said, "Being in *More of You* is kind of really big for me, though. It's super exciting."

Chelsea cocked her head. "Aw, that's so cute." I squeezed her knee under the table; I could feel she was getting bitchy. Ignoring me, she said, "You know *I* actually auditioned for Sarah?"

Chelsea!

I shot up straight and grabbed my drink from the table, hoping that would somehow cut through how unbearably uncomfortable I was feeling.

But Maggie didn't seem to care. Like, at all.

Without breaking eye contact with Chelsea, she said, "Really? Damn, girl. I'm sorry. I mean, we all know how that feels. It's the worst. But also, I always like to think ... *the right part won't pass by me.* And you know, it won't pass by you either, Chels."

She smiled at both of us ... and I almost dribbled my mouthful of drink back into the glass. She was so unfazed, and so *sure.* She was so right, too.

I smiled and put my hand on Chelsea's back, making a little circle to tell her I agreed. She shrugged me off.

Dom piped up, pointing between me and Maggie. "You guys should go meet Nic, or you'll be late."

Maggie bounced up, doing the rounds of goodbyes, and I turned to Chelsea, leaning in to kiss her.

Before our lips touched, she whispered through clenched teeth, "Don't forget you said you'd be home at ten."

I was sure I had *not* said that, but I nodded. "Okay. All good." I shifted the kiss from her lips to her cheek.

As Maggie and I headed out, Brooks shouted, "What's Australian for 'bye'?"

Maggie spun around, her face scrunched in confusion as she considered. Then she called back, "I don't know ... *Hooroo?*"

Through an over-enthusiastic wave, Brooks shouted even louder, "*Hooroo!*"

As we walked out the door of The Alibi, Maggie nudged me and said, "No one ever says 'hooroo' like, ever." She flashed the same cheeky grin, the one from our chem read. Then she giggled, which was lovely to hear.

Introducing her to Marco, my driver, she told him she'd call him "Sweet Marco" because he had a sweet face. He blushed; it was pretty cute.

On the way to the restaurant, I could see that Maggie was desperately searching through tangled thoughts in her mind. I was trying not to be weird and stare, but her eyes almost looked like they were ... *shaking*. Subtly, like she was reading something only she could see. She looked a bit panicked, like she couldn't make sense of herself.

When we arrived, Nic was waiting at a table. "My Sarah! And my Liam!" she called out the second she spotted us, and Maggie skipped straight towards her.

Throughout dinner, Maggie's face had a firm grip on my focus. I listened, too, but mostly watched. She was wearing this cream linen shirt that was tied up with three little bows down the front. I caught a glimpse of a white lace bra underneath. The second I noticed it, I forced myself not to look again and kept my eyes on her face.

I tried to take the opportunity to see if I could untangle even *one* thought going on in her head. It wasn't easy, especially in the way that she spoke. Her eyes would sparkle and widen in sync with her voice, and they pulled me right into the rhythm of her mind. The rhythm was fast, but it felt like a little adventure, so I was into it.

Sometimes, when Maggie would talk, she'd start one sentence and finish it with a completely different one. Then she'd correct herself, finish the first sentence, and start the third sentence with the end of the second sentence. Even though it could sound a little scattered, she was still confident, like she trusted herself and knew she'd get to the point. She was still in control.

Patting Mags and me on the hand, Nic said, "Well, my dears, I've got to run. I've got an overnight flight. But you should stay! Keep ... being excited!"

We said goodbye to Nic, and as she walked away, Maggie called out, "Love you!"

Maggie went to the bathroom, and as I eyed our half-full drinks on the table ... I considered the troubling consequences for me if we stayed to finish them.

I checked my phone. It was 9:52 p.m. *Shit. Fuck. Etc., etc.* It was impossible for me to be home in the next eight minutes.

When Mags sat down again, she said, "Well, we can't just bloody leave half-sipped drinks on the table, can we?" She held up her drink to meet mine. A subtle glimmer of mischief swept over her eyes, and she gave me that cheeky grin again.

In two seconds, I processed three thoughts:

One, I was a dead man when I got home.

Two, Nic was right, this was exciting.

And three, I hadn't untangled a Maggie thought yet.

I let number three be the one that stayed in my mind.

Picking up my drink and tapping it to Maggie's, I said, "You're right. *Cheers.*"

8

Dinner for Three, Minus One

Maggie

I didn't bother making small talk with Chris on the way to dinner; I'd Googled the distance earlier and knew it was only a few minutes. In my mind, I was desperately trying to write dot points for the questions I had for Nic, but I couldn't put the words together, and it was frustrating the shit out of me. *Cherie told you to write them down, Maggie.*

I should have listened to Cherie. I hit my head back on the headrest and succumbed to the acceptance that it was just *who I was*. I felt lighter, remembering that, but it didn't mean it wasn't frustrating.

I was also distracted because The Alibi was one of the dreamiest places I'd ever been! Being there felt more like being somewhere in Greece, the way the sunset cast a golden glow over the white-washed ... everything.

I'd never been to Greece, but from July through to August, my Instagram feed would take me there vicariously through people I knew.

When we arrived at the restaurant, I ran straight for Nic and gave her the biggest cuddle. She looked so glamorous, in a tailored, sky-blue jumpsuit paired with five-inch heels because she was short, like me. And she smelled like Christmas in Switzerland! I'd never been to Switzerland, either. It's just how I imagined it in my head, like fresh pine and cinnamon.

Nic had a booth table for us, and I scooted in across from her and Chris. The restaurant was only lit up by the candles flickering on the tables and the dim sconce lights on the wall by the seats. It felt cosy. A little bit sexy, too. The kind of place you go when you're in the mood to give away some charm and receive it right back.

I gave Nic a teasing smile, leaning across the table. "Nic, it feels like you're taking us on a date! This is so ... *romantic*." I added a quick wink.

Nic replied, "Well, I kind of am! I don't mean to move too fast, but ..." She held Chris's hand and reached across the table for mine. "I think I'm in love, with both of you." She returned my wink with a radiant smile, looking *very* proud.

Giving her hand a big squeeze, I mouthed, "Thank you." I could feel my voice would break if I said it out loud.

Chris didn't say too much, but I didn't mind, because I certainly did. I was sure I sounded rather off my chops, to say the least, but I let it bubble out and over me. I was excited! Nic was dazzling; she created Sarah, in her mind! It was fascinating and I hung on every single word she said. It meant everything to me to be her Sarah, and this was my opportunity to make sure I would do it well.

I was trying to take proper, deep breaths and remind myself to slow down and not babble. But I don't think it worked.

"Oh, I love that part, where they are in the cabin; it's just so ..." My eyes darted between Chris and Nic. "Like the part when they are in New York, did you base that off a real experience?" I paused, biting my lip, thinking about the cabin again. "Sorry, but the cabin scene is just *so* dreamy." I cocked my head. "And the real-life experiences, how much of the show is based on them? I want to make sure I carry that, too." I smiled, eyes wide and waiting for her response.

Nic glanced at Chris and shook her head, but she kept her smile, so I didn't think it was a bad thing.

"Maggie, Maggie, Maggie," she said, shaking her head again. "You are a treasure. So much like Sarah. And, yes, New York *actually* happened." She winked at me again, and I pretended to faint in my seat because the New York chapter of the book was utterly riveting. As a fan, I was ecstatic to know that it really happened.

Nic got up to leave because she had to catch a flight, and I told her I loved her as she walked away. I couldn't help it; it burst out from my lips. When I loved someone, I just ... told them.

Chris and I both had glasses half full, so I said, "Well, we can't just bloody leave half-sipped drinks on the table, can we?"

I held my drink up, and for a couple of seconds, I thought he was going to leave me hanging. He took an awkward extra second of consideration. I let my shoulders relax when he picked up his drink and tapped it against mine.

"Very true," he said, with a little smirk. "Cheers."

A little bit of awkwardness lingered at the table ... Chris was just ... staring at me.

It felt kind of intense, because his eyes really were like two, glowing orbs. Big, round, and a deep midnight shade of blue in the dim light. He was dressed casually, in a white T-shirt with a band name I didn't recognise, loose-fitting black trousers, and Converse sneakers. He'd tucked his sunglasses in the neckline of his shirt, and I noticed the necklace resting at the base of his neck. It was pearl, with little gold bits in between.

I really liked necklaces on men. Quite a lot, actually. Once I noticed it, I decided it was better to keep my eyes on the orbs instead.

Trying to embrace the awkward and lean into it, I said, "So, dinner for three, minus one, hey?"

Chris smiled. "Ha, yeah. I guess so." He shrugged, still staring.

Diverting us back to Sarah and Liam, I asked, "Do you feel like you're Liam? Like a bit, for real?"

"Oh, absolutely." He nodded. "Do you feel like Sarah? Nic looks at you like a mother, like she gave birth to you or something."

I giggled trying to swallow my drink. Looking into Nic's eyes did feel similar to looking into my mum's.

"Yeah, she basically did. I'm *very* Sarah."

"Yeah, I can tell," he said, tapping his temple. "What you wore at the read was exactly how I pictured her in my head in that scene. It kind of freaked me out."

"Oh," I said, my eyes widening. I was a little surprised, but not shocked. "Well, sorry for freaking you out." I leant my elbows on the table and cradled my head in my hands. "It's probably going to happen a lot."

He smiled, struggling to swallow his mouthful, too.

We stayed at the table and yapped for a while, tripping and falling into another three drinks each. Once Chris relaxed, he was nothing like I *thought* he would be. He was actually everything I *hoped* he would be. That was exciting to discover, and honestly, it filled me with a sense of relief.

He was generous in the way he told me so much about living in L.A. and being an actor. He didn't hold back the truth of it all, which was mostly that it's fucking hard. There was a slightly singed tone in his voice; I thought maybe he was a little jaded. But that would disappear when he'd talk about acting and not the Hollywood ring around it.

It mattered that we had chemistry, but acting with someone you could trust was even more important than that. And I knew I could trust Chris because I could tell he'd let me rip him off. He could laugh at himself, like he knew his life was ridiculous in a "fuck it, if you don't laugh, you cry" sort of way. It made my insides feel safe, like it'd be easy to just ... be myself around him.

Necking his last mouthful, he leaned right into me across the table. His gaze was intense. Piercing, even. The glow in his eyes was blazing.

"Maggie," he said, edging even closer. "I think you're kind of like a duck."

I almost spat laughing. *"What?* What are you talking about?"

He elaborated, "You're sitting here, right now, in front of me. And you're floating along in this ... dreamy way. But under the water, I can tell. Little feet are trying to go as fast as they possibly can." He moved his fingers back and forth in front of my face.

I pursed my lips to trap the bubbles of giggles from bursting in my chest. He took me by surprise because he was dead right. I wanted to tell him he was right, but I didn't want to give him the satisfaction of saying it plainly.

"Well," I said, acting smug. "Quack quack then, I guess."

I shrugged, downing the rest of my drink as he laughed, shaking his head. Then I grabbed my bag to make the "let's go" signal.

We left through a side door of the restaurant, which made me feel *cool* and *mysterious.* Those were two unusual feelings for a yapper like me, but I liked it. Sweet Marco was waiting in the car right outside the door.

"Marco will take you home. It's fine," Chris said.

"No, no, it's okay. I'll walk." I poked my head through the passenger-side window of the car. "But thank you anyway, *Sweet Marco."*

Chris wasn't happy with my answer. "Are you sure?" he asked. "Where are you going? Is it far?" He looked almost offended, kind of childish, like I was trying to take away his favourite toy.

I giggled through my reply. "I'm going to Cherie's; it's not far. I sort of live there, until we start and they put me in the hotel."

"Oh, yeah sure," he said, nodding. He briefly stared at me again, tilting his head. Then he shook it quick and said, "Okay, cool."

He put his arms out, and as I hugged him goodbye, he took a big breath in and held it … even after I let go. I started to walk backwards, waiting to see if he'd let out that breath.

"That was fun," I said, watching for the exhale. "I'm keen to start filming."

Chris replied, "Yeah, me too." Then he let out the breath in a quick, sharp exhale. He smiled and cocked his head. "What does 'keen' actually mean?"

I rolled my eyes, smiling back at him. "Don't worry, you'll be saying it soon." Then I blew him a kiss, and turned to start the walk home.

Almost at Cherie's, I thought about how my mum would always say that I'd been here before. I definitely felt like I'd met Chris in some strange past life. And now, we were here, colliding in the strange present.

Chris himself was very present. He met me where I was when I talked to him. He didn't try to take us anywhere other than the moment we were living in. I knew we would become really close, really quickly.

I felt thankful that it was him who was cast as Liam. It could have been someone else, someone who didn't like my silly little jokes, or someone who didn't like … wearing necklaces.

When I walked inside at Cherie's, she was awake with Jill, sipping a glass of red on the couch.

"Oh, may I join?" I asked, but I was already pouring myself one.

I plopped onto the couch and stared up at the ceiling for a few seconds, daydreaming about the night like it hadn't happened yet. *But it is happening, Mags. For real.* I turned to Jill and Cherie, beaming so hard my eyes welled up.

Jill asked, "So, how was it?"

I knew my voice would crack, but I managed to say, "It was *really* great. Like really, really, really …" As I trailed off, Jill wrapped her arm around me, popping a little kiss on my head.

"Good on you, Mags," she said. "Take it all in."

I knew I would *take it all in*, because every single night when my head hit the pillow, I'd get these feelings deep in my core. Like the little electric sparks I'd only ever really feel when I was acting.

Sometimes, when the feeling would course through my bones, it would hurt, like growing pains. But I'd let it hurt and do its thing, because I was ready.

9

La La Land

Maggie

Looking around on set for *More of You* felt like watching a big, kaleidoscopic collision of my daydreams and reality. From the moment we started filming, it was like there was no boundary between them! It made me feel sparkly and jittery, like the air around me had an electric crackle. Every so often, it would jolt me down to Earth, and the sensation would remind me that *this was real.*

It didn't take long to feel like I'd landed right where I was meant to be. Being *woo-woo* and a little *de-lulu* had paid off! And I was livin' la vida la-la land. *Big time.*

Alicia, who did my hair and makeup every day, was amazing. She wore these hot pink glasses and had short, fire-red hair. She told the story of who she was in what she wore, and I loved her for it. Her fiery personality matched her hair, too. She'd share a lot of hot takes, but she could back them up, and she wasn't fazed if you didn't agree.

Alicia didn't like Chris at all, which tickled my ribs because their interactions were always a little awkward. Chris mostly avoided her, but he couldn't when Chelsea was around. Alicia was also Chelsea's personal makeup artist, so they were close.

The rest of the crew were all so fun and smiley, and the energy was nearly always high. Chris, Dom, and a few others would zip around on skateboards. Chris was really good at it; he could do tricks, like the ones in the *Tony Hawk Pro Skater* PlayStation game.

I learned quickly that he was that annoying type of person who could just ... excel at anything. If you handed him a basketball, I'd make a bet he'd slam dunk it.

I wanted to know Chris's secret to being a jack of all trades, so on our fifth day on set I brought it up over lunch.

"I feel like you're the kind of person who can just *do* things," I said, narrowing my eyes. "Tell me the secret."

Chris smirked, amused. As he leaned across the table, the smirk grew.

Then, it vanished, and he said, "No." When he slumped back in his chair and crossed his arms, the smirk returned.

I huffed and frowned. "Why are you gatekeeping?"

He looked at me, poker-faced, swinging back on his chair. "You didn't say please."

I rolled my eyes, and with exaggeration in my tone, I asked, "Can you, *please*, tell me the secret?"

He chuckled, shaking his head. "There's not really a secret."

Rocking his chair forward, he leaned in, clasping his hands on the table. "You just learn a lot of tricks when you're a Hollywood circus animal."

I huffed again, disappointed, and he shrugged with an apologetic smile.

As the days went on, Chris and I continued to bond quickly on set the way most twenty-somethings do in the workplace. By sharing food. It started when he caught me pouring chocolate oat milk into my coffee.

"What the hell?" he said, astounded at the carton by the coffee maker. "You have *chocolate milk* in your coffee?"

"Uh-uh," I said, shaking my head. "Don't knock it 'til you try it. I'll make you one."

I made another shot of coffee, steamed the chocolate milk, and poured him one. I watched him take a sip, eagerly waiting for his reaction. He played it out, but I caught the glimmer in his eyes, and I knew he loved it.

"Yep," he said, with a quick, confident nod. "That's pretty genius."

Chris always made his coffee with chocolate oat milk after that, which was great for me because we never ran out.

The tables of food swapping turned on the second week on set. Chris was sitting with Dom, eating a quesadilla, and I noticed it had corn chips in it.

Pointing between their plates, I asked, "Does that have chips, like, in it?"

Dom was shocked. He practically shouted, "What? You've never had this?" I shook my head. "Maggie, I am making you one right now."

He meant it; he was at the stove prepping another one before I even sat down.

Chris chuckled and said, "He saw it on TikTok. It's pretty good." I wasn't entirely convinced. I also didn't have TikTok, so I'd never seen it.

After a few minutes, Dom set a plate in front of me with a fresh quesadilla on it. There was no way in hell I'd get through more than two bites. It was *huge*, and I was never hungry.

"*Bon appétit, ma chéri*," he said, in a near-perfect French accent.

"Bone apple teeth." I shrugged, taking a bite. They were on edge for my reaction. After a moment, I smiled. "Oh, shit," I mumbled through a mouthful. It tasted *so* good. "This kinda slaps."

I gestured a chef's kiss to Dom, and when I looked at Chris ...
I accidentally made a *Maggie in la-la land* mistake.

I blurted out, "That's, like, a solid fifty friendship points right there."

"What?" he gasped. "There are *points?*" His mouth hung open in one-third shock, one-third kind of offended, and one-third "this is hilarious".

Gosh darn it, Maggie. The friendship points thing was not meant to be a "planet Earth, say-out-loud" phrase!

Because my head was so messy all the time, I had to devise little organisational methods in my mind. They helped me cope with the scramble of picking up my thoughts and feelings about life and people.

Sometimes with people, I'd imagine a little points system in my head. The points would add up and, over time, solidify the friendship. It was silly and immature, and I didn't *rely* on it. It just helped me remember details about people I cared about.

"I mean, yeah!" I said, trying to sound like the blurt was intentional. "There are points." I shrugged again, smiling sheepishly.

Chris slumped back in his chair and folded his arms. "Right," he said, squinting at me. "So, what's the limit? What's it out of? One hundred? Five hundred?"

I threw my hands up. "I don't know! It's not a competition or anything. It's limitless, I guess."

Chuckling under his breath, he raised an eyebrow. "Interesting. What am I up to now?"

I immediately dropped my eyes. "I don't know. I can't remember."

He reached across the table and lifted my chin. At the moment our eyes met, Chris learned my *I am lying right now* face.

When I tried to think of a lie, my eyes would get stuck, round and wide like saucers. I'd hold a half-smile, mouth half-open expression. It was exactly the face that Chris was staring at.

He smirked, shaking his head just slightly, and he murmured, "You're lying." I scrunched my eyes shut, and he threw up his hands. "Just tell me! I want to know."

I shook my head and took another bite of the quesadilla so my face would do something else.

He wasn't giving up. "Tell me. I know you know."

I did know. It was five hundred and fifteen. But I didn't respond. I watched Chris's patience wear thin.

"Well," he scoffed, "I know what you're on. It's twenty-five."

"Twenty-five?" I almost spat my food in his face.

With a firm nod, he said, "Yep. It was five hundred and twenty-five, but I took five hundred off. Because you lied. So now it's only twenty-five."

I slapped my hands on the table. "Okay, fine!" Lowering my voice, I said, "Fine. I'll tell you." Chris leaned in close again, and I mumbled, "It's five hundred and fifteen."

He frowned, tilting his ear towards me. "Sorry, what was that?"

I sulked through a quick sigh, then I spoke up. "It's five hundred and fifteen."

He looked at me, nodded in acceptance, and smirked in satisfaction. "Cool. I've got catching up to do, then."

When he stood up to wash his plate, I felt satisfied that he didn't really take the points off my score. I heard Dom giggling next to me, reminding me he was in the room. I think he'd been staring at me, so I just smiled and shrugged ... again.

Before Chris sat back down, Dom said, "Chelsea's on her way, FYI. She messaged ten minutes ago."

Chris flopped onto the lounge by the table, letting out a sort of half grunt, half moan. I didn't let my giggle escape my chest because he rested his elbows on his knees, buried his face in his hands, and any silly energy in the air was instantly sucked right out.

Mumbling beneath his hands, he asked, "Did she say how long she's staying? Like, all night?" He lifted his head, his eyes closed. "And is there any possibility we can make that *not* be all night, please?"

I glanced at Dom, and he shifted in his seat a little, as if he expected the sharp look Chris shot him. He flicked his eyes to me, then down at his phone, and back to Chris.

Hesitantly and very softly, Dom asked, "Why don't you want her here, dude?"

I tried not to show a frown, but I'd picked up from day one that most of Chelsea and Chris's communication went through Dom. Chris and I had made a quick and solid bond, but the topic of him and Chelsea hadn't just organically popped up in conversation.

I honestly felt neutral about her. I mean, I knew she lied about seeing *Shattered Glass*. It was obvious; her voice completely changed when she said it. Lucky for her, I didn't ask what her favourite part was. I really wanted to.

My best friend from back home, Ben, asked about Chelsea over the phone after my first week on set. I told him how she came to set every single day, and how I noticed Chris would kind of change his mood when she did. His reply?

"I've always thought that relationship was like those fake Gucci bags people bring back from Bali. Like, looks cute and all, but if you look up close? Oh, *honey*, everything about it is just … *off*."

I completely agreed. Chris and Chelsea made my gut feel twisted. And that was a surefire warning sign of something that appeared one way, but really, it was something very different.

Chris hadn't responded to Dom's question. I thought maybe it was because I was there, so I scooted my chair out to leave.

"No, no, Mags," Chris said. He pointed to the table. "Sit and finish your food." He smiled at me, then added, "That quesadilla got me fifty friendship points, so you should eat it."

I softly smiled back and gave him a little nod. I felt like I was breaking a moment of trust if I left, so I sat down again.

Dom started to say, "She mentioned going to dinner at Travotti's with ..."

Chris cut him off. "Can you book that in? Please? Just book it for like eight tonight."

"Dude, you will definitely still be here then." Dom looked confused, shaking his head.

"Yeah, I know." Chris sighed. It was kinda dramatic. "Book it for her and whoever else."

I'd never heard Chris so *cranky*. He spoke sharper with every syllable. When Dom started typing on his phone, I think it made Chris even crankier.

"Dom," he said, his voice low and razor sharp. He had that piercing look in his eyes again, but I wouldn't describe it as *glowing*. When Dom looked at him, Chris said, "Just book it. Please, dude. I can't. You *know* I can't."

Chris shook his head, looking pained, and without a doubt in my mind, I knew what he meant when he said, *"I can't"*. It was exactly how someone would say they couldn't hold on to a rope any longer because it was burning the hell out of their hand.

Dom replied, "Okay. I'll do it now. But she's going to ask."

Chris retorted, "Just tell her I'll be there."

"But you *won't* be there." Dom shook his head slowly; I sensed a hidden warning in it.

In a matter of seconds, they had a conversation in their minds. Chris flicked his eyes to me, back to Dom, then back to me, and back to Dom again.

Then, through a deep exhale, Chris said, "I'll deal with it later. It's good. Thank you." He smiled like he was thanking Dom for doing something he hadn't even done yet. Chris's way of saying the conversation was over.

When Dom got up, Chris looked at me and moved to a chair at the table. He let out another deep exhale while holding my gaze, and I think I got it then. He wanted me to see that back-and-forth with Dom because he wanted me to *know* what was going on ... without actually having to tell me about it.

On his way out, Dom stopped at the door, turning to Chris. "You've spoken about, like, set rules, right? With her?" He flicked his eyes to me. "Chels just texted. She's here."

Chris kept a soft expression, but his words still had an edge. "Thank you, it's fine," he said. "And don't speak about Maggie like she's not in the room. She's right here, and she's not an idiot."

He gestured to me, and I dropped my eyes instantly, pretending I was deaf, blind, and mute.

He added, "This isn't her first rodeo, or kangaroo ride, or whatever they do in Australia."

I pressed my lips together, fighting the urge to crack into laughter at Chris saying "kangaroo ride" so genuinely. He was real for saying that to Dom, though. He was talking like I was invisible.

Before he vanished out the door, Dom glanced at me, shrugged, and mouthed, "Sorry."

Dragging his hands over his face, Chris groaned, "Ugh, *shit*. Maggie, Maggie, Maggie." He leaned across the table, clasping his hands again.

I had to know, so I asked, "What are the 'set rules'?"

He shrugged. "Just the normal, everyday ones."

"And they are?" I leaned in, mirroring him.

He was looking, like, *into* me … really deep in the eyes. "Well," he said, frowning a little, "Dom is referring to the whole *don't kiss in rehearsals* rule. If that's what you're wondering."

"Oh," I scoffed, realising it was obvious. "Well, duh. This shit ain't free." I pulled the most unattractive face I could muster.

He chuckled. "No, Mags. It's not." Then he shook his head, and his smile turned serious. "It's really not. So, yeah. Just … it gets messy. And weird. And trust me, I've done it. It's shit."

I put my hand on his shoulder and smiled. I appreciated him being real, but I was very sure I understood before he took it to that place.

Assuring him, I spoke firmly. "Chris, we're good. Trust me."

He nodded, smiling back at me. "I trust you, Mags."

Then I added fifty thousand friendship points for both of us. Mine on his behalf.

10

Rationalising Rational

Chris

Getting to know Maggie on set was so effortless. We just clicked, like we'd met a million times before, but it was only now that we had the chance to really ... connect. We became tight so quickly. Being around her just felt natural, and the chemistry we had definitely lingered. It always flickered, even between takes.

I was rational about it all, though.

In our first scene, I looked at her, and I was logical about how it felt. I knew she wasn't just there because I thought this would be fun and easy with her. She was there because a room full of people had decided that, too, even before I did. The same room full of people could have decided that the first woman was the one, or the second.

But they didn't. They chose Mags, and they chose me, because they loved us. Together.

And after *one* day, so did I. Like ... a lot.

We just had fun. *So* much fun. *Too much* fun. Astronomical amounts of outrageous, ridiculous, completely rational fun.

I'd get home from set, and my cheeks would hurt because unless we were filming a serious scene, we were laughing. Frankly, we'd laugh during serious moments, too, and get in shit for it. Cherie joked to the director that she had a title change to *Child Handler*.

Though Maggie really was the perfect Sarah. Sometimes, I'd watch when I wasn't in the scene, and she just dazzled. She was beautiful, honest, and radiant. She made Nic cry at least once every single day.

Most days when I'd ask Maggie how she was, she'd reply, "Livin' the dream! How 'bout you?" It confused me, because even when she seemed worn out, she'd still answer, "Livin' the dream."

After hearing it over twenty times during our first week of filming, she said it again on the morning we had a five a.m. call time … and I had to ask her about it.

Walking to set from our trailers, I said, "You always say that, but do you always mean it?"

She cocked her head. "Well, mostly I mean it, yeah! I mean, I *am* living the dream. But also, it's kind of a *meme*, I guess."

Still confused, I asked, "What do you mean? How is it a meme?"

"It's just an Aussie cultural thing." She shrugged. "The meme part is that it's very Australian to say it in situations when you're definitely *not* livin' the dream."

I frowned, trying to make sense of it in my head.

She elaborated, "Like, someone asks how you're doing, and you're sinking in shit. But there's a moment where you look at them before you respond, and you tell yourself … *don't say it, don't say it* … but then you say it anyway. That you're livin' the dream."

I chuckled. Australian sarcasm was a little absurd, but I thought I understood it.

A few days later, I'd filmed a scene where Liam was swimming at night, and even though it was filmed in an eight by ten-foot water tank, my lips were pure blue. I was jogging back to my trailer to have a hot shower when Maggie spotted me, and this is when I knew I got the Aussie phrase for sure.

From the steps of her trailer, she called out, "You good?"

I stopped in my tracks and faced her, making sure she knew how freezing I was. "Yeah, Mags," I called back. *"Livin' the dream!"*

She laughed, nodded, and I knew I got it.

I also thought it unfroze me a little, hearing her laugh. But I hadn't even had a shower yet, so I knew that wasn't rational.

In her downtime, if Maggie wasn't busy floating around, making coffee with chocolate milk, playing her Nintendo, or trading snacks with anyone who would swap her for something she found more interesting … she'd stay in her dressing room.

At first, I didn't understand her random disappearances. She was so charming, it seemed like it could never run out, like she just wanted to be around people all the time. But in the middle of a night shoot, at one a.m., I walked past her trailer and saw her lying on the couch, staring at the ceiling.

Popping my head in, I asked, "Mags? You good?"

"Yeah, I'm good," she said, sounding very sleepy. She propped herself up on her elbows to smile at me.

I confirmed, "Yeah?" She nodded, still smiling, so I followed up, "Whatcha doin'?"

She flopped back down on the couch. "Just recharging."

I leaned against the doorframe, just looking at her. She closed her eyes, and I got it, then. Maggie wasn't an unlimited fountain of charisma; she'd share it when she wanted to, and she knew her limits. She was smiling like she was watching her favourite movie, and I wondered what was behind her eyelids at that moment.

Taking one last, rational gaze at her, I said, "Okay, I get you. I'll leave you to it."

"No, silly," she chuckled sleepily. "You don't have to go. Come and sit." She patted the chair next to the couch, but she didn't move from her spot or open her eyes.

As I stepped into her trailer, she muttered, "Are you sitting, or did you leave?"

Sitting down, I replied, "No, I left. Sorry."

"Ah. Bugger." She giggled. And that giggle ... *my god.*

Maggie Marshall's giggle was the kind that, if you heard it, you were objectively an arsehole if it didn't make you giggle, too. Rationally, of course.

"So, what are *you* doing, Chriso?" she asked, still unmoving, eyes closed.

I thought I misheard her. "Did you just add an *O* to my name?"

"Yes, *Chriso.* It's your Aussie name," she confirmed.

"Right, right ..." I didn't love it, but I wasn't going to deny her a little extra letter on my name. Answering her original question, I continued, "I was just going to get something to eat. Do you want anything?"

She shook her head, a solid *no.* She still hadn't opened her eyes or dropped her little smile.

Too curious, I asked, "What are you watching right now? It seems good. Would I like it?"

She giggled again. "You wouldn't like it. It's boring. Too zen for you."

I scoffed. "Mags, I can totally be zen. What do you mean?"

She rolled over, opening her eyes and smiling at me. I coughed to cover up the breath it took away. I think she caught it, 'cause she changed the topic.

"What time do we finish?" she asked, sitting up slowly. She looked ready to sleep; her eyes were heavy.

It would be irrational to think about having a power nap with Maggie, so I stayed rational and just answered her question. "Probably three a.m. I asked earlier."

"Ah, *bugger.*" She huffed a little groan, sinking back into the lounge.

After a moment, I noticed her face shift into a small frown. She tilted her head, flicking her eyes over me a few times. There was something about me she was trying to read.

"What?" I asked, squinting at her.

"Chriso," she spoke gently. "Are you okay?"

Damn it. I immediately felt like I'd been caught.

Maggie saw through people. I knew because I'd seen her do it. She wasn't the type of person you could *not* be yourself around.

In an attempt at avoidance, I pretended to sound confused. "Yeah, of course. Why?"

"It's just ..." She sighed and sat up straight, smiling softly. "Sometimes you seem a bit cranky. And that's okay; people can be cranky. They can feel all of the feelings, all at once, if they want. But I'm not sure they should be cranky all the time about the person that they love, that's all."

Rational, Chris.

Through a forced, breathy laugh, I said, "I'm good, Mags. I promise."

"No, no." She frowned at me; it was a big frown, too. "We don't say *promise* when we don't really promise. Friends like us, we don't do that."

I couldn't help but smile when she said, "friends like us", and I instantly felt guilty about lying.

With a hand to my chest, I said, "You're right. I'm sorry. I am okay, though. I'm just figuring it out right now."

"Okay, good. That's good. I know you've got yourself. No one knows you like you do." She smiled wider and gave me a little nod. Then she asked, "But you know how you spotted me here, just now, recharging?"

"... Yeah?"

"Well, I've spotted you, too. And sometimes when Chelsea leaves, you look like you're ... *gasping for air.*"

I took a slow breath, holding Maggie's gaze. I wasn't surprised. Not one bit.

On our first late-night shoot, Chelsea came to see me on her way home from The Alibi. I was in my trailer, tired and trying to regroup. I couldn't be mad about her coming to set. I offered it. Admittedly, maybe stupidly, I didn't think that would mean she'd be there *every single* day.

When she walked into my trailer, wearing a pale blue mini dress I'd bought her for her birthday, I looked at her through the mirror. And I didn't feel anything. Nothing at all. It was like I was so drained, I felt empty.

I thought maybe it was just a moment of exhaustion, so I closed my eyes, hoping I'd open them and just ... be in love again. But when I opened my eyes and looked at her, the only thing I wanted at that moment was for her to leave. I repeated the process a few times, trying to snap out of it, but ... nothing.

She sat on my lap, slid her hands over my shoulders, and hugged me. I took a breath in, hoping again. Hoping that maybe it would fill what felt empty. I was tired, probably too invested in work, and the deep breath I needed would come back.

But it didn't. The air was all smoke; thick and suffocating.

Gazing at her through the mirror, I just knew. There was nothing she could do that would ever fill what was now empty. We'd changed. Well, I'd changed. I don't think Chelsea was ever going to change.

But I was rational, and I'd stay rational. I ignored what I knew, and chose the path *most* travelled. I wrapped my arms around her, felt the familiarity of her skin against mine, and let it bury what *I knew*, I knew.

When Chelsea left that night, I did *gasp for air*. I did it every time she left after that. Sometimes I'd physically clench my chest.

Whenever she left, it felt like she took every last inch of me with her, even the oxygen in my lungs. I dealt with it because it was all I had left to give her, so I didn't have a choice.

I'd walk back to set, see Maggie, and my lungs would fill up again. Just her presence alone would do it. She carried this joy, coated in that glittering, honeyed glow ... and I'd crave it. In between the lines of the complex rationales running through my head, Maggie felt soothing.

But then I'd consider the path *least* travelled, and I'd stay logical. And rational. Chelsea and Chris? We were endgame.

Maggie held my gaze from across the couch like she could carry it all night, patiently waiting for my response. It stung when she said Chelsea's name, and I think she knew it would, but she wasn't afraid of it.

Maggie was good at using words for their intended purpose— to tell the truth. Like she'd had a lot of practice, too much practice, for our age.

Eventually, I said, "Yeah, sometimes it just feels like I desperately need to breathe, I guess. Like, I feel it in my body. You know?"

She looked thoughtful and reflective, like she was trying to meet me in my own mind or something. She didn't want to speak unless she knew she could empathise.

Slow and steady, she said, "That must feel really ... lonely. And empty. And maybe you feel like you're ..." She paused, deliberating. "Like you're all out of love."

A gentle shrug fell from her shoulders, and her eyes didn't have any hue of sympathy. The way she held my gaze was steady, sure, and soft. Like her eyes could speak for themselves, and they said, *You'll figure it out, and when you do, I'll be here. And I'm here now, too.*

I mirrored her gentle shrug, and in response to her words, I said, "You're right, Mags." Then, responding to her eyes, I quietly added, "I know. Thank you."

Her smile grew; I knew she'd get it.

Twenty minutes later, we were blocking out a scene on set where Liam and Sarah have this passionate kiss that ends up on the kitchen counter.

Before the take, right when Liam and Sarah would start kissing, Maggie stuck her tongue out and babbled, "Blah blah blah, blah blah."

Then she giggled. *That frickin' giggle.* The sound of it was so angelic; I swear, something inside of me was healed. I don't know what, but *goddamn*, it hit different.

I giggled too, obviously, because I wasn't an arsehole. It was a rational response. It was logical; she was a bright light to me, and you can't see in the dark.

It made absolutely perfect sense to let her light me up.

11

Armour of All Your Fault

Chris

I don't know what the sign was for Chelsea, but when I tell you she found out that I didn't love her anymore ... I mean it. She knew. And from the moment she knew, she would go out of her way to make sure I couldn't breathe. It was like there was a virus in the air and, over time, it made my lungs *sick*. Every interaction felt poisonous.

I'd lie awake at night, looking at her asleep next to me, thinking of ways I could try talk to her about it. But I couldn't find the words; they didn't exist yet. And Chelsea would *never* accept that things *just changed.*

I'd work backwards in my head, trying to figure out when we checked out of the honeymoon suite and rationalise my way into what shifted between then and now.

It wasn't Maggie. I'd be lying if I said meeting her didn't give me a push, but it wasn't a push into her, it was a push into something else. What I was feeling hurt, and falling in love with Maggie wouldn't hurt. This was something even truer than the possibility of being with someone like Maggie. It was different; it was all me.

The guilt was so heavy when I'd think about how Chelsea would feel. She'd feel like it was overnight, but that wasn't true.

It was slow ... until it wasn't.

At first, I'd catch myself ignoring her, completely uninterested in anything she had to say. We'd be at dinner, and she'd be talking, but I just ... wasn't present. I'd try to tune back in because I'd feel like a jerk, but she became so predictable that I could check out. She never asked about me, ever, so I didn't have to worry about answering any questions about myself.

We'd go out, get too drunk, come home, and fight because I took a photo with a fan or bought one of her friends a drink. Then we'd have sex. And that was all normal, until the one time I didn't drink because I had an early call time the next day. That night, I saw it for exactly what it was.

Chelsea's favourite game.

Watching her, it was like it *turned her on* to scream at me, make me feel like I was going to lose her, then scramble my way back to her. I slept in the lounge that night, and she didn't speak to me for three days.

Honestly, those three days felt like I'd been born again.

Then there was the audition for Sarah. When she didn't get it, she cried, *a lot.* Mostly out of anger. She couldn't accept that it just wasn't meant to be. It had to be someone's fault. She built this steel armour around her, and no matter what anyone said to console her, it bounced right back off.

When her dad didn't answer her call after she found out, she turned to me and said, "You know this is all your fault, right? You're so public about our relationship. They'd never pick me, it would be, like, too obvious."

I was stunned speechless.

It wasn't even *what* she said, it was the fact that I believed her when she said it. I blamed myself, and I hated myself for it, and I'd get angry, too.

Before I could even process what was happening, I was sidestepping around her in the house like that awkward dance you do with someone on the sidewalk. I didn't even want to touch her, not even by accident, because it was so *toxic*.

It was probably then ... that she knew. It wasn't too long before I started on set for *More of You*.

She'd come to that set on a relentless mission to take all of my attention. One time, she stripped down into lingerie and waited for me in my trailer. I got caught up in conversation with Cherie, and when I got there, I only had five minutes.

I panicked, trapped under her gaze and hyper-aware of the consequences waiting if I didn't entertain her idea. So I surrendered, gave her what she wanted, and she'd take it like she knew it was killing me. But it kept her finger on my pulse, like I was still hers.

In a twisted way, thinking that she knew how I felt made it easier. I thought there was no way she could still love me, too. How could she? She *knew* she was the poison.

When Maggie noticed the cracks in my consistency at work, she wasn't the only one. Nic said something, even one of the guys in lighting said something about how exhausted I looked, all the time. The façade I was wearing had already fractured; then Cherie pulled me aside and pierced straight through it entirely.

Shoving her finger in my face, she said, "You need to get it together. I can see what's going on. Other people are relying on you." She glanced at Maggie, who was spaced out, staring at the ceiling again. "You're better than this. Sort it out. Now."

I nodded, assuring her. "I know. I will." I couldn't ignore Cherie's wake-up call. She was like a mom on set, and she was not mincing her words.

I booked a suite at the hotel, and I had to face Chelsea. All I needed was space. So I could breathe, figure it out, and think about what needed to happen next. There was no doubt in my mind, though ...

Chelsea was going to absolutely hate it.

I got home from set just after nine, which was already a bad start because I thought I'd be home at seven. After hearing me close the front door, she poked her head up from the lounge.

She called out, "You said seven! It went late again, what happened?"

I let out a tired sigh, knowing I'd have to silence any others, and called back, "Yeah, sorry. I'm not sure."

As I walked towards the lounge, she propped her head over the armrest to face me. "Are you excited to see me?" She smiled, waiting.

But I froze. I physically could not say yes. I'd never chosen the other option, and it felt like I was standing on the edge of a cliff.

... I had to jump.

"Chels." I sat in the armchair across from her and took a deep breath in. Through a tumultuous exhale, I said, "I need to talk to you."

She shot up, tapping the spot next to her. "Why are you sitting all the way over there? Come here."

"No, Chels. I'm good. I'm not staying long."

Through instant panic, her eyes darted all over me. "What do you mean? Where are you going?"

I held up my hands. "Chels, just let me talk, please." I looked at her, pleading. She nodded, so I continued, "I just need some space. I'm not ... feeling this. Us, I mean. And I'm not sure—"

"What are you talking about?" She spoke over me. "Chris, you don't mean that. You're just tired."

I could feel a small boil in my blood at the fact that she was cutting me off before I even began. But I knew I had to keep soft.

Speaking very delicately, I said, "Chels, please. Let me talk. I don't know what I feel right now, and I've been trying to figure it out. But I can't here, with you. I need space—"

"You're on set like all day and night. You're not even here with me." She glared at me, cutting me off, *again.*

"Chelsea, you are also on set, all the time. You know that it's fair to say that."

Her glare morphed into a fierce scowl. "And you don't want me there?"

I took a moment to respond. Holding her gaze steady, I made sure she knew the pause wasn't because I didn't have the answer. I needed her to understand how serious this was for me.

As I felt ready, I spoke clearly. "No. Not right now. I don't."

She kept her eyes locked on mine. I could see her trying to think of a plan ... so I tried to destroy the idea.

"This is happening, Chels. I'm okay with you staying here at the house. But I'm not staying with you. I need to breathe and figure myself out. I need space. And I'm sorry, but you can't change that right now."

She pressed her hands over her eyes for a moment, then snapped them back to mine. "Chris, you're not being logical right now. You know you're not. Think about this, please."

Right then, watching Chelsea try to poison my brain because she knew exactly how it ran, a little voice resurfaced in my head.

Maggie's voice, reminding me. *You've got yourself. No one knows you like you do.*

I let that thought wrap me in a little bit of light, and staying steady, I said, "This isn't about logic, Chels. Something has changed, and it's inside *me.* I don't know what that is, but I want to know, and I need you to support me. Please."

She tilted her head to the ceiling. "What about the event tomorrow morning? So you're not coming? I'll need to tell, like, everyone. And they will ask why."

"I already told Dom. He let them know. I'll be in a fitting, anyway ..."

She whipped her head back to me. "So, what, I just have to carry it then, do I? What do you want me to say to people? Like, 'Oh, he couldn't come. He woke up today and decided he hates me.'"

I shook my head. "Don't say that, Chels. That's not true."

"Well, what is true, Chris?" She threw her hands up and crossed her arms, waiting.

I kept her waiting, sitting strong, unmoving. I wanted her to see that I wasn't bending this time.

Before the silence became unsettling, I said, "Chelsea, please. No publicity, or press, or anything like that. We know, Chels. We know how hard it will make it for us both. I don't need some random person's opinion on this. I need to figure out my own."

I paused, expecting her to cut me off, but her lips were pressed together. I could tell she was internalising many reckless words, like they were burning the tip of her tongue.

While I could, I continued, "That's why I need space. I can't be smothered with other shit right now. I just can't."

To my surprise, she nodded. "Okay, I agree. You're right. So, where are you going to go?"

"The Bennett." She rolled her eyes, but I put my hand up before she could speak. "No, Chels, stop. It's so close to work. I've stayed there a million times. Don't twist it."

She scoffed, cocking her head. "You know what I don't get, Chris?"

"What, Chels?"

"I don't get why you treat me like I'm *so* stupid. You treat me like a child; you always have."

I sighed, considering the parts of those words that were true. "I'm not trying to treat you like a child. I'm not. I'm just trying to protect you. And us." I gestured in the space between us, but she rolled her eyes again.

"Oh, and you leaving right now is protecting us? Great idea, Chris. Real *man* behaviour." She jumped up and started pacing in front of the lounge.

I could feel my heart pounding in my chest. It was getting harder to breathe.

"Chelsea, I don't have anything else to say. I need space, that's it. I don't have any other words right now."

She burst into flames, furiously yelling at me. "So then get out! Just go, now!" She threw her arm out towards the front door. "I'm the one sitting here, trying to have a conversation with you, trying to give you what you need, and you've already given up! You're not giving anything back to me at all!"

My breathing stopped; I was suffocating. I immediately tapped out.

I jumped up, yelling right back, "I don't have anything left to give you, Chelsea! You've taken it! I've given every fucking piece of me to this. Chels, I am *suffocating*. I can't breathe in this anymore. I'm not asking you to give me anything; I'm just telling you I need space, *please*."

She took a step towards me, but I was done. Tapped out and tired of the same old shit. I stormed into the bedroom to grab my bag and get the fuck out.

She followed me, yelling and scrambling, "Chris! Please, I don't want this."

"I don't care what you want, Chels."

"I'm sorry, okay?" She tried to grab the bag from my hands. "I'm sorry!"

I turned to face her. "And what exactly are you *sorry* for, Chels? Can you tell me that?" She looked shell-shocked. I knew she didn't know; she had no idea. I scoffed and shook my head. "Yeah, that's what I thought."

Dipping her toes into desperation, she kept scrambling. "I'm sorry that I'm not enough for you, and that I can't give you enough, but I try!"

"Chelsea." I was sharp. "You don't *give*. You *take*. And you're just angry that I'm leaving because you're not getting what you want right now. You're acting like a ..."

I paused, tore my hand through my hair, staring at her. Scared to say it.

She crossed her arms, challenging me. "Like a what, Chris? Like a child?"

I couldn't let her win. "Yes, Chelsea! Like a *child*. Okay? I can't take care of you like this anymore. I can't." I grabbed my bag and gave her a sharp look of surety. "I'm done."

She followed me to the door, so I spoke over my shoulder. "I'll call you in a few days. Don't call me, don't text me."

"Don't exist? Chris?" Her voice cracked. *Shit. Here come the tears.*

The guilt pushed an exhale from my lungs when I faced her again. I softened my voice. "Chelsea, you know I don't want that. You know I don't mean that."

Her eyes were full of tears. "You're telling me that all I do is take, but you're taking everything right now."

As she said those words, I closed my eyes. I didn't even mean to. I just ... did. Like my body knew how sick this was making me, and if I let her look at me when she said that, I'd never get better. Because I'd believe her.

The way she could take life and twist it between her fingers until it became the reality that she wanted to believe was astounding. And every other time, every *single* other time, I'd let it be my reality, too.

The look in her eyes would make me feel like I could fall in love with her again, like she could switch it back on when she was desperate. She *almost* had me. I felt so guilty that she was upset, I wanted to drop my bag, console her, and fix it.

But I had to choose what I was sure I knew. There was nothing to fix, and I couldn't breathe in this smoke. I needed *air*.

I forced a deep breath in. It was agonising, but I let it hurt.

I put my hand on her shoulder and kept my voice soft. "Chelsea, I'm sorry. I need to do this. I'll call you soon."

She burst into tears as I darted out the door, closing it gently behind me. I could hear her sobbing from inside until the moment I closed the door of the car.

Marco asked, "Good to go, Chris?"

I nodded, fell across the back seat, and let out the exhale. Then I cried, too.

12

Livin' the Dream

The third Friday of October came around, which meant Chris and I had a big day of promo rounds for *More of You*. I was so excited and nervous that the feelings blurred into anxiety 'cause I couldn't tell the difference in my body.

It was really just a handful of interviews, mostly for social media. We couldn't even talk much about the show, because we were only half-way through filming. It was more like a hype-train, I guess. Like the studio wants people to watch bits of Chris and me together, hop on board, and feel like they've "pre-ordered" the show.

I glanced over at Chris, and he looked a little ... *elsewhere*. I didn't get an opportunity to ask him why, but we'd been filming for almost five weeks. That's a lot of time to spend with someone. He was doing that thing where you stare off into nothing and jolt when someone says your name, like a crash-landing back to planet Earth.

If I was to take a guess, I'd say he was way up in the cosmos, trying to ask the universe how to get a refund on the Gucci bag he realised wasn't, in fact, Gucci at all.

I really felt for him, though. Even if I was wrong, whatever it was, I could tell he was frustrated by the way it made him feel while he was working. Chris had been living the full-time actor life for a lot longer than me, and I wondered if maybe the whole "blink and you miss it" thing was starting to take its toll on his mind. Like he was opening his eyes and thinking ... *shit. I wish I didn't miss that.*

Being on set is like getting thrown into this weird bubble, where time doesn't work the same way as the world outside of it. The hours are long, and the days feel slow in the way you get familiar with all the subtle details of the people you work with. But when the bubble pops, you blink, and you have no idea what day it is. It's accelerating and exhilarating, but it's also a little ... dizzying and disorienting.

In between interviews, I was feeling the dizzying part, and my right knee was tapping out of control. Chris had eyed it a few times, and I knew I needed to go somewhere in my mind that felt a little safer.

For me, that meant *silly.* Being silly was my safe space, where I could just be me without overthinking, or performing, or needing to control my brain to make it make sense.

Leaning over to Chris, I asked, "Maybe we could play a little game? You know, keep it interesting?"

He jolted, crash-landing. When he looked at me, he raised an eyebrow. "I'm listening ..."

I inched a little closer, speaking right into his ear. "When the next interviewer asks us how we are, we look at each other and say, 'Don't say it,' until one of us breaks. Whoever breaks first has to look at the camera and reply, 'Livin' the dream.'"

I flashed him a sly grin. He gave the idea a little scoff, shaking his head and folding his arms.

"Well," he said. "They're definitely gonna ask us how we are, so ..." He trailed off, deliberating, watching me beg with my eyes.

Come on Chris! Please, be fun right now!

He met my sly grin with a playful one. "Game on."

Yes!

I looked away from him and smiled, my eyes fixed on the doorway, waiting for the next interviewer to walk in. I knew I was gonna win.

Cherie was trying to speak to me through her mind, I could tell in the way she was glaring at me. She was screaming *stop messing around* with her eyes, which I ignored. Chris kept his arms folded, acting all cool and nonchalant about it.

When the next interviewer, Mark, sat in front of us, we all shook hands, and the camera started rolling.

Mark began, "It's so great to meet you both! How are you doing?"

I whipped my face straight to Chris. He tightened his arms across his chest, flashing a big, wide, mischief-maker smile.

We started softly, rapidly mumbling, "Don't say it, don't say it, don't say it ..." As our giggles and smiles grew, we spoke even faster. "Don't say it, don't say it, don't ..."

Yes! Chris broke. *Knew it.*

He laughed, threw his head back, and shouted, "Damn it!"

Uncrossing his arms, he looked at Mark and smiled. "We're *livin' the dream.*" He whipped his eyes back to me and gave me a *screw you* look. I just smiled and gave him a smug shrug.

Mark looked a little rattled, so Chris said, "Sorry, sorry. It's an *Aussie* thing. We are good, though, thank you. Please, do go on."

Mark responded, "That. Was ... You two are wild." He chuckled, looking at us like we were two children in adult bodies. He continued, "Fans of the *More of You* book are so excited for this show. So tell me, how excited are you guys to be deep into the process of delivering for them?"

Chris answered, "Yeah, we are so excited, we are having so much fun. I mean, *clearly.*" He gestured to me. "We're on set every day with Nic, the writer, who is just brilliant. And yeah, it's been awesome."

Looking between me and Chris, Mark asked, "Do you guys get much time to goof off and kind of, do the type of thing you just did, when you're on set?"

Chris looked at me to offer the answer, but I wasn't entirely sure I heard the question right. I was distracted, assessing Mark's watch and trying to see if there were two *L's* in Rolex.

My eyes shot Chris a quick *no thanks.*

He answered, "Yeah, we goof off. But also ... we usually get told to cut it pretty quickly if we get too off track which, yeah, we tend to do."

Mark asked, "Who's the troublemaker? Chris, is it you? Or Maggie, is it you?"

Chris and I pointed at each other, answering in sync, "It's definitely you!"

"No, no," Chris spoke up, pushing my finger away. "Maggie, it's you. For sure." He looked past Mark, gesturing to the room. "Everyone in this room knows it's you."

I glanced around; everyone was nodding, Cherie's nod was the biggest. I dropped my jaw, acting appalled at their on-the-spot betrayal. When I looked back at Mark, I shook my head.

Assuring him, I said, "That's honestly shocking, and I'm feeling really betrayed right now."

We all laughed, and Mark asked Chris one more question, but I didn't hear it. I was too distracted watching Chris smile and glow. He was present again, and that made me feel too happy to pay attention to anything else.

Expectedly, in a blink and you'll miss it kind of way, by the time we finished up, it was already nine p.m. I felt tired, dizzy ... but exhilarated, too. So, I also felt very thankful.

I was impressed with myself, because I'd managed to tame the wild yapper within, keeping at least some kind of mystery about who I was from the world. I didn't think I was the type of person capable of doing or saying anything "cancel-worthy", but it was reassuring to know there was less of a possibility of that happening before the show even aired.

On our way to the car, Cherie turned to Chris and me and asked, "What are you guys doing now?"

I yawned, giving away my response. Answering anyway, I said, "I am so tired, so probably going to sleep, honestly."

Cherie looked at Chris. "What about you? Are you going to just ride with us?"

Confused, I glanced at him, too. "Oh, are you not going home?"

He shot a quick glance at me, then at Cherie, who immediately vanished. That made me realise there was intention in the *look* she got.

"Yeah, I, um ..." he stuttered, but he caught himself and took a quick breath. "I got a suite at the hotel. It's just ... easier, right now."

Quietly, I asked, "You and Chels?"

"Yeah, Mags. Me and Chels." He sighed. "I need the space. To breathe." He nodded, but there was sadness in it, almost like he was apologising for it.

I put my hand on his arm, smiling softly up at his eyes. Gently, I said, "I know. I'm sorry. It's a lot, I'm sure."

He nodded again. "Yeah, it's ... yeah."

"It's okay." I linked my arm with his, picking up a slow walk to the car. "You don't have to have the words right now; you don't need them. Sometimes things just are, or were, or aren't.

And that's okay. You don't need to figure it out right this second. You'll know, when you know, you know?"

I giggled at how silly my sentence sounded out loud, and he did, too.

"Yeah, you're right," he said.

He looked down at me, smiled, and I could tell he already knew what he needed to do. But I couldn't say it for him, he had to go through that on his own.

In an effort to keep his smile in place, I perked up the tone and said, "When we get back, I'll get a key for my room for you. You can come by anytime, if you ever need anything, or if you want chocolate milk, or something."

Chuckling, he replied, "Maggie, you are the cutest person. And thank you, that's so sweet. I'll get one for you, too. We'll be like real neighbours."

My eyes widened at that exciting prospect. "Yay, fun!" I stopped us in our tracks, bouncing in front of him. Then I frowned, pointing my finger at him. "No loud sex against the wall, though, please."

He scoffed loudly and shook his head. "That *definitely* won't be happening. Also, I don't think I'm like, literally your neighbour."

I rolled my eyes and they landed in a glare. "You got the penthouse, didn't you?"

"No, no! Not the penthouse ..." He laughed, reaching for my arm; I had already walked three steps away from him. "Maggie."

I turned back to face him and gave him my *go on, give me your best lie* face.

Sheepishly, he said, "Just, like, a little higher. Like a few floors."

"Oh my *god.* Blah blah blah." I waved my hand in front of my rolling head. Then I added a little impression. "My name's Chris and I'm rich and famous!" He laughed, but I'd turned around again, striding ahead of him.

From behind me, his tone ... changed.

"You really are so cute, Maggie," he said.

That electric crackle in the air, the one that reminds me when things are real? Right then ... I felt it. I hoped he didn't see me jolt.

He really meant it, when he said it. And I think it meant a lot more than *cute*. It made me smile, but I didn't want him to see, so I just kept my stride to the car.

13

X Marks the Spot

I was sleepy on the way back to The Bennett, resting my head against the window. Chris and Cherie were scrolling on their phones, and I was glad we were all at that cosy point of knowing each other where silence is comfortable. You can check out, go mute, recharge, and just exist without needing to apologise for being boring.

Teetering on the edge of being asleep, I heard a sharp whisper from Chris.

"What the hell? Cherie look at this."

I lifted my head off the window to face them, and Chris was showing her his phone screen. I sat up straighter, my sleepy haze lifting with a sudden spike of curiosity. Leaning over, he showed me, too.

It was a video of what appeared to be a ... house party? The air looked hazy, and people were jumping into a pool, but it was so quick I couldn't see who they were. When I looked up at Chris, he looked pissed, and I was confused as to why he cared.

Cherie scoffed. "Ha, well. When the cat's away ..."

Oh. That would be why. It was Chris's house.

I watched him swipe through a couple of videos, shaking his head, then he opened his contacts, tapped a name, and held his phone to his ear.

He snapped, "Brooks, are you at my house?"

I couldn't hear Brooks, only muffles of music in the background, but whatever he said in response ... I don't think Chris liked it.

"Dude," Chris said, pinching the bridge of his nose like he was trying to stop his head from exploding. "I am working. I'm not going. Also, I don't think I was invited."

He tore his hand through his hair, tapping his legs and scrunching his eyes shut while he listened. I was trying to soften my stare because I knew my eyes were wide, glued to Chris. Cherie's were, too.

"Yeah, I *know*," he snapped again, tilting his head up to the roof of the car.

Cherie and I exchanged a glance, and she rolled her eyes *so* hard. I couldn't hold in the giggle in response.

Chris shot his eyes to me, and I snapped my smile back into a straight line. We stared at each other, momentarily, then he dropped his shoulders, exhaled, and started to laugh.

With a little shake of his head, he half-laughed his way to ending the phone call. "Whatever, whatever, I don't care," he said. "Brooks." He spoke firm. *Very* firm. "It's good. We're good. Have fun." Then he hung up, chucking his phone on the floor.

For a few seconds, we all just darted looks between each other. Cherie looked kind of smug, watching Chris drag his hands down his face like she was holding back a big, loud, *told you so.*

Or maybe she shouted it so loud in her mind that Chris heard it, because he said, "Cherie, I haven't even been gone two days!" He threw his hands up and slumped back into the seat. "Like ..." I don't think he knew how to finish his sentence, so he just shook his head again.

Cherie huffed, crossing her arms. "Humans in their twenties aren't ever their actual age. It's like you either act eighteen, but in reality, you're twenty-four. Or, you act like you're thirty-five, when you're only twenty-six."

I nodded in agreement. She was kind of right, I got it.

Being in your twenties was a sea of constant contradictions. It's like adulthood mingled with lingering adolescence, and most people stumbled through the balance between real-life responsibilities and youthful impulses.

Like, your friends still had house parties, and you'd show up with a case of beer and a new vape … only to look around and realise there were three pregnant women, conversations about buying a house and fixed-term interest rates, and someone had to bring their toddler because the babysitter fell through.

So, you walk over to the esky, and you put three beers in it. Then, you decide you'll drive home instead of calling an Uber, and you keep the vape hidden in your bag.

I sometimes felt as if being in my twenties was like an entire second puberty. Your mind and emotions are running wild, caught in the spaces between who you thought you were, who you are, and who you're becoming. It's unsettling, weird, and very much like the jacked-up version of all the shit you thought you were supposed to graduate from after being a teenager.

But, without warning, you realise there was no graduation. And this time around, you don't just wake up, go to school, and get told how to live. In fact, it's more like you've been catapulted into an involuntary PhD, without a guideline or guidebook in sight.

Now, you had to make all the decisions on your own, and even though you never really get taught, there's a hidden pressure—

Those decisions must be *right*.

It was a constant navigation of paradoxes, and right now, Chris was a little lost.

There was no map I could give him, though. I knew that.

I knew, because I had already seen what X was, on that map. And I think anyone could find it ... if they searched in the mirror long enough.

14

Heavy on the Comedown

Chris

When I was sixteen, I was cast in a movie about World War II. Dom swindled me into it, somehow. He just knew people, who knew other people ... who knew people.

I wasn't a lead, and I didn't even have a name, just *Young Guy 2*. I only ended up with one line and twenty seconds of screen time, but it was my start. I was hyped about it.

It was my first taste of what it felt like to be real actor, and it tasted damn good. But I tasted something else, too. Something I decided, at sixteen, that I would never, ever, want to taste again.

I was walking to set when I overheard the lead actor's manager on the phone in a dressing room. It sounded intense, but I was sixteen and immature ... so I snooped.

Hiding behind a costume rack by the door, I heard him say, "He's going to burst. Be here at four, maybe even three. He will. Oh, he will. And trust me, you'll get the shot."

He hung up, so I bolted to set. When I saw Marcel, the lead actor, it made sense. I didn't know much about drugs at the time, but I know now. And that poor guy was comin' down *hard*.

He looked like shit. Really, he did. And his manager, the person that he trusted to take care of him, protect him, take his ten percent, and not be a dick about it ... was setting up paparazzi shots.

It infuriated me, and in my youthful arrogance, I took my bold arse straight to Marcel to tell him upfront. I was stopped in my tracks, though. Marcel was coming down hard and fast, and I think I watched him hit rock bottom in real time. Without a word, he stood up ...

And he punched the director square in the face.

Dom ran over to me and another young guy, *Young Guy 1*, and yanked us right off that set. I remember Dom sitting us down, scrambling and stuttering through some knock-off inspirational speech about how "violence isn't a measure of a man's worth," or something like that.

Dom was only twenty-four, and, ironically, still had bruising around his right eye from a bar fight he got caught in. But good on him for trying, I guess.

I looked up at Dom, scrambling and stuttering, and I decided, right then. Even though I loved him like he was my own big brother, he would only get *one* chance with me.

One.

If he, or anyone in my circle, ever tried to screw me over like that?

They'd be done.

After checking into The Bennett, my filming schedule really ramped up on the night shoots. Liam was quite the sly and sneaky type. Lived most of his life between ten p.m. and four a.m., so I was discovering.

I finally had a call time that was decent, nine-thirty a.m. I slept in, kind of, like my mind had woken up, but my eyes hadn't yet. I could feel my phone buzzing somewhere in my sheets. Someone was calling me, over and over.

Fumbling around until I found it, I opened one eye to see who it was.

Oh, gee. Thanks, Maggie Marshall. Mags had threatened to change Cherie's contact in my phone to read *Chez*, and clearly, she'd gone through with it. Chez had called me eight times.

When she tried again, I answered, "Yeah?"

"Oh, well, good morning to you too, sunshine." Her response was stone cold. Chez was *pissed*.

"Sorry," I said, smiling so my voice would sound chirpier. "Good morning, how are you?"

She ignored my question. "I need to tell you something. And because I can tell you're already lying down; I'm going to come right out with it."

I frowned, sitting up in bed. The first person I thought of was Mags. Something happened to her, and it was bad.

"Where's Mags?" I asked. "Is she okay?"

Sharp and direct, she replied, "It's not Mags. It's Dom."

Oh crap. Something bad happened to Dom.

"What happened?" I asked through a breath. My heart felt ... jumpy.

"Chris," Cherie started, but she paused. I felt my heart jump again when I heard her pained groan. "I am so frickin' sorry right now. I just ... ah, *shit*." I heard a loud slap of her hands on something hard.

"Chris," she repeated, her voice tight. "Dom slept with Chelsea. I'm sorry."

What? I couldn't get the word to escape my lips. It was stuck in my brain.

I blinked hard, forcing it out. "What?"

"You heard me." She was blunt, meaning no-nonsense.

I needed to hear it again, to be sure. "No, Cherie. Say it." My breath hitched. "Say it again."

Cherie's breath was heavy on the other end of the line. "Chris, Dom was at the party, at your house, and he stayed. With Chelsea. And they slept together."

Impossible. That's an impractical method of operation. Dom wouldn't do that.

My chest tightened. *How do I know he wouldn't?* Rapidly breathing, I tried to calculate, but I had nothing. *I don't … know that.* I couldn't think of one thing about Dom's life from the last three months.

I blinked. For too long. And I missed this. *I've had my fucking eyes closed.*

I never anticipated that a decision I'd made at sixteen would actually come to fruition, but here we were. I'd already decided, so without another thought, I knew.

Dom was done.

Cherie continued, "I just got off the phone with him. He was crying and blubbering about it, and …" She tried to talk me through what he said, but I didn't care. It was background noise at this point.

I cared about the one *fact.* Dom was my guy, my frickin' day one. And he'd just annihilated that.

And Chelsea? Well, I guess there were two facts. She didn't surprise me. I would bet that she thought she had, in choosing *Dom.* But she hadn't.

With Cherie still on the line, I ripped the sheets off me, grabbing the closest shirt and pants I could find. "Cherie, with love, I'm going to stop you right there," I said, pulling my shoes on. "I don't care. I don't give a single fuck what Dom said."

I picked up my keys, put on my sunglasses, and stormed out the door. Through a clenched jaw, I spoke low into the phone. "He's done, Cherie. Done."

"What do you want me to do, Chris? Fire his arse?"

Cherie being as pissed at Dom as me wasn't helping lower my anger, but I loved that she gave a damn. I didn't want a snoop in the hotel to hear me on the phone, so I waited for the elevator doors to close before I responded.

The second they shut; I raised my voice. "I said he was done, Cherie. I'm not dealing with it. Deal with it. Please."

Chelsea had already stripped every last fibre of my being, so she felt compelled to seize someone else I loved, too. It was as if she was trying to completely erase my existence. But she wasn't going to—I was going to let her know that.

With a tight grip on the car keys in my pocket, I said, "I'm taking my car, Cherie. I'm going home."

"Chris, you better show up today," she edged the volume up, almost daring me to argue. "Deal with it on the weekend, when you've got time. Just show up today."

"I'll be there." I climbed into my car. "But I'm going home first. Deal with him for me, please."

"Okay, consider it done."

I hung up on her as I started the engine, and for a split second ... I went numb.

Then, in one fast heatwave through my body, as my foot hit the gas, I was burning alive. This burning alive didn't have the type of flames I could shrink down through logical reasoning. There was no *think*. It was all *do*. I was only in my body, and it was on blazing fire.

The hour drive to my house took me thirty minutes, and in those minutes my hands didn't stop shaking once. When I pulled into my driveway, I slammed the car door, hoping it would wake Chelsea up if she wasn't already laying by the damn pool.

I was in my front door in five seconds flat, slamming it behind me, too.

"Chelsea!" I shouted, and it echoed.

A voice called back, "Hello?" It wasn't Chelsea's.

Moving through the house, I heard murmuring coming from the bedroom. Halfway down the hallway, Chelsea's friend Liv popped out and stopped me.

My jaw still tight, I said, "Liv, where's Chels?" When she shook her head, I took a page from Cherie's no-nonsense book. "Don't lie, don't mess with me, just tell me. Now."

Stepping closer, Liv held her hands up. "Calm the hell down, first of all. You can't come in here like this."

I took a step closer, too, narrowing my eyes in her face. "I can't come in here like this, Liv? Really? My own house?" I side-stepped her, she followed, and I pushed the bedroom door open.

There she was. Sitting on the end of the bed, crying.

I felt like a fucking psychopath, glaring at Chelsea. There wasn't any piece of my body, mind, or heart that felt bad for her in that moment. I didn't feel *good* about that. I didn't feel *good* about the growing realisation that I'd let this happen.

But I didn't know what I was supposed to feel, either. So it was more of a *fuck it, I'm already on fire, so let's just burn this whole thing to ashes.* At least, maybe that way, Chelsea would experience the heat for once.

Before I could open my mouth, Liv jumped in. "Chris, seriously, calm down."

My hands were trembling again, eyes darting between Chelsea and Liv. I doubted a *single* tear of Chelsea's could be verified. She could act. And pretty well, too. But it wasn't going to put me out, because so could I.

I turned to Liv and softly smiled. "Liv, I'm sorry. You're right." I even threw in a hand on my heart for good measure.

Then I whipped to Chelsea. "And Chels? Chelsea?" I kept my voice soft, almost sweet. She wouldn't look at me, so I took a few strides closer. "Chels? Why can't you look at me right now?" I dialled up the sweetness. "What is it?"

Throwing my hands up with an extra sugary smile, I said, "I heard I missed a fucking *rager* on the weekend, Chels!"

She didn't make a sound.

I crouched down to her level, ducking my head beneath hers, so she didn't have a choice but to look at me.

Low and sharp, I said, "Chelsea. I want you to pack your shit. Every last thing. Get the hell out of my house. Today."

Quietly, she stuttered, "Chris. I'm ..."

She paused, flicked her eyes to me, I caught them roll, and it took about one-and-a-half seconds for the chilli to hit sweet in the sugar I was dishing out.

I was on fire again. "You're what, Chels? Sorry? No, no ..." I scoffed, shaking my head. "*That* is impossible." I jumped up. "What, are you embarrassed? That Liv knows?" I pointed at Liv, who put her hands up and stepped back. "That Liv can see who the fuck you are?"

Chelsea looked at Liv, pointing out the door. "Liv, just go out there, it's fine."

Liv scampered away, awkward and shocked, but right then, I didn't care.

Looking at me, Chelsea continued, "Chris, Dom told me you knew. He said he told you."

I looked at her baffled. "I'm sorry, *Dom* said *he* told me? Really? And you believed that?" She shrugged, shook her head, like it was obvious.

I went on, "Chelsea, I am looking at you *fake* crying right now. You're on *my* bed; the *same* bed, too, I'm sure." I know she knew what I meant, and she confirmed it with her eyes. "Fucking spare me, Chels. Because even I know you've got to be smarter than that."

"Well, yeah." She scoffed. "That's what he said."

I shook my head. "I am not arguing with you about this right now." Raising my voice again, I said, "Maybe he did tell me, but it must be in a frickin' letter because it hasn't reached me yet!"

I crouched back down, head in my hands. I was exasperated, starting to only singe myself instead of her. I was so angry, I almost started to forget why.

Then, she reminded me.

"Chris, stop," she said, her voice soft.

Still crouching, I looked up at her. *Give it your best shot, Chels.*

She continued, "I meant what I said last week. I want to keep trying with you, and I want us back here together."

I shook my head, closing my eyes, and she panicked. Her voice shot up as she shouted, "You're just looking for reasons to tear that apart and take that away from us. This isn't worth throwing everything away, Chris!"

I stood up, my voice low. "I don't believe you." Crossing my arms, I shook my head again. "I just don't. I don't. And I never will." I shrugged. "So, pack your shit and get out. Liv's still here. She can help."

"Chris, I need more time, I don't have—"

"You don't have anywhere to go?" I cut her off again. I couldn't listen to it. "Chelsea, I am staying in a hotel, so that *you* can be here. In *my* house."

She burst into flames. Screaming at me. "*You* said you wanted space! *You* said you wanted to stay there!"

With her finger pointed in my face, I thought of all the times I'd give in, kissing her in this exact moment. We'd have hot sex and fake smile our way through until it happened again.

And that scared the shit out of me.

I knew there was no way in hell I'd come back to the house this week. The hangover from this shit show was going to come with an epic comedown, and it was going to hurt. Badly.

I took a step back. "One week, Chelsea. *One week.*" She just stood there, stock-still in shock at the twist of me not giving in to her again. "I'm done." I nodded. "For real, Chels. It's done."

I stormed out, putting my sunglasses on in the hallway so I didn't have to look at Liv on my way out the front door.

I beat my time on the way to set. Twenty-five minutes. I was still burning. Everyone I passed on the way in stepped aside like they could feel the heat bouncing off my skin.

I headed straight to Maggie's room. I needed her to put me out.

Passing Cherie in the hall, I didn't stop. I threw the words sharply over my shoulder. "Does she know?"

Cherie nodded. "Yeah, she knows ..."

I didn't let her finish the sentence. I flung Maggie's door open and slammed it shut behind me.

15

I'll Show You My Fire
if You Show Me Yours

A strange part of the set-life bubble was that sometimes you could be doing next to nothing, all day, for thirty minutes of filming. Other times, you were in front of a camera for, like, twelve hours straight. It could be brutal, but today was a "next to nothing" day, so I was in my dressing room sipping a lukewarm coffee. One that I'd forgotten about because I got distracted ... when I thought I saw a spider in the bathroom.

We were filming at a different studio this week, which is why I actually had a room instead of a trailer. My name was on the door when I arrived! It felt like an upgrade ... but I still wondered if Chris's was better. My room was pretty bare, I think they might have run out of personality after the nameplate.

Forcing down a mouthful of lukewarm brain juice, I whipped around to a knock on my door. *Aunty Chez!*

"Chez! Yay!" I smiled, gesturing for her to come in. "How are you?"

She stepped inside, closing the door behind her. Her expression was painted in all shades of seriousness. She sat on the couch by the door, and I tilted my head, trying to read her.

Her voice dropped low. "Maggie." *Oh no. Full name alert.* "I need to tell you something. It's not good."

That is not how you should start a sentence to anyone, ever! Just say the damn thing, no pre-warning. The pre-warning makes it worse.

Extremely alerted, my eyes chaotically searched her all over. "What? What? Are you okay?"

"I'm fine," she said. I exhaled. "Dom isn't, though." And … I sharply inhaled.

Holding in the breath, I asked, "Is Dom okay?" The words barely made it out.

"No. Dom is fucked in the head, is what he is."

My jaw dropped. The exhale fell out. Cherie barely swore, ever. I think that was the second *F* word I'd ever heard escape her lips. I stared at her, wide-eyed and panicked. *Spit it out, Cherie.*

She took a deep breath, her shoulders rising, but I let her take her time. After a moment, she said, "Dom thought it was a bright idea to attend the party at Chris's house on the weekend. And then, Dom thought it was a bright idea to sleep over. In Chris's bed. With Chris's girlfriend."

I should've just left my mouth hanging open in the first place. My jaw dropped again, and I looked at her in disbelief.

She could tell, so she added, "And no … they didn't just *fall asleep.*"

Shaking my head, I said, "No, no way, Cherie. Dom is, like, obsessed with Chris. He wouldn't do that to him. And Cherie … Dom has been here, this week. On set! The party was days ago, how could he come here and pretend …"

"Sorry to break it to you, sweetheart." She cut me off. "He did do it. He told me he did it. I imagine the guilt of it was a *burden* for him." She threw her hands up, and I caught the blur as they moved, shaking in anger.

Straightening her posture, she took another steadying breath. "As you can imagine, Dom's arse is fired. So, he won't be around anymore."

It hurt, badly, to hear her sound so sure.

I was afraid to ask, but I forced the question out. "Does Chris know?"

Cherie scoffed like I was a fool for asking. "Of course, Chris knows. There's no way I was keeping that from him. I called him this morning, right after Dom called me."

I appreciated how upfront Cherie was. I did. But it cracked my heart to think about what the other end of that phone call would have sounded like. Or felt like.

Through all the mixed emotions, I stuttered, "So ... so what? Chris fired him? Did Chris see him? Speak to him?"

"I don't think Chris *should* see Dom. Maybe ever. I don't think Chris will bother speaking to him. I told him I'd take care of it. And believe me, I have."

Cherie had a wrath inside her I knew I never wanted to be on the wrong side of, so even though I wasn't exactly sure what she meant, I wholeheartedly trusted her when she said she'd taken care of it.

I hung my head in my hands, feeling angry, and confused, and sad, and ... uneasy about Chris's current mental state.

"Is he coming here?" I asked.

Cherie frowned. "Who, Chris?" I nodded. "He better be. I told him to suck it up today, and deal with it on your weekend off this week."

"Shit, Cherie," I murmured. It was coated in concern. "Isn't that a little harsh? Like where *is* he right now?"

I meant physically, to Cherie, but to myself, I meant his mind.

Where was he right now? It would have been dark, that's all I knew for sure.

Sighing, she stood up. "I'll go call him. He should be here soon, he told me he was going home first." She gave me a *look* on her way out, and I remembered ...

Chelsea was still living in his house. Chris was going to see her. *Yikes. What the hell was Cherie thinking? Letting him go like that?*

I slumped back into my chair, took a big, deep breath, and tried to start the process of ... *processing.*

I picked up my Nintendo and started playing *Stardew Valley.* I needed something to make my brain slow down. I couldn't process further without knowing Chris wasn't in jail for burning his house down, so I was running lines in my head, trying not to think about Dom being the worst person in the universe.

Then ... the room got *hot. Fast.*

Chris flung open the door and slammed it so hard it shook the walls, startling the crap out of me. My Nintendo flew off my lap and onto the floor.

"Slam the door a bit harder, yeah?" I snapped, giving myself whiplash at how quickly I turned my neck to face him.

"Mags, I'm sorry." His voice was rushed and panicked, his chest heaving. "I didn't mean to slam it." He shut his eyes and shook his head. "Or I did, I think. I'm sorry. Did I scare you?"

"Uh, yeah!" I threw up my hands, jumping up to grab my Nintendo off the floor. "Yeah, you friggin' did, Chris! What the hell!"

Chris's eyes grew wide, blazing. "Maggie, why are you angry at *me*, right now?" He helplessly gestured, pacing in front of me.

"Aren't you angry at *them*?" He stopped, pointing to the door.

I watched the way his chest moved quick, lifting with each breath, in sync with his shoulders ... I half-expected smoke to start blowing out his ears.

Slowly, and very deliberately, I sat back down. I knew he wasn't done. I also knew he needed to get it out, and not be judged for it.

"I know you know," he said, pointing at me. "Cherie just told me you know. I saw her, just then, when I came in. She said you know." His hand ran through his hair, tugging at the ends. He still wasn't done.

"It's fucked up, Mags," he snapped, pacing again. It was quickening. "Don't try and tell me that this isn't. It is."

He stood still for a moment, staring at me, his breath heavy and uneven. I think he was waiting for me to disagree. He expected it so much, he pretended I did ...

And he blew up.

"The one person, Maggie! The *one fucking person* she knew I'd suffer the most without! In my house, Mags! What the fuck?"

His hands tugged at his hair again, eyes wide and locked on mine like I was hiding the big secret he desperately wanted to know ... *Why?*

But Chris didn't even give me a chance to speak.

"Mags, why? *Why* does Chelsea hate me *so* much? I just, I can't deal with this fucking cycle over, and over, and over." His voice was starting to crack. "I should have ended it. I should have ended it last week. I should have ended it before it even fucking began."

He dragged his hands up his face, through his hair, and clasped them tight at the back of his head. "Two years, Maggie. And like, ten years, with Dom. Gone." He backed against the door, crossing his arms.

My heart was jackhammering wildly in my chest. I took a slow breath, trying to gather and organise all the thoughts, words, and feelings in my mind so I could share something that wasn't scattered and jumbled.

While I was searching, Chris tilted his head, squinting at me.

Under his breath, he muttered, "How long have you known?" He sounded accusing.

I scoffed, dismissively. Glaring at him and shaking my head, little bubbles of heat boiled under my skin.

He shook his head right back, speaking through his teeth. "Don't mess with me, Mags. Tell me."

I stood up, calm and steady, looking him dead in the eye. Squared right up to him, I said, "Ten-fucking-minutes, Chris." I didn't move.

His gaze narrowed. "That's a load of shit, and you know it."

He let out a sharp, bitter breath, and as he broke our gaze … I smiled. It was laughable. He really thought he was invisible.

I yanked the front of his shirt so he'd look at me. "You think I can't see you, right now?" I asked. "That I can't *feel* what you're trying to do?"

"What am I doing, Maggie?" He tightened his arms across his chest.

"You want me to feel what you're feeling," I said softly, a gentle smile on my face. "And you're afraid that I won't."

He looked at me like he was a bull, and I was a bright, red flag.

A few years ago, if this happened, if Chris showed me his fire like this, I would have tempered it. I would have done anything I could to agree, make peace, calm him down, and put it out. All because *I* felt uncomfortable with it. I would have felt scared, like I'd lose him if I didn't go along with it, if I didn't meet him where he was.

But I'd grown up. I wasn't scared. And Chris needed to meet *me*, where I was.

Gritting his teeth again, he said, "Maggie ... Don't do this right now."

I took a step back, throwing my hands up. "What are you gonna do, Chris? Light me on fire? Isn't that what you want? For me to feel what you're feeling?"

He shook his head. "That's not what I want."

"Please! You're melting right before my eyes!" I gestured wildly in his direction. "And I can see that it hurts, and it burns. But you don't get to come in here and just hand it all over to me, Chris."

He shook his head again, gently, over and over. His eyes completely softened. I almost thought he might burst into tears. Slumping against the door, he slowly sank to the ground, burying his head in his hands.

I think he might have realised that I could see him, very clearly, and he couldn't hide.

Before I sat down, I gave him a warning I hoped he would remember. "I've got my own fire. And I'll show you mine, if you show me yours."

He didn't reply, but he lifted his head and nodded. It was a sure nod ... he got it.

I kneeled in front of him, sitting on my feet, and I knew he'd hate it, but it was a waste of my time to say anything other than the truth. I wasn't wasting my time, on anyone, ever. I cared about Chris too much and too deeply to help him waste his time, too.

Like I knew for sure, because I did, I said, "Chelsea doesn't hate you, Chris."

"Maggie, I don't think I can handle this," he said quietly.

"No, you can." I smiled, nodding. "She doesn't hate you. She hates herself. And right now … You hate *yourself*, too." I let it sit; it was harsh, but it was true.

Chris closed his eyes so he didn't have to look at me. I knew he'd close his eyes. I was hard to look at, but I didn't move. When he opened his eyes, I was right there, waiting to look into them.

Through a vacant gaze, he said, "I don't know who the fuck I am, right now, but it's a piece of shit, Mags." Then he covered his eyes with his hands.

"No, you're not, Chris. Hear me, you're not." I reached over, moving his hands from his eyes. "You're angry at yourself, but you're angry at yourself because you know, deep down, you're *not* a piece of shit. You're mad at yourself for acting like one, because you know better. You knew better, weeks ago, maybe months, whatever. But you didn't listen."

He tried to cover his face again, but I gently stopped him. "No, don't. You're okay." I smiled and nodded again, continuing, "You're not just mad because other people betrayed you. You're mad because you betrayed yourself. And I think, maybe … that hurts a little more."

I held up my finger with a stern look on my face. "I'm not saying that what they did isn't horrible, and that they aren't stupid little … *weenie heads*." The corners of his mouth twitched upwards, and it did sound silly, that *that* was the moment I chose *not* to swear.

Leaning in, I placed my hands on his knees. "If you're going to get out of this, and prepare yourself, because it's corny, and you might cringe, but …" I scrunched my nose a little. "You're *really* gonna have to forgive yourself."

His eyes softened another smidge, gazing at me. He was present again. I liked the way it felt, to feel him here. But he needed time, and right now, he just needed someone to sit with, while that time passed.

He took a deep breath in and released it, slowly.

With the heat dialled down to a simmer, in a soft voice, he said, "I feel like I can't even process Dom, right now. But Chels ... Mags, *two years*. And I loved her, I did. And I know that I haven't for a while; I can admit that. But for a long time, it was everything I ever wanted. Like, I don't know ... what do I do with that?"

"Do you want me to write you a receipt?" I asked.

He rolled his eyes, but I interjected his thoughts before he'd dismiss me. "I'm not messing around. Haven't you heard of that? That 'grief is like love's receipt'. I think it was Glennon Doyle ... Yeah, it's Glennon Doyle, who says it. Have you read any of her books?"

He shook his head, pressing his lips together.

I giggled. "Well, yeah. I guess it's hard to read when your head's up your arse." I gave him a cheeky grin; he didn't like it.

"Ha, ha, Maggie. Are you done?"

"No," I said, crawling to the coffee table. "I'm going to write you a receipt." I grabbed the notepad and pen, sitting cross-legged in front of him. "So ... describe it to me."

"Describe ... what?"

I swirled the pen in the air. "The relationship."

"I don't know ..." He hesitated, trailing off into thought. After a moment, he said, "I loved her, a lot, at first. We have a lot of history, and fun memories ... But after a while, it just ..." He sighed deeply. "It just changed. Everything became like a competition. And we stopped making fun memories, and only made painful ones."

He frowned, continuing, "And it got worse, like, way worse, when she didn't get Sarah. She was just angry, all the time." He clenched his fists at his knees. "She'd yell at me; I'd yell at her. And then we'd, like, force smiles at each other for a few days."

"I'd try, Mags." He looked me sharp in the eye, so I gave him a little reassuring nod. "I'd try and be kind even when I wanted to leave because I *cared*. I just kept caring, even when I knew I should stop. I just didn't want it to feel like it failed, like *we* failed, and I wanted to protect us from that feeling."

He took another breath, punctuating it with a chuckle. "I was too late. Way, *way* too late."

As I wrote the total on his receipt, I said, "That's a lot, Chris. And it mattered, and it still does matter. You loved, hard. That's not bad, it's who you are. And this ..." I ripped the page off the notepad and handed it to him. "Is your proof. What you're feeling, right now, is the price you pay for caring, and for loving the way that you do."

He took it from my hands, and I smiled. He smiled back. It made me smile even bigger.

"Don't hate the feeling," I said, putting my hands on his knees again. "It's probably time you start making friends with it, because you're a beautiful person, and I don't think you'll ever stop loving people as hard as you do."

I watched him read his receipt, and I hoped he could read my messy handwriting.

But mostly, I hoped he could see himself. In the same way I was seeing him, right now, through my eyes.

16

The Everything Smile

Chris

Maggie handed me the piece of paper, the receipt, watching me as I read it. On it, she had written:

2 years loving = $1 billion

fun happy memories = $1 billion

painful memories = $1 billion

the times i yelled = $1 billion

the times i got yelled at = $1 billion

being kind when i didn't want to = $1 billion

wanting to protect someone I loved at the expense of my own self = $1 billion

subtotal: changing, realising I am better and the better me deserves better!

AND I am onwards and upwards to brighter days, baby!!!

TOTAL = PRICELESS!!! ♡

(no refunds)

The way the smile grew on my face, like as it grew bigger, every shitty thing I was thinking and feeling shrunk at the same time ... it was the *best* feeling.

I would never be able to thank her enough. For doing this, for being here, for making me smile like that. It hurt to think I'd always fall short. But when I looked up at her and saw how calm and sure she was, I knew she wouldn't want me to feel that way.

She didn't want anything from me. There were no conditions, nothing in a size four font that I couldn't read.

When I brought the fire into her room, hoping she'd put it out, I could feel that she wasn't going to. And I think at that point, I just hated how angry I was, so much, that I wanted her to feel it. Just to validate it, somehow.

But she wouldn't, and I get it, now. For sure.

Instead, she lit me up in a completely different way. It didn't burn or leave smoke. It wasn't suffocating.

It just glowed.

Looking at Maggie, smiling and sitting on the floor, right with me ... she really was so lovely to look at. I wanted to tell her she was my best friend, *the best* friend I'd ever had. But that didn't feel like enough.

I thought of the first day I met her, joking about *Stepbrothers* at the chemistry read. I thought about that day a lot. It made me smile, and breathe easy, and it reminded me of all the reasons that I loved being in love.

I think, also, it reminded me of who I really was ... or, who I wanted to be. I'm not sure.

I smirked, leaning in towards her. Then I held my thumb over my shoulder, and I asked, "Do you wanna' go play karate in the garage?"

Her smile in that moment was *everything* to me.

She threw her head back and laughed, *"Ab–so–fucking–lutely!"*

17

The Butterfly Effect

I spent the rest of the week on set being an absolute *ratbag*. I went full-feral goofball. My best friend Ben was coming to L.A. for a few days, and we had a full weekend off from filming. I was buzzing, excited, and I let everybody know about it!

Chris was ... up and down. I think he was struggling to process it all, especially the Dom part. He really didn't speak to him, not once, and he wasn't going to. It was an intense choice to make, but Chris was an intense guy, so ... he just cut Dom loose. I guess it was his way of protecting himself, his work, his mind, and figuring himself out without needing to figure anyone else out.

Chris did have therapy, though, which I'm sure helped. And rich people have therapists come to them!

His therapist's name was George, but in my mind, it was Grandpa George. He had the same vibe as a grandpa who gives out life advice while you feed ducks at the park. Chris and George would go for long walks around set. Sometimes George had a clipboard, it was a whole thing.

Whenever Chris would get a little *too* down, I'd play this silly game where I'd try to embarrass him by saying, "I got your letter," and then follow it up with something ridiculous.

In one of the moments I chose to be a ratbag, Chris was chatting with Cherie, and it looked heavy. So, I trotted over, giving Cherie an awkward, cheeky smile.

"Sorry, Cherie," I said, completely cutting her off. "Sorry to interrupt."

I shifted to Chris. "Chris, I got your letter. It said, 'To Maggie. I'm sad because I can never grow a nice moustache. I wonder if it's possible for you to somehow make me one, so I can feel what it's like, just for one day. Love from Chris'."

Then I pulled out a big, thick handlebar moustache I'd stolen from costumes and stuck it right on his face.

Stepping back, I cocked my head to the side, taking in the ridiculousness. At this point, I'd played my little letter game a few times, so Chris just went with it.

He glanced at Cherie, then back to me, before pulling out his phone to check himself.

Cherie, looking nothing short of baffled, snorted into laughter.

Chris turned to her. "What? Does it not look good?" Then he looked at me and flipped his hair.

"No, no," I said, fanning myself dramatically. "I think it looks *hot*, actually."

As I walked away, I heard Cherie ask, "Did you really write her a letter?"

That made me burst out laughing, too.

So, yeah ... it was goof week.

We'd just wrapped our last day on set before the weekend off, and Chris, Cherie, and I were having a cheeky bevvy in Chris's dressing room. I kept checking my phone every two minutes to see if Ben had landed yet, completely tuned out of their conversation.

Then I got his text:

Bitch ... ... your King has arrived!! omw to hotel x

I burst up from my chair and squealed, "Yay!"

Chris and Cherie stared at me, realising I hadn't listened to a word they'd said.

"Sorry." I shrugged. "Ben's here. He's on his way to his hotel!"

Smiling, Chris said, "Mags, that's amazing. I'm excited to meet him."

I sat back down, leaning into Chris. "Would you say you're ... *keen*, to meet him?"

Chris's eyes narrowed slightly as he leaned closer, a little smirk tugging at the corner of his mouth. "Very *keen*, Maggie," he said, adding a quick brow raise.

I'd been trying to get Chris on the "keen" train for a while, so I was satisfied to hear him say it. I didn't know it was such an Aussie thing until I came to L.A. I'd say it and people would just stare at me, so I'd have to self-correct with "excited" or "looking forward to it".

Cherie chimed in. "Maggie, did you hear anything we were *just* discussing? About Sunday night?"

I stared at her blankly ... then smiled sheepishly because I was a terrible liar.

Chris answered on my behalf. "That is a solid *no*, Cherie."

She sighed. "Mags, you and Chris need to go to the GQ thing. It's booked. I know it's last minute, and Ben will still be here, but I locked it in. It's necessary that we keep you both out there." She waved her finger between me and Chris. "This is an unmissable opportunity."

We locked eyes, glaring at each other. I frowned, wide-eyed, setting my jaw. I thought my face might have been enough to tell her I wasn't doing it, but her expression didn't change. She wasn't budging.

My time with Ben already felt fragile; I knew it would go by fast. Now it felt threatened entirely.

Crossing my arms tight to my chest, I squeezed my eyes shut. A little shaky, I said, "I'm not doing it, Cherie. I can't do that to Ben." I snapped my eyes open, locked back in the glare-off. "I've got *four* days. You're not taking a second of that."

Flicking my gaze to Chris, he looked awkward, like he was watching me fight with my mum for the first time. I looked back to Cherie, her face set in stubborn lines … and one tiny, fluttering thought darted into my mind.

You don't get a choice, Maggie.

I gasped a little, trying to stop it … but like a butterfly, it darted in anyway, hovering and whispering for my attention on the colours of its wings.

Cherie probably told you days ago. You forgot. Because you always forget.

Cherie leaned into me, resting her hand on my knee. "It'll be a few hours, Mags."

I pushed her hand away. "Cherie, it's never a few hours. And it's not *necessary*. It's not."

She crossed her legs, clasping her hands on her knee. It was confirmation. I knew there was no hope. I had to go to the event, and I had no control over that. I had to tell Ben our precious time was being taken from us. And with the feeling of knowing I had to let him down …

My face fell in sync with my heart.

I glanced back at Chris. He was watching me so intensely, like he could feel exactly what I felt in that moment.

Without thinking, tears welled up in my eyes, so I flicked my gaze up, trying to stop the emotion from slipping down my cheeks.

The feeling of guilt was so heavy, it made me feel helpless, and weak, like I wasn't strong enough to have any ounce of control over this dizzying, disorienting life I'd chosen for myself.

It had only been seconds, but I'd already run through a hundred different ways to tell Ben. Trying to accept that I didn't have control was tying anxious knots inside my chest.

My mind instantly fluttered through hundreds of darting thoughts, scattering through speeds so sporadic ... I couldn't keep up.

The world is happening to you, Maggie. You don't have control.

Swirling and scrambling, all my thoughts and feelings were tangling together, and I couldn't make sense of any of it. I couldn't catch a single word.

This is what you wanted. Smile, Maggie. Be grateful. Be an adult.

Without a pause, my mind spiralled into a pattern of chaos. I tried to take a breath, closing my eyes, but all I could see was a fluttering, frantic, kaleidoscope of butterflies.

I knew what was coming, because when my mind scattered like this, erratic and uncontrollable, it stirred up a certain ... effect.

The butterfly effect.

They say a single flap from the wings of a butterfly, anywhere in the world, can cause a tornado on the other side. Because inside chaotic systems, something that seems so small and insignificant can lead to uncontrollable, unpredictable outcomes.

In a system as chaotic as my brain, just a tiny thought can flutter in and steal my focus, even if it doesn't belong in the present moment. Before I could blink, my mind would overflow with hundreds of other thoughts, each one distracting me from the last.

Losing control, I'm overwhelmed by the twists and turns of all my darting thoughts ... and I spiral. It's like the chaos of my scattered mind takes over my entire body.

And that's when I start to *panic*.

Keeping my eyes closed, I tried again to take a deep breath, desperate to catch and tame even just a few of the swirling butterflies. But with the patterns in my brain, Cherie's unwavering gaze, and the dizziness of knowing if I closed my eyes too long, I'd miss something—I couldn't take the breath.

My eyes shot open, and I watched Cherie's lips move, but I couldn't hear her anymore. My right knee tapped out of control, and the chaotic rhythm of my heart pounded against my chest. Once I could hear it, loud in my ears, I knew it was impossible for me to catch even one, tiny, butterfly.

My lungs strained, trying to breathe, and the more I tried, the sharper my breaths came. Blurred and foggy, my eyes glazed over ...

Maggie, you're having a panic attack.

18

I Got Your Letter, It Says Ben

Chris

I was watching the two fiercest women I'd ever met in a standoff I didn't expect ... and I had no clue what to do with my face.

I empathised with Mags; I really did. When she said she wouldn't go to the event, I was shattered. I didn't want to go without her. But she didn't want to be without Ben, and it would kill her to give even a moment with him away to Hollywood bullshit.

I hadn't seen it yet, but I knew their bond was special. Maggie's eyes would light up at the thought of him. Honestly, I didn't like talking about Ben because I'd get jealous. He was gay, it wasn't *that* ... it was the face she made when she talked about him. It made me wonder if she could ever think of me like that, or if she already did.

I could see that Maggie was trying to take deep breaths, but they were hitching rapidly, and they sounded like small, panicked, sharp ones.

I had to step in. "Mags, Maggie," I said gently. "You don't have to go. I will go." I looked to Cherie, pleading with my eyes. "Cherie, it's fine," I murmured. "I can just go."

Without thinking, I reached forward, resting my hand on Maggie's knee. But Cherie yanked it right back off, shooting me a stern look that said *don't touch her.*

Looking into Maggie's eyes, it was like no one was home; they were vacant. Tears glazed over the pale green, and she wasn't looking *at* me and Cherie, she was looking right through us. She was out of this world, but not in her dreams. Her little white knuckles had a tight grip on the armrests of her chair.

The second I saw them, I knew—she was caught in her nightmares.

I wanted to jump straight in and rip her the hell out of there, or just do something, *anything,* to keep her safe from getting lost in whatever was filling her mind.

Glancing back at Cherie, I felt a low-key panic creeping in, pleading with my eyes again.

What can I do, Cherie?

She ignored me, leaning forward and inching her hand to Maggie's chest.

In a soft, smooth voice that I didn't know existed in Cherie's range, she said, "Maggie, it's okay. You are here. It's just me, and Chris, and you. We are here. Just breathe, Mags. You're okay." She didn't move a muscle, steadfast in Maggie's gaze.

Maybe it was melodramatic and too dark, but for a second, it kinda felt like I was watching Maggie die. The way she flicked her eyes between me, Cherie, and her nightmare made me sure she was lost somewhere dark. To me, Maggie was *only* light, but that light had completely gone out, and I didn't recognise her without it.

Keeping her voice smooth, Cherie said, "Maggie, breathe." Then she took a deep breath in, eyeing me to do the same, so I did, too.

As Cherie gently dropped her hand and leaned back in her chair, Maggie flicked her eyes to me again. She held my gaze for an extra second, and in that second—

I think I might've found a source of her light.

In her mind, she'd lost all control, but in mine, I realised ...

Maggie always had control.

From when she walked into the room at the chemistry read, to every time she walked onto set as Sarah, and all the moments in between ... Maggie claimed a space, and she lit it up. It wasn't in a way that needed to control the people or places around her. It was in the way she carried herself.

She'd glow like a halo circled around her entire body, captivating an entire room, and she wasn't afraid of it. Her control came from knowing exactly who she was, and that was a source of light for her. It made her feel safe. She relied on it; she relied on her light to get through. And it was hers alone to keep.

Maggie would never, in a million years, want to hurt someone she loved. And I don't think Cherie would, either. But to Maggie, it felt like Cherie was forcing her to. That would make her feel weak, dim, and far from the person she knew she was.

When Cherie took a little piece of her light, I think Maggie felt like she lost a piece of herself. So, she lost control ... and went dark.

That's how it looked through my eyes, anyway.

Cherie leaned, whispering to me. "We should help her lie down. She's okay. Move slow."

I nodded, eyes fixed on Mags, trying to remain low-key about the amount of stress her struggle to breathe was giving me.

Cherie put her hand on Maggie's shoulder. "Mags, let's lie down. You're so tired. Let's go to the couch."

As Cherie helped Maggie out of the chair, she glanced at me, then jolted her head towards Maggie's back. I thought it meant

Maggie was going to pass out, so I jumped up, nearly tripping over my own feet in the rush to get behind them.

But Cherie shot me another look, shaking her head slightly, and I realised she just wanted me to help guide Maggie to lie down. I also realised I should probably relax. You know, just a touch.

Maggie's little body melted into the couch, and the moment her head hit the pillow, she burst into a puddle of gasping sobs. Her hands shook as she wiped at her eyes; I had to catch myself before I reached out to do it for her. The way she looked at Cherie, the way her eyes said *help me* ... tore my insides up to watch.

Through scattered breaths, Maggie said, "Cherie, I don't want to miss a moment with Ben."

"I know, Maggie. And you don't have to." Cherie sounded assuring, but I knew she was lying, and it was hard to stay silent when I heard it. Cherie continued, "It's okay. You're here right now. You're not missing a thing."

I shot a disapproving glare at Cherie, but she was waiting for it, because she gave me a firm look, warning me to drop it.

Slowly, I crouched down next to the couch, sitting cross-legged in front of Mags. She rolled away from us and cried, but her breathing slowed; she was more ... *here*, than *there*.

Cherie spoke up. "I'm going to go and get Ben. Mags was meant to. I'll bring him here. What are you going to do?"

"I'll wait." I nodded, eyes on Maggie. "I'm not leaving, I'll wait right here."

I couldn't imagine the feeling of being alone after a panic attack. I'd never had one. I was sure Maggie would know, and I was also sure it would be painful. There was no way I was letting her switch her light back on alone.

Cherie looked at me like she saw directly into my heart, which made me want to hide because she was intimidating, but I let her, anyway. She nodded at me, smiled, and closed the door on her way out.

I sat in silence as Maggie's crying softened. I wanted to touch her so badly … rub her back, stroke her hair, completely wrap her up in my arms. Even without Cherie eyeing me the *rules of a Maggie panic attack*, I knew it would be breaking them if I did. So I just waited for her to come back.

I was trying to think of what to say to her if she turned around to face me. I blacklisted the thought of asking if she was okay; that felt pointless. Maybe I'd just say something simple, like … *hi*. Or maybe *"Welcome back"?* No, I loved teasing her, but not now.

Before I could decide, Maggie slowly rolled over to face me. She looked into my eyes, and I let out a big, deep breath.

There she is.

Her voice still a little shaky, she said, "You didn't have to wait. Your back must hurt, like, so badly right now." She giggled, looking at me sitting on the floor like I was eight years old.

I almost rolled my eyes. *Of course, she'd be worried about me, right now.* Sometimes she was predictably beautiful, but most of the time it was shocking—a sharp inhale.

"No, Mags." I shook my head. "I did, because …" A smile grew across my face; I knew exactly what to say. "I got your letter."

She giggled again, sniffling. "Oh, really? What does it say?"

I opened my mouth to answer, but before a single word left my lips, the door burst open like an M80 exploding into the room.

And there *he* was.

In all his glowing glory, illuminating the room so brightly it almost burned my eyes …

Ben.

"My beautiful, cotton candy, cherry drop, sunshine, badass little hoe … *Daddy's home!*"

He stood by the door, arms open wide. I could have sworn he was about to bust out into song or shower us all in confetti and glitter. It was one of the grandest, most radiant entrances I'd ever seen.

Ben winked at Maggie, and they both cracked into laughter and tears at the same time. He lunged onto the couch, smothering her in cuddles in an outpouring of affection.

Cue the jealousy pangs in my chest.

I sat on the floor, a little awkwardly, laughing at their reunion. Scanning Ben all over, I had to admit it—the guy was frickin' flawless. He had a jawline that could surely cut glass. Blonde ringlets cascaded over his forehead, short at the back, and he looked sun-kissed. Far too bronzed for having not long come out of Australian winter.

Once they collected their excitement, Ben stuck his hand out to me.

"Oh, how rude of me," he scoffed, acting shocked by his own audacity. "I'm Ben."

His eyes softened when I shook his hand. "Chris. I've ..."

"Heard a lot about me? All *terrible*, I'm sure." He winked at me.

I shook my head and frowned. "Oh, so terrible, awful ... truly." I gave him a wink back.

Then Ben shifted his tone, and I knew Cherie had told him what had gone down.

He looked at Maggie, stroking her hair. "You're okay, Mags. It's not real. It's not you. *We* know who you are." He glanced at me when he said *we*.

I'd met him ten seconds ago; how could he know that?

... Oh, that's how he knows.

Ben was just like Maggie. He burst into the room and lit it up, but he was reading it at the same time. He took in all the energy, ran it through some kind of "good or bad" filter, and released it back. Just like Maggie, when he did, it was brighter and better than he found it. I felt deeply satisfied, knowing I'd passed his test.

Maggie grabbed one of my hands and one of Ben's. "I'm so happy right now!" She squeezed our hands. "Here with my two favourite boys!"

"Geez, Mags," Ben said, fanning himself. "Take us out for dinner first." He stuck his tongue between his teeth and winked at me again.

We sat around for a while, laughing and talking about plans for the weekend. Watching Maggie bounce back how she did was really cool. I could just feel that she'd already accepted it, moved on, and completely let it go.

I don't doubt having a panic attack makes her feel awful, but once her light's back on, I think she knows that awful feeling doesn't have a place to exist. Under the light in Ben's eyes, she seemed brighter than ever.

19

Benny from the Block

Maggie

Having Ben with me felt like warm rays of sunshine on my nervous system. It was ultra soothing, cosy, and instantly revitalising.

We stayed up until two a.m., laughing, yapping, and carrying on. Also crying, because he cracked open his bottle of Maggie worries, the ones he'd been holding inside since we last saw each other.

In the morning, I took Ben to meet Roy at Bronte's. I wanted to show him where I'd been working, so when he'd think of me here, he could have the visual, too. And because Roy was a bloody legend, obviously.

We sat outside in my favourite spot, facing the beach. The chipped, wooden chairs would leave loose threads on your pants, so I took cushions from the couches inside to avoid Ben having a whinge.

Waiting for our coffees, I gazed at Ben, trying to solidify the memory of his first visit to L.A. in real-time. Both our faces were puffy with dark rings under our eyes, but I didn't care. It was worth it. I knew the colours and swelling on our faces told a little story about what it's like to see your best friend after six months, and I liked that story.

Ben was humming J–Lo's *Jenny From The Block*, which, when he'd sing, he'd always replace the Jenny with Benny. He was so gorgeous; his tanned, smooth skin made his blue eyes pop.

Roy brought our coffees to the table, and I gave Ben an apologetic smile because I knew he'd think it was terrible coffee. When Ben took a sip, his eyebrows shot up, and he pressed his lips together, like if he didn't, the mouthful would ... dribble back out. When he swallowed it, he gave me the finger, but I just shrugged.

"You're so tanned," I said. "It looks really good."

He gave me a cheeky side-smile, keeping his eyes on the beach. "Thanks," he muttered. "It's Bondi Sands. Ultra-dark. Just one coat."

He kept giving judgy eyes to an influencer, who was getting photos in a bikini on the beach. It made me giggle, but it was becoming a little obvious.

"Oi," I snapped, slapping his arm. "Stop that! You're so obvious about it."

He threw up his hands. "What? I wasn't judging. I was ... admiring. Everyone here is fucking hot."

I laughed and rolled my eyes, but he was right. Walking around the streets in L.A. felt like walking through the gates of heaven ... if heaven were only made for people with symmetrical faces, long thin legs, and YSL sunglasses. It was definitely fun to admire.

Ben scooted his chair to face me and pulled his sunglasses to the bridge of his nose, peeping at me above them.

Continuing with his previous thoughts, he said, "Chriso included."

I shook my head. "Yeah ... nah."

Then we looked at each other, nodded, and in sync, said, *"But yeah."*

"Yeah, nah" was the one Aussie phrase I'd almost eradicated from my word bank not long after moving to L.A. It meant "yes" but it also meant "no". If you flipped it and said "nah, yeah" it was different. It meant "no" and also "yeah" but also ... "no"? The phrase was confusing and contextual, but it felt good to talk to someone who understood it.

"Mags," Ben said, forcing a hard swallow of coffee. "I can't believe Chris, like, waited. Like in the room, when you were having your little ... *menty b.*"

"*Menty b?*" I rolled my head to face him, unimpressed. Then I slapped his arm again. "It wasn't a mental breakdown, Ben! I was just ... upset ... and unable to breathe at the same time."

I straightened up in confident denial ... then slumped back down in reluctant acceptance.

Ben scoffed through a giggle, shaking his head. "Okay, fine. You were just ... *upset.*" I nodded, thankful for his participation in my denial. He continued, "But still! I mean, Chris is famous! Doesn't he always have somewhere else to be?"

Now I was the one scoffing. "Ha. I guess ..." I said, thinking it over. "Not really, though. He's booked and busy, you know, with filming the show. We don't have time for other stuff."

Still peeping over his sunglasses, Ben looked me deep in the eyes. I could tell; he was trying to read my mind.

"Were you surprised?" he asked. "Did you know he was there?"

"I mean, yeah! Yeah, I was!" I replied, trying to be mysterious, but very likely failing.

"Oh, Mags, that was basically rhetorical, my love." He pushed his sunglasses up and looked back towards the beach, pursing his lips. "I know you weren't surprised."

I sighed, grabbing his hand. "Honestly, Ben, I was just thinking about you." I gave his hand a little tug. He looked back at me, and I whispered, "I'm *so* sorry. About Sunday."

He smiled and patted my hand. "Mags, Aunty Chez told me Chris loves you, you know. In the car, when she came to get me. She said she knew when she left to pick me up, and he said he was staying."

I sighed again, deeper this time.

Ben, like me, wasn't afraid of words. He didn't hold them in his chest. If they were there and ready, he'd just say them. Although sometimes, he'd say them *before* they were ready, just to stir the pot a little.

Sliding his sunglasses down again, he leaned back in his chair. "And you know, I can see it." He nodded. "You've rubbed off on him. I saw your little 'don't say it, livin' the dream' bit. And when you rub off on someone, Mags ... well, you know."

He shrugged and sipped his coffee. But I didn't know what he meant.

"No, I don't think I do know. What?" I asked.

Gesturing over me, he said, "You don't just rub off. You, like ... *stain*." He smirked, knowing he sounded silly.

I scrunched up my nose. "What? That's so weird and kind of gross!"

"No, Mags! I just mean that you're ..." He held my hand, smiling. "Unforgettable. You leave a mark. And the mark is pure sunshine, wrapped in glitter. And the glitter gets, like, everywhere ..."

I joined the rest of his sentence. "Like Mardi Gras in 2019."

"Exactly, my love." He nodded, patting my hand again.

I did like feeling glittery and sunshine-y and warm. It made me feel nice, and I guess other people could notice it. But I wasn't just giving it away, or at least I didn't think I was. And if people remembered me, that's lovely, but I didn't really care if they forgot me. I just hoped they would remember themselves. I wanted people to feel like they could just be who they were around me.

After thinking through Ben's words again, I said, "You and Chez might be right."

He piped up. "Oh? And?"

"And … it's fine?" I held my shoulders up, half-smiling.

Ben slumped back down, and I got it. I'd given him a disappointing response.

I continued, "I don't know, it just *is*. Like, we got on from the moment we met, we spend, like, a million hours a week together now. We are having this crazy, shared experience together and it makes the time move *so* fast and I just … get it."

I shook my head quickly, like I really was *just getting it.*

Leaning across the table, I said, "Like, if Chris loves me, that's great. I love *him*, too."

Ben was interested again; his mouth was in an "O" shape. "Mags isn't that, like, *huge* news right now?"

"No, it's not, really. I'm not saying I've *fallen in love* with … *Chriso*." I smirked. "I just love him. Because he's my best friend. A person that I love."

Looking unconvinced, but trusting my honesty, Ben pursed his lips into a straight line. "Hmm," he huffed. "Well, poor *Chriso*, then, I 'spose."

I rolled my eyes again; that was enough *Chris and Maggie* talk.

Strolling back to Ben's hotel, I daydreamed about how much I wished he lived here, too. I could visualise our little apartment, with lots and lots of plants. Mostly dead, and brown. But the green cushions on the black lounge would trick your eyes.

Nudging me, Ben said, "*Earth to Mags*, come back down, babe."

I jolted back. "Oh, sorry, what?"

"Can we get into The Alibi? Or not?" he asked. "I want to people watch, but better, *celebrity* watch." He shot me a double brow raise.

"I don't know," I said, hesitant. "I can ask Chris, but I think Chelsea always goes there with ..."

I wasn't sure how to finish, but Ben was.

"With their *groupies?*"

"Yeah, kinda," I giggled. "I'll call him and ask."

As I pulled my phone from my back pocket, Ben said, "No, FaceTime him. He doesn't get much time with me. He needs to see me."

I let out a belly laugh. Ben was every single colour wrapped into a human body.

Still giggling, I said, "Because I love you *so* much ... sure."

Ben wrapped his arm over my shoulder, and we stood on the sidewalk, waiting for Chris to answer our call.

20

Oi, Nah, Yeah

Chris

Running on the treadmill in the hotel gym, I was thinking about how badly I didn't want to do the YouTube segment for *Vice* that Cherie had arranged for the following night. I hadn't let myself get excited, like Mags, for the weekend off because I knew how quickly things changed. I was used to it.

I couldn't be mad at Cherie, though. Technically, Dom had sorted it out; she was just picking up his pieces by locking it in. And it was just easier to blame Dom right now. For, well, everything.

Lost in thought, I almost slipped off the back of the treadmill and broke my damn leg when I saw Maggie was calling. I hit the stop button, realised it was a video call, and felt an exciting surge of intrigue.

Slightly exasperated, partly from running, but mostly from seeing her call, I answered, "Hello?"

"Hi! Hey, sorry," she replied, but I barely caught a glimpse of her.

Ben snatched the phone, and his face filled my phone screen.

"Hi, lovely," he said. Noticing I was in the gym, he repeated himself, adding a raised brow. "Oh, *hi*, lovely."

I felt a little awkward. Moving right along, I asked, "What's up?"

Ben smirked. "I got your letter."

Shit, him too? God, they love to mess around.

I went along with it; I had to. "Right, sure. And?"

Ben's smirk grew cheeky. He spoke fast, like he knew he was about to get slapped. "It said, 'Dear Ben, I would like to take my shirt off while I run on the treadmill, and—'"

"Ben, shut the fuck up, you *perv!*" Maggie snatched the phone back, and as expected, slapped his arm.

I'd never heard her voice sound so Australian. I liked it.

Looking at her on my phone screen, I asked, "So what's actually up?"

She flashed me her cheeky grin. "Oh, you know, the birds, the sky ... and can you come to The Alibi with us later so we can get in?"

I didn't have to consider it. It was a *hard no.*

My face dropped, and Maggie said, "Please? For Ben?"

She looked so pretty; her eyes were bright and glowy. She almost had me.

"Mags, do you really wanna go there? It's not even that fun."

I sort of lied. I would love to see Maggie and Ben after necking a few Triple S's. I had no interest in bumping into Chelsea or Dom, though.

Ben called out, "Don't worry about Chelsea, Chriso! Stop being a bitch!"

I laughed, but I wasn't budging. "Mags, for real. And yeah, that's *partly* why ... but also, let's just chill. There's a small wine bar, near a good club. We can go there."

Ben snapped, "Ew, Chriso. That sounds like we are over thirty years old."

I snapped back, "Uh, yeah? We're closer to thirty than twenty."

Mags laughed and I could see her looking at Ben, mouthing to him.

Her face filling my screen again, she said, "You're allowed *one* more suggestion. No wine bars."

I honestly couldn't come up with anything. I was a *tell me the time and place, and I'll be there*, kind of a guy. Not a *I'll make all the arrangements and let you know*, kind of guy.

"I don't know ..." I said, shrugging. I felt kinda guilty. "Just come to my suite later. We can go from there."

Maggie looked at Ben to confirm; I saw them exchange a nod.

"Okay! Yay! Ben wants to go full-feral, so get ready, I guess." She blew me a kiss, then they hung up.

Feral? I knew what it meant, but only in the literal sense, like a feral cat.

I laughed when I realised. I think she *did* mean literal.

The evening came around, and I'd smoked half a joint, so, rationally, I changed my shirt three times. I convinced myself that it was to avoid smelling like weed, but, on a deeper level ... I knew it was because I really wanted Ben to like me.

On an even deeper level than that, was the reason *why* I really wanted Ben to like me. But I wasn't fully ready to deep dive into that just yet. I considered it was maybe more of a ... full joint, type of thing.

Just as I finished adjusting shirt number three, they knocked on the door of my suite. I swung the door open, and it was like being splashed in the face with two, large buckets of sunshine-soaked tequila.

"Oh, wow!" I said, ushering them in. "The feral Australians appear!"

Mags giggled, giving me a little side-hug, and Ben pushed past me to check out the room.

"What the hell, Mags!" he said, scanning every corner of the suite. "Is the pay gap really still *that* bad here?"

Mags looked up at me, shrugging sheepishly at his audacity. I felt a bit awkward again. He was probably right, but I figured I'd set the record straight in this case.

"Yeah," I said, scratching my head. "I kinda chose to be here, so ... I'm paying for this."

Ben cocked his head and pulled a sad face, but I don't think there was much sympathy behind it. I shrugged; it was fair enough.

Changing the subject, Ben asked, "So, where's the bar?"

I made us each a margarita with the mixer they brought because Maggie insisted that I use it. I knew the ones in the hotel would be better, and I did offer, but she was having none of it. Ben winced when he took a sip; I knew I'd made it too strong. I was distracted when I did it.

I was about to apologise, but Ben said, "Mm. I like you. You're my new best friend, call me every five minutes?" Then he smirked. It was a real devilish smirk, too.

Ben was one of those people who said words as soon as they hit his chest, and it could be hard to know how to respond. I just laughed, revelling in the feeling that he liked me, and guessing he liked his margaritas strong.

While I was in the kitchen fixing myself another drink, they were dancing around the living room. Ben was wearing a short-sleeve black button-down, and the buttons looked sparkly, like sequins. They reflected light onto the walls, and Maggie's eyes darted around, chasing the little glimmers. It was so fun to watch.

Ben wasn't feral, but he was singing along with Charli XCX very loudly, so I chuckled knowing he was well on the way.

And Maggie?

Maggie looked *stunning*.

I had to try not to peek too much when I was near them; I'd suck a breath in and give away the thought.

She had on this short, bright pink dress that tied up around the neck, and her hair was out in big waves down her back. I loved that she paired it with bright blue Gazelles; she was ready to dance. Even just watching her dance with Ben, the way she moved her body was almost hypnotic.

She was alluring, but not in a way that was immediately obvious. It exuded from her gently, then it'd hit you all at once. Like the contours of her body were just understated enough, they left a halo of mystique around her. It was undeniable; the woman was a petite powerhouse.

Letting my eyes wander a little too much over Mags, to the point it was her with the dress *off*, not *on* ... I ditched the drink and took a shot instead.

I called out, "You guys good? Let's go!"

"Oi ... Oi, Mags." Ben grabbed Maggie's hand and they scurried right up in my face, looking in my eyes. Ben murmured, "Chriso's gone full-feral."

I gave him a shove. "Shut up, I definitely haven't." Which was true, I knew I hadn't. "I just thought we were pretending we weren't closer to thirty?"

They looked at each other and laughed, saying in sync, "Nah ... *yeah.*"

I couldn't be bothered to work out what it meant, so I headed for the door.

The club, The Havana, had a massive line, as always. I had a hunch Brooks and some of the others would be inside because, as always, that's what they did after The Alibi.

Eyes wide and gazing out the window, Maggie said, "Oh shit, we're going to be waiting for so long."

Ben put his arm around her. "Yeah, but Mags, we've got *all* night. Please?"

I knew Maggie would do whatever Ben wanted; she was already losing a day with him. I also knew, I could kind of be a hero right now. They'd rip me to shreds over it, but they were giving me so much fun … I wanted to give them something back.

I texted Brooks:

Havs?

He replied instantly:

YES

I sent a follow-up:

Chels?

He shot back:

NOPE.

I smiled, exhaling. Then I sent:

I'm here. Mags and Ben too let them know?

And instantly again, he replied:

ON IT

Sweet, that was easy. We were in.

Leaning into Marco, I said, "Marco, go around the side, down there." I pointed down the side street, immediately feeling like a dick because Marco had done this trip a thousand times.

I turned to Mags and Ben in the back. "We aren't lining up; we'll go in the side." I smiled, impressed that my life choices had led to a little moment like this. I looked to Maggie and said, "When you see Brooks pop out, just run for the door."

She took a quick breath in. The idea made her anxious, which I understood. We hadn't really been wise with our timing; there were a lot of paparazzi lingering around. Not that you could ever really pick it. But if I had a choice, it would never be to cause Maggie any type of anxiety.

Like Ben was born to do it, he snapped Maggie right out of it. "Oh Mags, look at you!" he said, tossing her hair. "You shot for the moon … and landed among the *stars.*" He gestured to me, clearly mocking me.

Admittedly, I loved it. So, I owned it, smiled and put my sunglasses on.

Marco pulled up, and we waited until I caught Brooks' head popping out the door.

The second I saw it; I reached into the back and shook Ben's knee. "Sweet, let's bounce."

In excitement, Ben flung open the car door and shouted, "Fuck!"

I stood by their door, my hand out, and Ben slapped his hand in mine, his other hand pulling Maggie behind him. I led us up the stairs and through the side door. I was fairly certain there'd be a photo of Ben and me holding hands somewhere on the internet in under fifteen minutes.

I'd barely even greeted Brooks when I spun around and realised Mags and Ben had disappeared. I shook my head, a little astonished at their speed, but I let them go. It was their weekend.

I had many more to come with Mags.

21

Going Through with Reckless

Chris

There's always that point of drunk where you're feeling reckless enough to think of stupid ideas, but not quite drunk enough to go through with them ...

And that was about the point I was at.

From where we hung out on the landing above the dance floor, the music was loud enough to feel the bass thumping in your chest. But there was kind of a disconnect to the energy below. All the bodies packed together under the strobe lights blurred, twisting into one another in slow motion.

Brooks called this spot the "Sweet Nothin' Special". You could actually have a conversation up here and hear each other talk, usually when you were ... *ready to go home.*

The Havana pulled an eclectic crowd, and I was casually people-watching, enjoying it. The flavour of the dudes was bland and cut copy: jeans, Jordans, a graphic tee with an unbuttoned button-down. But the girls, gays, and theys? That was always a strict serving of sugar and spice. I had to try kick back and relax each time I remembered Mags was somewhere in this club, looking like a total knockout in that pink dress.

Unclench your jaw, Chris.

I was sitting close with Chelsea's friend Ash on one of the lounges. Too close, probably. One of her legs hooked in front of mine, like she was trying to lock me down. She was being super handsy, flirting, batting her lashes, the whole show.

It was hot, but I didn't think it was gonna go anywhere. Her long, blonde hair was too much like Chelsea's ... actually, her whole face was.

The rest of Ash and Chelsea's posse were keeping the boys thoroughly entertained, and I glanced around at them, wondering how long we'd do this. How long we had left. Messing around, sneaking off into bathrooms when the high dipped, telling pretty girls sweet nothings so we wouldn't be alone the next morning when it all felt shit.

I'd been with Chelsea for two whole years, and it shouldn't have, but it surprised me that it felt like I was picking up where I left off before I met her. It kind of made me feel sick. There was a hard line to draw here, but ... I'd keep that pending, for tonight.

I took another shot with Ash.

Ash knew Chels and I were done. Brooks told me everyone had already discussed it at The Alibi a few hours earlier. For a split second, I felt bad for Chels. None of these girls were loyal. They were deeply invested in whatever *this* was. The shiny stuff. Fame, attention, and money.

I got it; it could be addictive. But it runs out fast. And when your tank is empty, you're so disillusioned into thinking that the only thing that can fill it is the same shit. Fame, attention, money. So, you seek it out again. Like the sneaky bathroom run when the high dips.

Chels was exactly the same. The guilt vanished. *Fuck her.*

I wasn't stopping Ash, so *fuck me too*, I guess.

Her hand snaked around my neck, and right in my ear, she said, "I can't believe you weren't at your own house party last weekend."

She gave me a sad, puppy dog face. I cringed a little bit.

I mumbled back into her ear. "Yeah, I don't really ... partake, when I'm working. You know?"

Her hand was still glued to my neck. "Tonight's different then?"

"Yeah, it is." I picked up another two shots, handing her one. "We got a weekend off, so ..." I met her eyes, tapped my glass to hers. "Cheers."

As the burn hit the back of my throat, I think I might've hoped that drink would black me out.

Ash continued in my ear. "It was better you weren't there. At the party. You might have walked in on ..." She trailed off, leaning back just enough to catch my reaction, her eyes scanning my face.

Did she really think she was going to be the hero to break it to me?

I felt compelled to entertain the idea, though.

Purposely avoiding her eyes, I asked, "Walked in on what?"

She went all in on her performance—tossing her hair, sipping her vodka soda, and putting a hand to her heart like it hurt to be the bearer of bad news.

I could feel a smirk tugging at my lips, so I took an extra-long sip of whiskey while I waited.

Leaning back into my ear, she said, "Chelsea. Chelsea and Dom." She snapped back to catch my reaction again, but I didn't look at her right away.

Someone else had caught my attention.

Maggie and Ben were dancing in the middle of the dance floor, right underneath the disco ball that hung from the ceiling beams. Their eyes were closed, hands on each other, laughing, sweat shining on their foreheads.

It looked so *fun*. Like real, deep, child-like fun ... just in a different context.

They were radiant, and infectious, and I felt the deepest jab of envy. It was like they were *untouchable*. Nothing was disrupting their orbit of euphoria.

I telepathically begged for her to look up and see me. As the song ended, my mind begging paid off, because she did. Her and Ben both did. I wanted what they were having, so I held up my drink and waved at them to come over.

Ash caught me waving at them; her face soured in disappointment. I leaned back in close, deciding I'd be her co-star for a few extra moments.

"Yeah," I said, shaking my head. "That would've been bad. Really bad."

"It must be so hard for you." Her voice was soft, sweet, and yet ... anything but sympathetic. "I'm here for you."

She slid her hand up my thigh, the other snaking up my neck again. At that point, Ash may as well have written *let's have sex* on her forehead.

It was a reckless idea, that I wouldn't go through with ... but I knew if I grabbed her hand, we could head to the bathroom right this second.

Ben cut her performance short, flopping beside me onto the lounge. My eyes shot from Ash, darting around in search for Maggie.

Ben caught me, shouting, "She's getting us drinks!" He grabbed a napkin and started fanning himself. "I was too parched to wait."

My eyes found Mags as she headed towards us, and I wanted to tell her exactly what Ash was doing. I wanted to ask her what I should say, and what I should do, but I also felt like I already knew her answer.

If Maggie were me, she would say, *"I know you want to have sex with me, and you think that if I think I'm getting back at Chelsea by doing it with you ... I'll want it too. But I don't. So, bye!"*

Then she'd tilt her head and smile sweetly. Maybe she'd shrug, sipping a drink like she hadn't just crushed your ego with her pinky finger.

I had to call cut on Ash's scene before Maggie could sit down, so I called into her ear, "Ash." She jolted, flicking her eyes to my choice of hand placement, firm on her knee. I continued, "I know what you're doing. And I'm not interested. I'm here with my friends. And that one, right there, remember her?"

I paused, glancing at Mags. She'd stopped to talk to Brooks on her way to us. Subtly, I pointed, and Ash's eyes followed.

I went on, "If she finds out you're messing with me like this right now, she'll ..." I laughed and shook my head.

Ash rolled her eyes and shoved my hand off her knee. "What, Chris, scratch my eyes out?"

I was oblivious to the look on Ash's face; my eyes were locked on Maggie as she set a tray of glasses down. Ben picked up a drink and downed it in one go.

I chuckled and turned back to Ash. "No, she won't." I pointed to Ben. "But he might."

Ash stood up abruptly. "Chelsea is so right about you. Fucking toxic." She pointed her finger in my face. "You know, I *tried* to tell her not to do the podcast. But I'm *so* glad she did."

Then she threw her drink at me! It was only ice, but still, it was hilarious. My cheeks puffed out, trying to stifle a burst of laughter that I knew wouldn't end well for me.

She stormed off, grabbed Brooks by the forearm and dragged him towards the bathroom. He shot me a look that said, *what the hell?* I just shrugged and slumped back onto the lounge next to Ben.

Maggie pretended to pull at a collar on her neck, also stifling laughter, which made mine burst at the seams.

Ben snatched some of the ice off my chest. "Give me some of that!" He shoved a few cubes down his shirt.

As I watched Ash and Brooks disappear into the crowd, I felt a flicker of … *what the fuck* … at the mention of Chelsea on a podcast. I frowned; I had no idea what Ash was talking about. But the flicker of fucks was fleeting, and I snapped out of it, because Mags stood up, holding both her hands out. One for me, one for Ben.

She was beaming. "We have to dance to this song before we go!"

Within two minutes, we'd shoved our way back under the disco ball, in the middle of the dance floor. Somehow, we'd hung onto the drinks in our hands that we definitely didn't need, but by then, there couldn't have been a single person in the club who hadn't gone full-feral.

There were maybe 2% of pupils left that weren't dilated, which was likely made up of me, Mags, and *maybe* Ben. He'd snuck off two or three times, so I wasn't sure. Mags wasn't into it. She told me weeks ago over a lunch-break quesadilla, when she voiced her wonder about living where weed was legal.

I learned the lesson on work and play years ago. I was strict; a minimum 24-hour window was required between partaking in drugs and working. I had *Vice* tomorrow, so I was out.

Necking my last mouthful, I reached for the empties in Maggie and Ben's hands, stacking them with mine to take to the bar. Maggie frowned, grabbing my wrist and shaking her head.

Pointing to the bar, I mouthed, "I'll be back." But Ben fiercely swiped the empties out of my hand, and they instantly disappeared into a sea of dancing feet on the floor.

"Oops!" Ben shrugged. "My hand slipped!" I caught glimpses of their boozy, devious smiles in snippets through the strobe lights.

More under the influence of Ben and Maggie than the booze, I felt like I'd been slingshot into their orbit of euphoria. I had my sunglasses on, and they were both mocking me, but I loved it.

We were dancing, and I spun away, peering over my shoulder and pulling my sunglasses down to the bridge of my nose. Backing up into Maggie, she was sandwiched between me and Ben. She laughed and wrapped her arms around my waist, with Ben gripping my shoulders from behind.

Maggie slid her hands under my shirt and over my stomach, and *ho-ly shit* ... it felt all sorts of *reckless*. Likely the kind of reckless that, with just one more drink, would have me following through on the ideas it put in my mind.

I spun back around to face her, crouching at her eye level. We smiled in each other's faces, our noses inches apart. Then Ben yanked my sunglasses from my face, but I snatched them back, pointing at a group of girls with their phones out. I knew they were trying to get a picture or video just moments earlier.

Ben screamed, "Oh, shit!" He ducked down, pulling Maggie and me with him. Panicked, he shouted, "Mags, we need sunglasses! We're going to look so cooked!"

I shouted back, "I have cash, I'll buy someone else's from them." I peeked up, scanning for an easy target.

Ben yanked me back down. "No, Chris, that's fucking embarrassing! I think I saw some, on the table over there!" He pointed through a sea of legs to a roped-off table that had two pairs of sunglasses on it.

I yelled to them both, "How is that less embarrassing?" They were laughing so hard there was no way they heard me. Or cared.

Mags grabbed my hand. "Don't let go, stay down!"

Ben grabbed my other hand from behind me, and Mags pushed through the crowd, but someone stepped back onto Ben, breaking our tight grip.

"Mags! Wait!" I shouted ahead.

Ben screamed back, "Just go! Save yourselves!" He was wetting himself laughing; I doubled over, cracking up.

I followed Mags and stood up again when we got to the rope at the table. She whipped around, saw Ben wasn't there, and her face dropped into panic.

I yelled into her ear, "He's fine!" I pointed to him hooking up with the guy who had knocked him over twenty seconds ago.

She smiled and shook her head, then grabbed my face, pulling it closer so her lips could meet my ear. "Okay, so do we like, just take them?"

I threw my hands in the air. "I don't know. What would Ben do?"

Looking me in the eyes, she took a second to consider her decision. Her pale greens were glassy; she was *so* drunk. I'd never seen her this drunk, but I couldn't tell if she was more drunk than I was.

She stood on her toes to shout in my ear, "Give me the cash, in your wallet."

I pulled my wallet out and handed it all to her. It was a few hundred bucks, maybe a thousand, but I didn't think she'd notice. She hadn't memorised American cash.

Ten seconds later, she popped back up in front of me, wearing jet-black sunglasses and swirling the second pair in her hand.

I called out, "Stunning!" Even though they were too big for her, sitting crooked on her face. I tried to straighten them up, but they fell crooked again ... it was perfect.

I took the second pair of glasses and tucked them into my shirt. Grabbing Maggie's hand, we shoved our way back to Ben.

I slid the sunglasses onto his face like I was placing a crown on his head. In response, he slapped his hands on my cheeks and smacked a kiss on my lips. He spun to Mags, pouted, and tapped his lips—she smacked a kiss on him, too.

In his face, she shouted, "Love you!"

Ben turned away into the arms of his newfound L.A. lover, and I looked down at Mags, giggling her little head off at him. I couldn't stop laughing, either. Ben was wild, *full-feral,* and it was absolutely brilliant.

Then, Maggie spun to face me.

She smiled. Pouted. And tapped her lips.

I blinked hard in disbelief. *Was she asking me to kiss her right now?*

She started giggling again, dancing in a slow-motion blur. She grabbed my hand to dance with her, and I thought maybe the moment had already passed.

But then I thought … *fuck it.*

It was reckless, but I was *definitely* going through with it.

I yanked us down low, and I kissed her—a little longer than I should have—because she pushed me off and laughed, pulling us back up, dancing like it didn't happen.

Now I was in euphoria.

22

I Can See You

Maggie

Gosh, I am so hungover. Turns out, twenty-six is not the same as being twenty.

How did we used to do this for, like, four days straight?

I lost count of drinks within thirty minutes of arriving at The Havana, and now, it was four in the afternoon, and I was trying to "sweat it out" by jogging on the treadmill.

I snorted, glancing at the stolen sunglasses perched on the treadmill tray. They were too big for me, and I think they sat crooked, but wearing them was like retelling a joke with a punchline that never got old.

Dom had tried to call me three times. I'll admit … I declined all three calls. I'll also admit … I wasn't jogging. I was walking. I'd been highly unwell, all morning, and Ben was *still* nursing his hangover. So, it was more of a recovery walk, I guess.

My phone buzzed, and yet again, it was Dom. Honestly, Dom could rack right off. He was disrupting my daydream, and I didn't have any words for him yet. I only had a big, fat, middle finger to shove into his face.

I'd barely tossed the phone back onto the tray when it buzzed *again*. But this time it was Cherie, so I answered.

"Hello?"

"Where are you right now?" She sounded agitated.

"I'm in the gym." I hopped my feet on either side of the treadmill. "Why?"

"I've tried knocking on Chris' door, like, twenty times today. His phone is going to voicemail; he's probably broken it again. Don't worry, I've already ordered a new one, but the front desk said he hasn't come in or out. He has to be in there." Cherie was rushed, all her words tumbled over each other; I could hardly keep up.

I yanked the emergency stop on the treadmill, and feeling a little jolt of panic, I asked, "Why wouldn't he answer you?"

"Oh, I don't know, Mags. Because I can't control the internet? Because he thought it was Dom?" She spoke like I was a moron for asking. I felt bad ... Cherie wasn't really into sarcasm, so she must have been seriously stressed out.

Sharply, she asked, "You've still got a key, right? I need you to go and get him out before tonight."

I tried to sound cool and calm because she sounded hot-headed and flustered. "Yeah, okay. I'll go. I'll go right now."

Cherie snapped at me. "Yes, go. Right now. We have *literally* thirty minutes to let the people at *Vice* know if his arse is going to be there tonight."

"Okay, Cherie! Seriously, I'll let you know." Mimicking her tone, I added. "I'm *literally* going there right now."

The way she said "literally" was like the climate crisis or feeding a starving nation depended on getting Chris out of his room. I had no choice but to mock it.

I grabbed my stuff from the treadmill, tossed it into my bag, and scurried to Chris's suite. By the time I got there, my pulse was racing, and I didn't know if it was from the scurrying, or from the fact that I had no idea what I was walking into.

My hand hovered, about to knock, but my heart was pounding so hard it was making my ears ring. If I knocked, maybe he'd tell me to go away ... then it was a bad start. If I didn't knock, and just went in, I could ask for forgiveness later ... *at least I'd get a word in?*

I swiped the room key to the door, it clicked unlocked, and I slowly inched it open.

As I crept inside, I spoke soft. "Chriso? Cherie's been trying to call you."

Ho-ly crap.

I accidentally gasped a little bit. I didn't know where to look.

My eyes rushed around the room, trying to put pieces together of what the hell happened. The only light in the suite was from his laptop screen, open on the end of his bed. Chris was lying in his boxers, upside down with his head hanging over the edge of the bed. It smelled so strong of weed; pretty sure I was second-hand stoned when I opened the door.

Creeping my way in like I was walking through a minefield ... I saw his phone on the floor near the wardrobe. The screen was smashed to shreds. *Cherie knew him better than I thought.*

When I reached the bed, I saw a YouTube video of Ariana Grande on his laptop. I didn't want to imagine how cringe it would be to walk in on Chris watching porn, but for some reason, this felt worse. YouTube rabbit holes were *only* embarrassing.

Chris didn't move. He cracked one eye open, barely, and let out a low, half-assed groan. Almost like he couldn't decide if he was annoyed I was there, or too lazy to care.

I read the title of the video; it was an acceptance speech from some award ceremony.

"What the hell are you watching?" I asked, slapping the laptop shut. "Why the heck are you watching this? This is so random."

I giggled; but he didn't. I reached for the blind and lifted it an inch to sneak some sunlight into the room.

I poked his thigh. "Are you getting inspo for your future acceptance speech or something?"

Chris dragged himself upright, rolling from his awkward upside-down position to flop face-first onto the mattress. He tucked his arms under the pillow his head sank into.

With a bit more effort, he groaned again, mumbling incoherently.

"What was that?" I asked. "I couldn't hear you because you were literally talking into a pillow."

Shh, Maggie. No sarcasm! Why did sarcasm have to be my native tongue? I regretted it instantly when I heard how my voice sounded.

I sat myself cross-legged at the end of his bed, and he slowly sat up, kneeling to face me. His eyes were so red and squinty. I'd never seen eyes look like that, except for maybe when my brother had conjunctivitis when he was twelve. I knew Chris would freak out if I freaked out, so I just pretended he looked normal … and fully clothed.

Under his breath, he mumbled, "Why did I have to meet you at the worst possible time?" He was barely audible, slowly shaking his head.

Before he continued, he dragged his hands down his face and waved his fingers towards the laptop. "It's what she says. What she says, in the speech."

"Oh, yeah? I haven't seen it. What does she say?" I asked, smiling gently.

"She says that at the peak of her career …" He sighed and shut his eyes. "Her personal life is at its fucking worst. And that it's weird, how that happens."

I tilted my head. "And that relates to you … how, exactly?"

Chris's eyes snapped open; his jaw clenched. *Oh shit. That pissed him off.*

For a second, it looked like he was going to say something, but instead, he just shook his head sharply, like I'd let him down, *big time*, by even asking.

He spat back at me, "Because that's me, Maggie! That's *me*, that's … that's my life! And I want to have it all, Mags, I want to. I want to have it all, and I can't. I fuck it up." His hands moved kinda wildly, like they were trying to keep up with the rush of his words. "Right when I catch it, in the palm of my hand … it slips through my fingers."

I pressed my lips together to stop my mouth from falling open in a silent gasp. He was skipping so many breaths, scrambling his way through his monologue. I was just staring at him, I couldn't pin down a thought, let alone a word to speak.

He stuttered, "I do everything I can to make it right. To *be* right. I do everything I'm told to do. To be good, and to be liked. And it just … doesn't work."

He buried his face in his hands, and I opened my mouth to say something, but before I could, he snapped his head up and locked his eyes on mine.

"Did you see it, Mags?" he asked. "Did you? Did you see what she said?"

I had to shut my eyes, for a second. His were so full of pain, it was starting to hurt a little just to look at him. And …

I had seen it.

"It" was Chelsea going on a podcast, saying Chris was … *evil.*

She chose *that* word. "Evil". I wanted to clock her when I saw it.

I wanted to respond to every single comment, from every single keyboard warrior on every single corner of the internet and tell them to shut the hell up. But we just couldn't do that. It's not how my friendship with Chris got to work. I couldn't just clap back and expect Chelsea's fans not to paint me as a villain, too.

It was becoming obvious Chris had fallen deep down a rabbit hole, and the second I walked into this room, I think I might've tumbled in after him. I wasn't sure I could get him out of it. Not right now, anyway.

His fists were clenched at his sides, and he was staring at me like he was choking back tears, I think. I caught the rapid rise and fall of his chest, and it made my own breaths quicken, like they synced up with his.

Unsure if I'd be stepping on a mine, I kept my voice soft and low, and said, "No one believes that bullshit, Chris."

His sapphire orbs were on the verge of hysterical, wild and frenzied. "Yes, they do! They do, Mags." He threw his hands up in a helpless shrug. "And you know why?" He exhaled sharply. "Because it's true."

Raising his voice, he continued, "And now I have to sit here, looking at you, knowing that all of this bullshit is gonna scare you away. That *I'm* scaring you away by being so ..." He covered his mouth and shook his head, trying to pick a word. Through gritted teeth, he said, "By being so, fucking, dramatic."

I looked at him, completely puzzled, and I couldn't help it ... I rolled my eyes. Not to upset him, but because it was so ridiculous that he actually believed that he could scare me away.

I let out a sigh, halfway between a laugh and a breath.

Chris shook his head. "Maggie, no, don't." Raking his hand through his hair, he closed his eyes, and spoke razor sharp. "Don't. You're trying to be chill right now, and I fucking know you're not, and it's driving me insane."

The way he said it sent a little shockwave through my body. I panicked, my mouth opening, but no words came out ... just a stuttering mess of noise.

Part of me wanted to wrap him up in my arms and lie in this room until he said so, even if it was weeks. Another part of me wondered if I should just try slapping him out of it.

Slowly and carefully, I asked, "What do you need me to do right now?"

When he looked at me this time, his gaze was so desperate, like he was begging for me to give him something to make it all go away. But I didn't have it. I didn't know what it was. I tried to organise my brain, to figure it out, but I couldn't.

I felt guilty, and horrible, and stupid for not checking on him sooner. I just assumed he wouldn't care about any of it, because I assumed he saw himself the way I saw him. And that wasn't anything like this. But he didn't, and he couldn't. He couldn't see himself at all.

Something about that just made me feel overwhelmingly sad. It sent silent, hot, and uninvited tears streaming down my cheeks.

Chris panicked. "No, no, no," he stuttered. "Mags, please don't cry. I'm sorry, I'm sorry." He reached forward and wrapped his arms around me tight. He was cold, covered in goosebumps.

I pushed him away and stood up. "I'm not crying because I'm scared. I'm crying because I'm sad for you." I wiped my eyes with the sleeve of my jumper. "You're my best friend, and I *feel* what you feel. I see you carrying this pain and I want to make it lighter and I feel like I can't."

I paused, taking a shaky breath, wiping my eyes again. "I just don't want you to feel alone. And I'm sad that you've been in here alone ... this whole time."

His eyes pooled with tears, but he tilted his head back to stare at the ceiling and blink them away. I reached out, holding his cheek.

When he met my eyes, I said, "I'm right here. And I just ... I *know*, Chris. I see it. I can see you."

I caught a little tear on the tip of my thumb, and when he noticed, he fell back onto his bed, crossing his arms over his face. Then he cried. Hard.

I opened the blind another inch, letting in a little more light, and picked his blanket up from the floor, laying it over him.

I texted Cherie:

cancel tonight. trust me.

Cherie must've had her phone in hand, waiting, because she instantly replied:

Done. I trust you.

Then I crawled into the bed next to Chris. I just lay there at first. I still didn't know what he needed. I figured a moment to cry about it was probably necessary.

After a little while, he turned his face towards me.

Soft and shaky, he said, "I don't want you to think I'm just ... an angry, crying, door-slammer." He chuckled at himself, just faintly, wiping his eyes. "Because I'm not. I'm not usually like this. I just ... am. Right now."

I helped him wipe his eyes. "I don't think that. Not one bit. And you're not evil, or toxic, either."

His voice so sniffly I wasn't sure I heard him right, he said, "I don't think I could be. Not with you around."

It wasn't a proper smile, but I saw the dimple on his left cheek. He was searching my eyes for solace, so I softened them, smiling back.

"You can't have it all, anyway," I said, propping up to my elbow and resting my head in my hand. "Not right now, at least."

Chris scoffed. "Yeah, because my personal life is always—"

"No." I cut him off, tapping his nose and half-smirking.

"Because you're not at the peak of your career yet." He smiled, his face looked puffy and sore, but it was still perfect.

I flopped back down and got my head comfy on the pillow, putting on a silly reporter voice. "So, Mags, how are you and Chris handling all this?"

Then I answered, "Honestly, random reporter … I'd say we're handling it like champions."

Chris laughed; I'd never heard that laugh before. It was a real belly laugh.

"Fuck you," he said, still chuckling. I decided it was my favourite laugh of his.

There wasn't anything Chris could do to scare me away. I thought it was admirable, really, to experience his intensity. It made me feel like maybe he was just … feeling it all. Like me. I hadn't met a lot of people brave enough to live like that. To let things matter. And hurt. Shifting your heart in different directions than you thought you were heading.

Lying in bed by his side, silent and comfortable, my eyes felt heavy. I caught myself drifting off. I think he caught it, too, because he tossed half the blanket on me and pulled it up over us both.

I really did like the way it felt, to feel Chris here. Relaxed and sleepy in the peace of his presence, I shut my eyes to fall asleep.

Right before I did, I heard him whisper, "You're my best friend, too, Mags."

23

Doctor, My Eyes!

Chris

In the lift at The Bennett, post-kissing Maggie Marshall at The Havana, I caught my reflection and squinted, trying to focus.

Am I swaying?

I checked the time—2:36 a.m.? Sheesh.

I slowly blinked, and I swear to God, I almost didn't open my eyes again. I gripped the handrail, because if I lost my balance and fell flat on my drunk face, that security video footage would be on TMZ before I even woke up.

Fumbling my keycard, I stumbled into my suite and flopped onto the bed, limbs heavy, ears still ringing from the club. As I stared up at the ceiling, it felt like I was still caught in Maggie and Ben's orbit ... the radiant, *untouchable* one.

My head was spinning just enough to make me question gravity, but not enough to question kissing Maggie. I smiled, replaying it in my mind. I mean, it was a bit reckless, or whatever ...

But she was the one who tapped her lips. What was I 'sposed to do? *Not* kiss her? *Please.* It was a rational response.

In a haze, I plugged my phone in to charge. There must have been over a hundred notifications on it. I think at least fifty were from Dom, which I ignored.

The first message I opened was from Jordan. All it said was:

Bro... surely not?

But he'd linked me a video. I tapped it open, leaving it to load on the nightstand while I stood up to get undressed.

Halfway through unbuttoning my shirt, the video started playing ... and I froze.

"I mean, I don't want to go into details 'cause, like, I'm always going to want to protect him. But like, Chris is toxic. He's basically evil."

Is that Chelsea?

I snatched my phone off the nightstand, eyes glued to the screen.

It was Chelsea. On a podcast. Just like Ash had said.

"He's just not who everyone thinks he is. It's honestly sad."

What. The. Fuck.

My gut twisted; hearing her voice was *sickening*. It was syrupy sweet, but it was insidious, calculated, and viciously laced with venom.

Stupidly, I scrolled down. I started reading the comments, and at blinding G-force, I was catapulted straight out of the untouchable orbit and body-slammed back into reality.

called this months ago. Toxic.

I always said his shit would come out!!

take the trash out chels

I was at an amber-fucking-alert level of panic.

> when is he gonna disappear?

> thought he was gonna dip again and get away with it. glad she called him out..

There were hundreds ... and hundreds ...

But there was one that sent me.

> who's gonna warn maggie marshall? like girl, you next. Run!

I hurled my phone across the room. *"Fuck!"* The way it hit the wall, you'd think I'd thrown a frickin' hammer.

I was shaking, pacing, borderline hyperventilating. I wanted to rip my own head off.

What the hell was she thinking? Chelsea was still living in *my* house! And we agreed—no press. No publicity.

I couldn't deal with this bullshit again. I sparked a joint, inside. I could pay the cleaning fee. Wouldn't be the first time.

Dom will fix it. I'll call him. Shit, no—he fucked my ex when she wasn't my ex yet.

Mags ... I'll call Mags. She can ask Cherie, and Cherie will help me.

I picked up my phone, but I'd completely butchered it. The screen was shattered. I threw it again, harder.

Sitting on the edge of the bed, rolling another joint, my eyes flicked to the laptop on the desk. I *could* open it, check everything, and do a bit of practical preparation for damage control. I shouldn't, but ... I could.

Parts of me screamed *not* to open it. I even heard the voice of George, my therapist, telling me not to in my head.

Don't do it, Chris. It's a trap. You know better. What are you trying to achieve? Ground yourself. Walk away ... Blah, blah ... blah ...

The resounding voice of my altered mind was tenfold louder.

I sat at the desk and opened the laptop.

Sorry, George.

Losing track of time, I spiralled down a deep, dark rabbit hole of "Chris Rowan is toxic" content. It felt like everyone on the planet had a contribution, an important voice with something to say, and a big, bold reason to agree.

The way they wrote it, you'd think each comment stemmed from an intimate knowledge of who I was, during every ruthless moment with Chelsea. It didn't take me long to buy into the collective consensus.

I'd dare anyone; just imagine it.

Thousands of people telling you who you are. Then another thousand, screaming with them in agreement.

Oh, and no. You don't get to utter a single word. No explanations, no defences, not even a solitary syllable. You don't get that. You don't deserve that.

Do you want to know how it feels to find out that the world knows who you are, and they *hate it?*

I'll answer for you.

No. You don't. You don't want to know.

I needed a frickin' doctor. I'd tell them, *"Doctor, my eyes, I think they're going. I can't see clearly ... I'm too young to go blind!"*

But I didn't have a frickin' doctor, so every now and then I'd watch a video of Mags. It was like I'd left a lamp on in the room; just enough light to see a bit more clearly.

Then I'd remember that she was next, or whatever ... and I'd shut it off.

The more stoned I got, the less it hurt when I read something new. I was stoned out of my mind. I didn't sleep at all.

"Chriso?" Even when she added the *O* to my name, it had a melody when she said it. I barely noticed the door creak open, but I knew it was Maggie.

If I wasn't floating somewhere between exhausted and stoned, I'd be so embarrassed. There's no way I'd let her in. *Why did I give her a key? Idiot.*

I couldn't move. I also didn't want to move. I just stayed where I was, praying that she'd think I wasn't here and leave.

Don't come in. Don't come in. Turn around and walk out.

I was silent. *Turn the hell around, Maggie. Please.*

I opened one eye, and I knew I had to give up. She wasn't leaving.

I squinted like I was looking directly into the sun, watching her move slowly and cautiously. She was pure light. It burned my eyes, so I kept them half-shut at first.

Her light was blinding, but also somehow deafening all at once. I couldn't hear what she was saying, but her lips were moving.

I winced when she slapped my laptop shut. *Did I leave it on a video of her?* I couldn't remember, but my face felt hot, so whatever it was, it was fucking embarrassing. I let out a weird, half-hearted groan, dragging myself into a pillow as she sat on the end of the bed.

Then, Maggie said, "What was that? I couldn't hear you because you were literally talking into a pillow."

She didn't leave the sarcasm at the door. I probably deserved it, but it kinda pissed me off.

When I looked at her, she had this gentle little smile on her pretty little face, and I could see inside her head. It was a tangled maze; one I'd seen before. She was trying so hard to be chill, as if I'd believe her if she said she walked into this shit show every day and had seen it all before.

Why couldn't Maggie ever just *be?* Her body was here, but everything inside her wasn't.

She tried to tell me no one would believe Chelsea's bullshit like it was something to shrug off. I knew she was starting to freak out, and that freaked me out, too. But it was better that way. She could forget I was in here, I could just see her tomorrow; she'd be safer. She wouldn't be next.

I had to tell her that it wasn't bullshit, that it was true. So, I explained it all to her on a silver platter, hoping she'd believe me and walk out.

But she rolled her eyes. And I wasn't seeing clearly enough to know she didn't mean it. Even before I spoke, I felt guilty about how I was about to sound.

I was practically hissing, "Don't. You're trying to be chill right now and I fucking know you're not and it's driving me insane."

I was ready to flinch; I swear she could have slapped me square across the face.

But she didn't, because ... she was Maggie.

She asked me what I needed her to do, and gazing deep into her pale green eyes, I was begging in my mind.

Stay in this room. Leave the light on.

I needed to see clearly, through her eyes, and shift my perspective out of the blind spot. I needed to be pulled back into her radiant orbit, covered in light in a way that didn't hurt or burn, because she was *Maggie Marshall.* She could make everything glow, without leaving a trace of ashes.

Her face turned sad, my chest wound up tight, and when I caught a tear rolling down her cheek, my breath got stuck. It was a sudden shift, a wave of panic; I thought I'd surely scared her away.

That wasn't *really* what I wanted, and the last thing I *ever* wanted was to be the reason Maggie cried. I reached for her, wrapping my arms around her tightly, but she shoved me off and stood up abruptly when I tried to hold on.

Then, she told me I was her best friend, in the entire world, and held her hand on my cheek. That little hand against my skin felt like a balm to whatever wounds had been split open in the hours since I saw her.

And it was in the way she said, "I'm right here. And I just ... I *know*, Chris. I see it. *I can see you.*"

Her light had absolutely covered me, and I completely melted into a puddle. I couldn't hold it—I was sobbing.

She climbed into bed next to me for a while. She could hold so much space, waiting for me to come back, just like I waited for her when she went dark. She could have offered me advice, or some type of band-aid, or a slap across the face.

But instead, she made me laugh. Hard.

In a way, I resented her for it because I was settling comfortably in this rabbit hole, and she pulled me out. I adored her for it at the same time, though. I let the feelings co-exist.

I wasn't ready for the light to go out, so I pulled the blanket up over both of us and prayed again. This time that she wouldn't leave.

Right before I felt her falling asleep, I made sure she knew.

"You're my best friend too, Mags."

24

Heartbreak Hotel

When I woke up, it was just past six in the morning, and Chris was still asleep beside me. We'd fallen asleep before it was even dark, which was probably the most sleep I'd had in weeks. So even at six a.m., I felt fresh. Bright-eyed and bushy-tailed.

Plus, I was a little supercharged when I remembered I didn't have to race around my suite, throwing everything in sight into my bag so I wouldn't be late to set.

Not wanting to wake Chris, I carefully shimmied out of bed and slipped out the door.

From the windows in the hallway, I could see the beach. The sun was just starting to rise, casting this pretty, soft glow on the water. It looked calm, clear, and perfect.

Watching the way the ocean sparkled gave me an idea. A silly and corny idea, but ... I was going through with it.

I turned back towards Chris's suite and, at first, I knocked gently, trying not to wake the neighbours. After no answer, I thought ... *stuff it*, and I knocked three times, loudly.

An older man poked his head out of the room next door, glaring at me. I stared back, straight-faced.

"Sorry, sir," I shrugged. "Welfare check." He huffed and shook his head before retreating back inside.

With my ear to the door, I heard Chris. "Mags?" he asked, his voice half-asleep. "Is that you?"

I cleared my throat, ready with my best Valley Girl accent. "No, sir. I'm from the front desk. We need you to check out immediately."

"Uh, just a sec." I could hear him scrambling for clothes ... *I think he bought it.*

Less than thirty seconds later, he flung open the door.

"Mags," he sighed, relieved. "What are you doing?"

I smiled, but not too big; I was in character. "Sir, as I said, I'm from the front desk. The front desk of Heartbreak Hotel." I paused, holding my smile, and gave him a moment to catch up to speed. "We're going to need you to check out immediately."

He crossed his arms and leaned against the doorframe. "And why is that, exactly?" His eyes frowned, but his mouth smiled.

I huffed; hands firm on my hips. "Well, the issue is ... Heartbreak Hotel is completely booked out for the rest of..." I glanced at my bare wrist. "For the rest of forever."

"Right ..." He tightened his arms. "And where am I supposed to go?"

I nodded, beaming so hard I accidentally dropped the accent. "You can follow me, sir!"

I grabbed his hand and made a break for the fire exit, dragging him behind me.

We sprinted through the hotel lobby; I figured the faster we ran, the more blurred it would appear, so people wouldn't know it was Chris. And it wasn't even about the whole *toxic* thing, either ...

He just didn't have any shoes on, running through a fancy hotel. It made him look heaps bogan, and he didn't need that added headline.

Once we got across the street, he let go of my hand and ran beside me. At that point, I think he knew where we were headed. We stopped when we hit the sand, both of us grinning at the sunrise. My cheeks ached from smiling so wide.

Chris shot me a look; his brows were raised. With a quick flick of his head towards the water, I heard the words in his mind: *Dare you?*

I stared back and threw up my hands. My face said, *duh*, and my mind said: *Obviously!*

In a race, we legged it for the ocean, pulling our shirts off as we ran.

Diving into that water was like getting a brain freeze that runs all the way down to your toes and loops back up again. Except, on the way back up, from your toes back to your brain, it turns hot, like *fire*.

I loved the way it felt—to *feel it all*.

I watched Chris dive under a wave, and I really hoped he felt the same way.

Sitting up on the beach, wet and sandy, we were far enough away from people so they wouldn't know it was us, but close enough that I could keep an eye out for anyone trying to get a picture with their phone. People were sneaky. I reckon we had roughly five minutes left to savour the sunrise before the L.A. chaos woke up and wreaked havoc ... directly onto Chris.

He checked his phone and I thought he might be thinking the same thing, but he asked, "What time is the thing tonight?"

"Five." I nodded. "I've got Alicia from, like, one or two, though. Maybe earlier. I can't remember."

He sighed a deep exhale, stood up, and held out his hand to me. "That's just enough time to get Chelsea's shit out of my place. You coming?"

I cocked my head, my face turning baffled as I raised an eyebrow.

What the heck? It was dangerously immature, borderline psychotic, and teetered right on the edge of audacity! So, naturally ...

I slapped my hand in his!

Then I said the most classically bogan, Australian phrase of agreement I could think of. *"Fucking oath* I'm coming!"

Chris cracked up, hauled me to my feet, and started to jog backwards to the hotel.

He called out, "Amazing! Meet you in the lobby in an hour!"

25

Theatrics

Chris' place was about an hour from the hotel, and Sweet Marco drove us. Chris stayed quiet, sitting in the front seat, his gaze fixed out the window. I didn't mind; most of the drive hugged the coastline, and the ocean views weren't hard to look at.

I imagined Chris was rehearsing the exact words he'd say to Chelsea, running through the conversation like a script. I didn't have the heart to remind him that no matter how many times he rewrote it in his head, Chelsea wouldn't remember her lines. He'd have to improv.

I wasn't entirely sure what my role was here. Moral support, I guess? I hoped it wasn't bodyguard. Chelsea wouldn't fight clean. And as much as I wanted to see the inside of Chris's house, because I had some guesses on what it looked like, I really didn't want to go in. This wasn't my fight. If he asked, I'd say no. But if I could be a fly on the wall ... that'd be a heck yes.

We pulled up to Chris's gate, and as Marco punched in the code, I leaned forward, perched in the centre of the back seat. The gate slowly inched open, and it echoed a creak that dragged out the moment I was waiting for. It felt like it was holding its breath along with me!

When the house finally came into view ... I slumped back.

Ugh. Gross.

It was just a big, grey box. That modern, boring, prison-like style. Everything about it looked so lifeless and sterile. *Has this bloke ever spent more than two days here?*

It was pretty friggin' big, though. I thought of the Netflix show *Outer Banks* and let a little giggle out. *Chris is such a Kook.*

Chris unbuckled his seatbelt, nervously glancing at me. "Okay," he huffed. "I'll just go in. I won't be long. I just need to make sure, you know? If I'm not back in twenty minutes ..."

"Burn the place to the ground," I said, deadpan. "Yes, Chris—I know." I rolled my eyes.

"Oh, good," he said, running a hand through his hair as his eyes darted back towards the house. "You remembered the plan."

I gave him a sure nod. I loved it when Chris went along with my silly little jokes.

With another huff, he nodded at Marco, jumped out, and slammed the door. I knew he did it on purpose, making sure Chelsea heard someone was here. The car windows were tinted so dark, I was sure she wouldn't see me, so that was a relief.

Ten minutes passed, and I'd already counted all the cement tiles around his pool to keep my brain busy. There were forty-seven. The balcony above it was boring, but I did try to peek inside. I couldn't see much, only the edges of a massive TV on the wall.

I wondered if he had one of those cinema rooms. Then I wondered if he had a popcorn machine, or a fairy floss maker ... I couldn't imagine Chris eating fairy floss.

I thought it was an odd design that the pool was at the front of the house. I mean, it was hidden behind a towering grey Colorbond fence, but it all still felt backwards.

I hadn't made small talk with Marco yet; I figured it was time.

"So, Marco," I said, climbing into the front seat next to him. I cradled my head in my hand on the centre console. "Sweet, sweet Marco," I added, smiling.

"Yes, Miss Maggie?" He returned the smile, but he narrowed his eyes, looking suss.

I inched a little closer. "What's the bet they're having wild, passionate make-up sex right now?"

He winced like he was grossed out. "No, Miss Maggie!" He shook his head, waving his finger at me. "No bets. Chris is in pain. Do you know how many times he's cried in this very car? So many. *Too* many." He winced again; I think he was having flashbacks.

Sweet Marco had his serious pants on today. I peered into the back, picturing Chris as a puddle of tears, snot … and weed.

Slumping back into my seat, I raised my hands. "Fine. No bets."

About fifteen seconds of silence passed before I turned to him again. "Wanna play eye spy?" The anxiety made me sound whiny, but thankfully, Marco agreed!

We'd each had a few turns when I realised it had been twenty minutes since Chris went inside. We didn't *actually* have a plan, here … I thought a few more minutes would be fine.

It was my go, in eye spy, but Marco spat, "Starting with P! Starting with *P!*" He slapped my knee, pointing behind us above the gate.

… *Paparazzi.*

When I saw them, I gasped. "Oh shit!" I threw my little body into the back, sprawling flat across the seats. If I was pictured here, I'd be done for.

"Reckon they can see me?" I asked Marco.

"No, Miss Maggie," he assured me. "Stay still. I'll call Chris."

I craned my neck just enough to still see the balcony over the pool. The door was open, and I did that thing where you say a person's name a hundred times in your head, hoping it will get their attention.

Chris. Chriso. Chris.

It didn't feel like it was working. At all.

I felt like the paps could hear me, so I whispered, "Hopefully he just walks back out. There's not much of a story in that."

Right as I finished my sentence, Chris stepped out onto the balcony. Marco and I gasped in perfect sync, and my jaw hit the goddamn floor.

Chris didn't look angry, but his arms were flexed and veiny, gripping a very large, very full suitcase. Marco's eyes stayed glued to Chris like he was predicting the next twenty seconds, so my eyes stayed glued, too.

To me, the moments that followed stretched out in slow motion.

Chris had his back to us, facing Chelsea, who was red-faced and *screaming* at him.

But when he spun back around ...

He pegged that suitcase as hard as he could, launching it over the balcony and into the pool.

A kaleidoscope of fabric and colour filled the air, and when time sped up again, the suitcase, and everything inside of it, were floating on the surface of the water.

Well, most of it. Everything else sunk immediately.

I slapped both hands to my mouth. *Oh my god.* My heart raced so fast, I felt my hands shaking against my face. I would have described Chris as a little dramatic, but this was a whole new level of theatrics.

With his mouth hanging open, Marco said, "Miss Maggie ... It's payday for the stalkers today."

I burst into laughter—it had me in stitches! I was clenching my belly, trying not to roll around too much. Mere seconds had passed, and I was already replaying it in my head, wiping my eyes and jittering through the laughing knots in my chest.

Then I felt the car door swing open and slam shut.

Marco closed his mouth, staring at his steering wheel, but I kept my mouth hanging open, eyes still wet, glued to Chris. I remained silent, unsure if we were laughing about this … or crying.

Leaning around the front seat, Chris looked at me lying flat on my back, stiller than a statue. He burst out laughing, and in sheer relief—I was in stitches again.

Cutting us off from cracking up, Marco shouted, "Chris! Open the gate. I will drive. Now." He pointed to the paps.

Chris hit his head back on the seat when he realised. "Oh, you've gotta be fucking kidding me."

As soon as the gate was open, Marco was pedal to the metal. He wasn't Sweet Marco when he drove like this; he took a sharp turn and it flung me to the floor.

Chris nudged Marco's shoulder. "Shit, Marco. Chill. It's all good; they've already got the shot now." Turning around to me, he asked, "You good?"

I could have just said yes and sat back up … but I didn't.

Lying on the floor of the back seat with my hands in the air above me, I said, "I can see it now. Front page of the Daily Mail: *CONFIRMED Chris Rowan—Evil, Toxic, Sad Boy!*"

Chris chuckled, shaking his head. "Thanks, Mags. Thanks a lot." Smirking, he added, "Cherie is gonna *love* this."

Sure enough, fifteen minutes later, my phone was ringing. It was Cherie, of course.

"Speak of the angel," I said, then I answered the call. "Hello?"

Cherie spoke sharply. "Tell me you are in your hotel room with Alicia right now, Mags." She sounded *pissed.*

"Okay," I said, nodding quickly as if it would help me lie. "I'm in my hotel room right now with Alicia."

She started yelling, "You little liar! *I* am in your hotel room right now, with Alicia. *You* are not here! So, tell me, Mags, where are you?"

She was speaking so loudly that Chris could hear her through the phone. He turned to me, shook his head, and held one finger to his lips.

I looked back at him, panicked. *Chris! You know I can't lie!*

"I ..." I started shakily, glaring at Chris desperately, but I choked. "I'm on my way. Running late, sorry! See you soon!"

"Wait!" Cherie shouted. "Mags, don't you *dare* hang up this phone."

Terrified, my voice went squeaky. "... Yes?"

"Tell Chris his arms looked hot when he threw that suitcase!" My body relaxed; it wasn't Cherie. It was Alicia.

I giggled. "I will! See you soon!"

When I hung up, Chris passed his phone to me and said, "You called it, Miss Maggie."

I read the screen, and there it was, posted by Page Six:

Chris Rowan puts on a toxic display at his L.A. home.

And yes—his arms looked hot in the photo.

I scoffed, a little shocked at their speed. "Damn. They are quick!" Mumbling, I added, "I liked my title better."

I saved the photo and texted it to myself. Flashing Chris my phone when I handed him his, I said, "This will remind me to be a badass every time I see it." I'd set the photo as my wallpaper.

Feeling extremely satisfied with myself, I smiled and gave Chris a little nod.

He rolled his eyes—*so* hard.

26

Forced Confrontation

Chris

Standing at the front door of my own house, one hand on the door handle ... I had a few thoughts:

Oh, shit.

Walk away.

This is ridiculous.

I'm fighting fire with fire.

They fucked in my bed.

And I did tell her—one week. It had been a week. This was fair.

I need a new bed.

Maybe I should start an actual fire.

Maybe Mags could go in for me.

What does fucking oath even mean?

Before I could move, the door flung open, and Chelsea stood right before me.

"What are you doing here?" she asked, eyeing me up and down. Her tone was surprisingly gentle.

Forcing my voice to match her level, I smiled and stepped through the door. "Chels," I said, "I just wanted to see if you needed a hand, you know, moving out of my house." It sounded kind of sarcastic, but it really wasn't.

She shrugged dismissively and headed back inside, so I followed her in.

"I'm leaving today, Chris," she said, spinning to face me, arms crossed. "So no, I don't."

I thought she was lying, then I saw a packed suitcase on the coffee table. *Good.*

I followed her into the bedroom and sat on the end of my bed, watching her pull clothes off hangers. She didn't look back at me once, just kept packing from the wardrobe. It felt painfully awkward. There was a big elephant shitting in the room, and we were just … pretending it wasn't.

What was I *doing?* She was leaving, I had evidence … I should just go.

Standing up, I spoke louder so she'd look at me. "Well, I'll leave you to it. I'll be back here soon. Home, I mean. I just wanted to make sure you had …" I paused. Finding the words was hard.

Packed your shit and left? Gone so I never had to see you again? I settled on one, a non-evil one.

"… Vacated." I smiled. "Before I'm back."

She looked at me with a harsh, cold glare. I could smell that elephant shit now.

How was she mad at *me?* She had been living in *my* house, after fucking my manager, and *after* telling the world I was a toxic piece of shit.

I opened my mouth to say it, I could have screamed it. *Fuck you.*

But it wasn't worth it. I wasn't proving her right; I wasn't giving her an inch. I just shook my head, scoffed beneath my breath, and walked towards the front door.

She called out, "Chris? Wait."

I felt her behind me. I should have kept walking right out that door. It felt like I'd deeply regret it, but … I turned around.

"Chris, what are we doing?" she asked, trying to grab my hand.

I flinched and folded my arms across my chest, tight. She tried to hide her disappointment, but I could see it.

She went on, "Why are we doing this? I don't want to leave like this. I want to be here when you're back." There was something twisted in her tone. It was almost *flirty*.

I just stared at her. I don't know what my face was doing, but I don't think I'd ever made that expression before.

"Chris," she said softly, putting her hands on my shoulders, stepping closer. She was begging for my attention, so I closed my eyes.

She whispered, "I'm so, so sorry." Then she leaned in and kissed my cheek, near my ear.

Keeping my eyes shut tight, I took a long, shuddering, deep breath in.

She stepped back and snapped, "What, you have nothing to say? Like, at all?"

My eyes shot open. Two daggers meeting hers.

I thought I'd see her. I was ready to see the real her. Calculated, vindictive, manipulative. Driven by anger and a relentless need for attention.

But I didn't see the real Chelsea.

In her eyes, for the first time—

I saw myself.

And the reflection was crystal clear.

Every juvenile, reckless, shitty thing I'd ever done met me in a single, damning instant. The forced confrontation of it shook me through my core, deep into my bones.

Maggie was right. I didn't hate Chelsea. The only person I hated in that moment was the person I saw in her eyes.

Myself.

Chelsea had infected all the reasons that I loved being in love. I wanted a love story so badly that I let her do it. I let her consume me, burn away everything that made me ... *me.* Like I loved the idea of being in love so much, I just ... became her. Mirrored her. Her anger, her greed, all of it.

We'd been feeding off each other all this time. Every time we screamed at each other; we were really screaming at ourselves. It was all a toxic cycle, a song and dance of co-dependency. And I had nothing left to give, nothing to keep feeding it.

I'd changed. I'd grown out of whatever that version of love is, or was. I didn't know what my reflection would be without her, but I had no doubts. Chelsea was in the way of me finding it.

Looking at her glaring at me, it just felt so definite. So final. I was done. Done with living like this, done with feeling trapped in a life that didn't even feel like mine anymore.

Underlined, in bold letters. **<u>Done</u>**.

I hung my head. I wished I didn't have this revelation with Chelsea, of all people.

She'd never get it. She'd never face herself. If it were someone else, someone like Maggie, I'd be loved through it. We'd talk about it. And we'd grow up. Together.

Chelsea hadn't stopped talking at me, but I couldn't hear any of it. When I looked at her, all I saw was a broken little child. I wasn't her person; I couldn't love her through this.

I took a quick, final look at my reflection in her eyes. If that had been who I was yesterday, and all the days before that, it sure as hell wasn't going to be who I was today, or tomorrow, or in all the days that followed.

I felt it in my chest, like the weight of a heavy burden lifting from my heart. And for the first time in a long time in Chelsea's presence, I took another deep inhale ... and a long, true exhale.

For a second, I felt bad for her. She'd be sad when I walked out.

But then I saw that the balcony door was open, and her suitcase, on the coffee table, was also open …

Fine. One more day to be a dick.

Chels was screaming at me now, but it was wasted on my deaf ears. I didn't hear a word. I pushed past her, grabbed the suitcase off the coffee table and headed straight for the balcony.

She kept screaming. "Chris? What the fuck! Chris, what are you doing? *Stop!*"

I saw her hitting my arms, but I couldn't feel it. I had one thing to do, then I was out of there.

I glanced back at her; she was completely ablaze in unchecked fury. Before she could get any closer, I hurled the whole damn suitcase over the rail and into the pool. She leaned over the edge, wide-eyed, watching all her shit fly through the air.

… Welp, that's me.

I was out of there.

Halfway to the front door, if she saw the smug look on my face, I'd be a dead man.

She chased after me, grabbing at my arm. "Chris! What the fuck is wrong with you? You're psychotic! You need fucking help!"

I kept that grin plastered on as I opened the door. I slid on my sunglasses, turned around, slammed the door in her face, and legged it for the car.

I jumped in the front seat, and Marco and Mags were silent. Marco stared straight ahead; mouth clamped shut.

Shit. They watched that.

I turned to Mags, lying across the backseat, mouth hanging open, eyes wet from undoubtedly giggling so hard, and I couldn't do anything else but burst out laughing.

Even after I knew the suitcase ordeal was snapped by L.A. vultures, I still changed my mind about turning around to face Chelsea.

I didn't regret a damn thing.

When we pulled up at The Bennett, I was thankful they had a carpark. There were so many cameras camped out front, Mags would have been caught, for sure.

As we got out of the car, she asked, "Before we're in front of cameras later, how did it *actually* go?"

I took a second to consider how I wanted to respond right then, and she smiled, trying to colour the empty space.

"It went well." I sighed and smiled, nodding like I was convincing myself. "I think I might have just met myself."

She looked excited. "Whoa! Deep!" She squinted, her voice turning sultry as she continued, "Is he, like, the dark and mysterious type, or ..." She flashed my favourite cheeky grin. "Is he more of a cool cat? Knows a few facts, fun to have a party?"

I scoffed, chuckled, and gave her a shove. "Neither."

"Well, do I get to meet him?"

I knew she was messing with me, but when she asked that, I also knew it was underlined earnestly. I looked her in the eyes, considering again before I spoke.

Raising an eyebrow, I said, "You?" She nodded, and I shook my head. "Never. Ever, ever." She frowned, but I chuckled.

I didn't want Maggie to meet that arsehole ... he was a dick.

I walked ahead of her into the elevator, holding the doors open to say bye to her because I knew she'd take the stairs.

"See you in two hours, Miss Maggie."

I winked, and I was certain I caught her peek at my arm against the doors before they closed.

Certain.

27

Clickbait

I'd managed to squeeze in time with Ben while Alicia did my hair for the GQ event. He was *still* nursing a hangover, even though it had been almost forty hours since we went out. We laughed about being old and young at the same time, and how weird that felt … but mostly, we just laughed at what Chris had done a few hours earlier.

Ben had made plans with an ex, which we also laughed about, so he left. After I watched him close my door, I sighed at myself in the mirror.

How am I still living the same day?

It was only three p.m. and I was completely spent. My brain processed the simple action of taking a shower the way a neurotypical brain would process an entire day, so when actual events happened in my life, it was completely and utterly exhausting.

When I met Cherie and Chris in the lobby, Chris had sunglasses on, and a second pair dangled from his fingers.

"Yeah, you're going to want these," he said, handing them to me with a sorry smile. "There's a bit on out there." He nodded towards the entrance. Where the view of the ocean should have been, there was only a sea of flashing cameras.

Cherie gave a quick nod. "He's right. Wear them."

I sighed and slipped them on, instantly feeling like the biggest wanker. I'd never felt like a wanker before, and I wasn't keen on the feeling.

Realistically, there were only four to six strides between the front door and the car, but now it felt like we were about to embark on the world's longest hike. One filled with paparazzi … and bad angles.

Chris said, "You go first, with Cherie. I'll be right behind you."

I just nodded. Why couldn't I speak?! *Say a word, Maggie!*

I felt frustrated and anxious and panicky. We'd done press before, but that was before the world considered Chris's life interesting enough to dissect. Cherie quickly linked her arm through mine, she knew not to speak to me, because she knew I was overstimulated.

It was over in four seconds. Literally.

We were already driving away, and I tossed the sunglasses onto the floor of the van. I stared out the window, taking long, deep breaths.

Chris leaned over to say something to me, but Cherie stopped him. "Just give us a sec." I loved the way she said "us", even though I knew she wasn't bothered at all. It was comforting.

Chris looked anxious, and I remembered, this was the first time he was doing this without Dom. I had to get it together for him.

I sat up straight and pulled myself out of the slump. "Damn, sorry." I giggled. "There's this Aussie saying, and I feel like it's really relevant right now."

There was just enough sarcasm in my voice that a smile tugged at Chris's lips, but he still looked a bit anxious.

I knew he'd be okay, though, because in my thickest Aussie accent, I said, *"Geez Louise!"*

His mouth fell open in a baffled grin. Through genuine confusion, he asked, "What the hell does that even mean?" Laughing, he added, "Who the hell is *Louise?*"

I shook my head. "Honestly, Chris ... I don't think anyone really knows."

It always felt relaxing to laugh about ridiculous things, like our lives. I felt my light switch back on. Dim, but it'd last me a couple of hours.

The event was the Breakthrough Hollywood Industry Awards, hosted by *GQ* magazine. Chris mentioned that once you're inside, not much happens at these events. Still, I was curious, and more than willing to play the role of an anxiously nosy spectator.

We were invited to support Michael Lesley, the casting agent who'd cast us both in *More of You.* And you know what? He bloody deserved an award, I reckon. He was a proper legend, like Roy, so I was hoping he'd win.

Being there to support Michael really just meant Chris and I were there to yap about the show, draw attention, and be visible. To do that, I'd learned, you become a walking billboard for a well-known brand. You wear what you're told to wear, you talk about who you're wearing, and you try your best to serve face for the cameras.

Six months ago, if someone had told me I'd be going to an event with a brand, I probably would've guessed Cotton On, at best. So, when I found out that we were going with Tommy Hilfiger, it felt like a moon landing. Totally outta this world!

Chris looked *damn* fine, annoyingly. Like he just got out of the shower, gave his hair a little zhoosh, and rocked up where he needed to be. He was styled in baggy grey trousers, a pale grey button-down, a loose red and navy tie, and a black varsity jacket.

He kept his sunglasses on in most of the photos, and he wore the same white sneakers as me.

I was dressed in an oversized cream-coloured knit vest with red stitching along the edges. The dark grey, oversized wool trousers that matched were secretly pinned at the back. My hair was out, tucked behind my ears in big, loose waves.

Our whole vibe was giving ... "going to my rich Grandpa's penthouse overlooking Central Park, where perhaps we'd have a stroll after we got tipsy on his fancy wine".

We were getting photos, which was the easy part. Smile, move a bit, but not too much. Smile again, maybe throw a hot, serious face in here and there ... you get the gist. It was especially easy for Chris because he carried an effortless aura of undeniable sex appeal. I think he knew it was there, but he knew how to handle it. *So annoying.*

We were separated to talk to reporters, and my anxiety was peaking. I felt jittery. And a little nervous about the butterflies in my belly and brain. Cherie stayed at my side, standing between Chris and me, like her right ear was on me, and her left ear was on Chris. She could be such a boss. *Eat your heart out, Kris Jenner.*

I razzle-dazzled my way through, talking about the show, Tommy, my cosy knit vest, and not even mentioning Chris's name. I shot Cherie my *I'm done, please* face and we headed off the carpet.

I figured I'd save Chris on the way, when I heard a reporter ask, "So, Chris, you've had an emotional week. How are you holding up now?"

I took a step towards them, eyeing the reporter. *That friggin' mole.*

Cherie grabbed my arm and yanked me back. She muttered in my ear, "He's a big boy. He's got this."

Chris smiled, and in a calm, cool voice, he responded, "Yeah, I mean, I'm feeling great! Like, this is a really exciting night. Maggie and I owe a lot to Michael Lesley, who is being honoured tonight, and yeah … The weather is perfect, I'm decked out in Tommy. Just happy to be here." He flashed the reporter a grin, gave her a thank-you nod, and bee-lined for me and Cherie.

And *that* is what they call answering a question, without answering a question. If it were a sport, Chris would be the Michael Jordan of it.

We were getting mic'd up for a quick sit-down interview with GQ when Chris leaned into me.

"You look really pretty," he said.

It was so sweet, he sounded so cute. It made me feel nice. I just wanted to grab his face and plant a kiss on his cheek. But I didn't, because … cameras.

The journo's name was John Gettin. Chris had met him before because he gave him one of those "pat on the back, no-hip-contact" bro hugs. Naively, I felt a little relieved. If John knew Chris, he wouldn't ask any invasive questions.

I quickly found out that John didn't give a fuck, because he led with—

"You two! So happy to have you here. Everyone is so hyped about this show, and we already know that you two together is going to be phenomenal."

Chris and I both mouthed a quiet, "Aww, thanks," knowing John wasn't finished.

"But Chris, my dude." He glanced at Chris and whipped out his phone. "You've gotta talk me through this photo." Shoving the screen in our faces, to no surprise, it was Chris throwing a suitcase over a balcony.

I glanced at Chris. We half-politely, half-awkwardly laughed, and Chris shook his head.

John wasn't giving up. He asked, "Bro, what was it, a scene in the show?" His eyes darted between us.

This dirty dog. I was still smiling, but my lips were pursing. We couldn't comment on specifics of the show, or we'd be in big trouble.

My eyes flickered to Chris, then to Cherie who was about to step in, then back to Chris. But then I thought ... *screw you, John Gettin.*

"Mate!" I scoffed, putting on a boyish voice. "That's literally my phone wallpaper!" I was sitting on my phone, so I pulled it out, showing John and the camera. I continued, "I love it! It's so funny, because it was such a small thing."

I was trying the whole "it wasn't even a thing, the media made it a thing" route. Like making it a joke would minimise the pain of it.

I went on. "But now, I have this really funny wallpaper, and when I look at it ..." I looked John square in the face, tilting my head. "It reminds me not to take any shit from anyone." I smiled and shrugged. "So, yeah. That's why I love it. And! It also kinda reminds me I should work out my arms more."

If my eyes could talk, they were saying: *next question.*

John fake-laughed, too hard, and it made Chris and I *real* laugh. I think, on camera, it would have looked fine ... *or so I hoped.*

Chris had his arm behind my chair, pretending to look kicked back and relaxed. It must have given John the impression we were a team, and it was two against one. He asked a random question about Michael Lesley casting us, we answered politely, and John's time was up.

I guessed they'd still make the video title *Chris Rowan Talks Us Through That Photo,* and it would get a million clicks, at least. Jokes on everyone who gets hooked on the clickbait, because they'd get thirty seconds of my chaotic bullshit instead.

I did briefly think of Roy saying that the business could "spit me back out", and felt a quick itch of fear that it was about to happen to me. But then I looked at Chris, and remembered he was living *in* that place, now. It meant a whole lot more to me to be his best friend than it did to be his co-star.

When we were walking to our table inside the event, Chris leaned into my ear and asked, "How many John Gettin jokes have you come up with?"

I spun to face him. "A few." I shrugged. "You?"

"Yeah ..." He smiled. "A few." He shrugged.

I smirked. "Yeah, like, John Gettin? More like John's-Getting-a-punch-in-the ..."

Chris flung his hand over my mouth, choking back his chuckles. "I know, Mags. Trust me. I'm thinking the same thing. Just *shh* about it, though." He released his hand and put a finger to his lips, repeating, "*Shh.*"

When we sat down, he leaned into my ear again. "Thank you, though. For before. You're kind of the best."

I felt a little glow in my body, like when he said I looked pretty. I turned to him and smiled. I didn't say anything, because it felt happy and lovely just as it was—as a thank you.

28

In Your Dreams, Mate

Maggie

The rest of the event was nice, which we all know means one thing and one thing only ...

Boring.

They barely ever feed you at these things, but they give you unlimited booze. And because you're bored, anxious, and awkward, you consistently sip away. The glasses just keep on coming! There's no way to know how much you've had.

When it was over, Chris stood up, accidentally kicked the table leg, and knocked a few glasses over.

"Oh, shit!" he said, glancing around at the mess he made and the others at the table. "Sorry, guys. So sorry."

He gave me this shocked look that said, *Maggie, I am so drunk. Help me, help me, help me!* I helped him pick up his mess before the bartenders came rushing over, chewing my cheeks to stop myself from laughing.

I felt a little tipsy, but Chris? Well, if I could use another classically Australian term, I'd say ... Chris was *munted.*

Cherie whispered sharply in my ear, "Car. Now."

I nodded to Cherie, then spun to the bartenders to say thank you ... and sorry.

I decided it was rude to interrupt the others at the table and say bye, which was just an excuse to dip without small talk.

We were waiting at the back of the venue for our car to pull up, and Chris was leaning against the wall with his eyes closed. He had a slight sway to his stance that made me giggle under my breath. Pick-up areas at these events were a tight ship, heavy on security and absolutely zero cameras, which was highly convenient right now.

I poked Chris's waist. "Had a bit much, did you, doll?" The question sounded patronising, but it was on purpose.

He opened one eye. "How are you not drunk right now? You're like, less than half my size."

I shrugged. "Chris, it's literally cultural for an Australian to be able to binge drink."

He pushed himself off the wall and slumped over my back, hugging me, but mostly resting all his weight on me so he wouldn't fall down.

Holding on to his arms over my chest, I muttered, "I also didn't have two glasses of red wine to "pep me up" when I started to feel tired."

"Ah, drats." He clicked his finger in my face. "I drank red *wine?*"

I nodded. "Uh huh."

"Damn. I think I meant to ask for Red *Bull.*" He sounded so slurred and tired, chuckling sleepily in my ear.

"Ah, *drats.*" I clicked my finger in front of my chest. He was too easy to mock.

Cherie texted:

Out the back.

"Oh, this is us," I said, shrugging Chris off me.

I dragged my feet towards the exit. Thank goodness there were fancy people there to open the door because I was too tired to pull it open, and Chris was incapable.

Dragging his feet behind me, Chris asked, "Did I already tell you that you look really pretty?"

I turned to him. "Yes, but if it's a two-for-one deal, I'll take it." I put my hands under my chin like a toddler posing for dance photos.

"Oh, good." He giggled. "You look *really* pretty."

When we got to the car, I opened the door and practically shoved Chris in. He flopped onto the seat, his head lolling to one side with a goofy grin. He was being a brat; a wine-soaked, cheeky one.

Cherie rolled her eyes and scoffed. "What the hell, Chris? Was it really that sort of event?"

I shot her a look, silently telling her to *cool it.* I explained, "He asked for red wine, instead of Red Bull."

She was baffled. "And you just ... drank it?" She quickly realised that he had, rolled her eyes again, and answered herself. "Well, obviously you drank it."

Back at the hotel, I walked Chris to his room. It was for the best, even though I had to take the elevator, which I hated. But I was genuinely unsure if he'd make it to his suite. I thought maybe I'd find him in the lobby, asleep on the lounges by the concierge the next morning.

Riding in the lift, he was swaying again, his eyes half-closed. He leaned against the handrail, then he pointed at me and said, "You made that reporter stutter. I saw it." He circled his finger in the air.

"Who?" I asked. "John Gettin?"

He frowned and shut his eyes tight. "No, no. Not that arsehole." Then he held a middle finger above his head. "Fuck him."

I snickered. "Then who?"

Opening one eye and squinting the other, he said, "The one at the photo spot, with the cameras. He asked you a question, and your pretty eyes made him stutter. I saw it." He closed his eyes and smirked, almost like he was rewatching it.

"I think you're making that up," I replied.

He shook his head. "I'm not." Then he briefly opened his eyes. "You do it to me, sometimes." He shut them tight again, crossing his arms. "I'm just too cool to stutter."

Giggling at himself, he wobbled and almost lost his balance.

I giggled with him. It was cute. And cute was kind of my ... *thing*, you know?

When we got to his door, Chris had a revelation. "Oh, Maggie." He patted all his pockets. "I don't have my key."

I gasped. *"You what?"* I was mockingly shocked, but truthfully, I was unsurprised.

His drunken giggle was slurry and silly, and he slapped his hand to his mouth.

"I'll have to stay with you," he said. "There is no other option." He held up his hands and shrugged.

"Oh, I do have another option, though ..." I said, offering a smile tinged with regret.

He looked intrigued, and a little aroused, raising an eyebrow.

I sighed. "I have the other key." I waved it in front of him and swiped it to his door.

When it clicked unlocked, I opened it for him without stepping inside, making it clear I wasn't going in. I handed him the key, and his cheeky, bratty, drunken smirk instantly dropped into a straight line.

"Stay with me?" he asked.

My breath caught a little. He was standing so close, the tip of his nose almost touching mine.

He snaked his hand behind my back, twisting his fingers in the ends of my hair. "I'm going back to the house tomorrow. It's *so far* from you. Please?"

Why did he have to be a cute drunk? *Why!* There were so many other types he could have been! Angry, obnoxious, too sexual, too sad, too reckless, the list goes on. But *cute?* It was melting me ...

But not enough.

Chris threw his ex-girlfriend's stuff over a balcony and into a pool, only a few hours ago. I couldn't meet him where he was in his mind, right now. Intellectually and emotionally, anyway. Physically, sure ... but I wasn't really the type to feel satisfied without all three.

Narrowing my eyes, I whispered firmly, "No." I smiled confidently, mostly at myself.

He threw back his head and sulked. *"Pleeeaassee?"*

I stepped back, folding my arms. "No." I giggled.

I started walking backwards away from him. He looked so boyish. *And so cute.* Before I could turn around, he smiled, pouted, and tapped his lips. No doubt reminiscing on the two of us at The Havana.

I laughed and shook my head. "In your *dreams*, mate."

He looked grumpy, but in a wistful way, half smiling again. As I turned to walk away, I heard his door close.

When I got to my room, I considered just flopping into bed exactly as I was, rented Tommy outfit and all. But I dragged myself through the whole makeup removal, skincare thing. I didn't want to take any avoidable acne back to set life, with cameras on me all day.

Lying in bed, like most nights in the past few months, I let my brain catch up to my body.

Chris just asked me to sleep over!

He may have been munted, but there was an undeniable magnetism in his eyes. I pictured his sapphire gaze in my mind, and it was piercing. I don't think it was the first time he'd looked at me that way. It was just the first time I felt it.

Chris loved, *hard*. I'd seen it. I couldn't say for sure if being on the receiving end of that was something that I ever wanted. If I was swallowed whole by its enormity ...

Where do *I* go? What would happen to ... *me?*

The concept of "falling" in love never appealed to me. The falling part felt like perpetually hearing the boss music on a Nintendo game, but never seeing the threat. So I'd look away, before the music crescendoed into something too overwhelming to face.

It would have been silly to step foot inside his room tonight. That's not to say he didn't look very delicious. I imagined myself perched on the edge of his bed, watching him loosen his tie, effortlessly slip off his jacket, and slowly unbutton his shirt with his gaze locked on mine ...

It sent my pulse racing. *Sheesh.*

He'd probably whip out a move of seduction to drive me wild, just because he knew he could. Maybe he'd crawl over me, but he wouldn't kiss me all over. He'd only let his warm breath graze against my skin.

Just the daydream of it filled me with a heady mix of thrill and appetite. My breathing was hitching, so I gave my head a quick shake. My life, much like my body, was feeling a little unhinged.

I chuckled to myself, and texted Ben what Chris said.

He replied in seconds:

Brekky tomoz?

I felt sad remembering I only had a couple of days left with Ben here. Then I felt a little extra sad that Chris wouldn't be here in the hotel after tomorrow. But I was happy he felt okay to go home. I thought of Michael Lesley winning his award and smiled, and thought of John Gettin being a dick, and frowned.

Closing my eyes, I thought of lots of other things that made me happy, and sad, and everything in between. I could feel the mid-twenties growing pains again, the ones that start at age twenty-two or twenty-three, and stay until you've learned what you need to learn.

I didn't try and make them go away, I just let them be ... until I fell asleep.

29

Define Untouchable

It was Ben's last day in L.A., and Mags invited me to go up Runyon Canyon with them. My schedule for the last week on set was mostly night shoots, and my only other plan was to sleep, so it made sense to go. The weather was perfect; the kind that makes you think … *I should get outside more.*

Plus, I kind of loved Ben. He was impossible *not* to like. Him and Maggie together was something I couldn't miss. Even though part of me wondered if they only asked because of the whole Americans drive on the wrong side of the road thing …

I sat in my car outside Ben's hotel, waiting to pick them up.

As they bounced towards the car, hand in hand, Maggie waved to me. She was beaming and it wasn't even eight a.m. I'd say she was a morning person, but I'd spent time with her at all hours of the day, and she was also a night person. I think she was just … a *life* person.

She looked adorable in a pink flowery hat, her hair in two loose braids. Both of them wore their stolen sunglasses; I chuckled when I noticed as they hopped into the back seat.

"Good morning!" Maggie said, bright and chirpy.

Slightly offended, I turned to them. "Whoa, whoa. I'm not an Uber. Are you two seriously going to sit in the back?"

They looked at each other, clearly having a full-on conversation in their minds. Whatever method they used to decide who had to ride shotgun ... Ben lost.

"I'll sit in the front," he said, climbing over the centre console. "But I'm DJ."

"Good." I nodded, hiding the disappointment on my face. "Thanks, *mate.*"

"Gross." Ben shuddered, jolting back. "Don't say *mate.* It doesn't suit you."

I scoffed a chuckle. "Yeah. You're definitely right."

On the way, Mags mostly looked out the window, chiming in on Ben and my small talk every now and then. I stole a couple of glances at her in the rearview mirror, but she seemed a million miles away. I'd do anything to know what filled her daydreams.

As we pulled up, Ben squinted at the Hollywood sign, looking absolutely appalled.

"Wait—" He threw his hand against my chest. "It's *all* the way up there?" His jaw dropped when I nodded. "Isn't there somewhere closer we can park?" He turned to Mags, visibly panicked. "Mags, seriously. It's so hot today."

She reached for his cheek and gave it a tap. "We'll be fine!"

Whipping back to me, he asked, "Chris, how many kilometres is it?"

"Uh ... it's not even three miles."

"That means literally nothing to me." He glared at me like I'd just spoken in another language, then slammed the car door as he got out.

I turned to Mags and smirked. "Not a morning person?"

"Definitely not." She giggled. "But also, Chris, we can't understand you. Speak *Australian.*" I rolled my eyes and stuck my tongue out.

Maggie jumped out, skipped over to Ben, and linked her arm through his. "Yay! Let's go!" It took him a total of two seconds before he started skipping with her.

Before it could even hit eight a.m., we were already sweating bullets. Ben was right. It was frickin' hot. California heat was no joke. Even in fall, the sun felt like it was clinging to summer, beating down like it didn't get the calendar memo.

Mags had walked slightly ahead, so I hung back with Ben, who was fanning himself with a paper *I ♥ L.A.* fan. We hadn't spoken much, both of us panting a little to keep up with Maggie's stride. Watching her, I wondered how her little legs were striding so fast …

Then I caught Ben giving me side-eye. "Take a picture; it'll last longer," he said.

I blinked, caught off guard. "What?"

"Stop checking out her arse." He smirked. "Grow up."

I spat a shocked laugh and shoved him. "*What?*"

"Um, do not touch me right now," he retorted, glaring. "I will literally combust."

He took a step back, holding up his palms, and I chuckled. Ben had every single colour in his personality.

"Besides," he continued. "It's just an observation. You keep taking little *peeks*, and for an actor, you lack any subtlety."

"I'm not taking peeks, I'm just …"

"Chris, Chris. *Shh.*" Shaking his head, he grabbed my arm to stop me and placed a finger on my lips. "You cannot lie to me. I see all." He tried to hide it, but I saw the corners of his mouth curl up.

I didn't really know how to respond, so we kept walking, the only sound the crunch of gravel underfoot.

"You're not going to get in," Ben said. "In her head, I mean, not her ... you know."

Snorting through an awkward laugh, I tried to reassure him. "I know what you mean. No need to clarify that."

We took a few more steps in silence before I broke it with the burning question.

Slowing down a little, I asked, "Why not?"

"Because she's just ..." Ben began, his eyes drifting to Maggie. He looked at her with such clear affection, it made me wonder how much real-life shit they'd been through together.

"She's just Mags," he said. "She's in love with the little dreamy life she built for herself in her head. She worked so hard for it. I think she's just ... enjoying it."

"Yeah," I said, looking up at her. I could see it. "That makes sense."

It felt like the most immature thing I could have asked at that moment, but I was desperate to know if Maggie had a boyfriend before I knew her. She'd never mentioned it. She'd never talked about dating, or her love life, at all. It was part of the halo of mystique that surrounded her, I guess.

I held my tongue, but Ben really did "see all", because he said, "I get, like, mad. She's always been so desired by guys, but never really loved all the way through."

The way he said it was layered, a mix of pain and beauty. It sent a flood of questions to the forefront of my mind.

Carefully, I asked, "If she's always a million miles away, how could they?"

"They just would!" He snapped in defence. "Because they wouldn't leave."

I gave a quick nod, ditching any follow-up questions.

Ben went on, "Everyone she's ever dated just takes some big life lesson from her, and then they leave. It's fucked up." He shook his head, tapping a finger on his chest. "That's why I always tell her, 'Maggie, the right ones won't leave'."

He paused for a moment, frowning in thought. I waited, hoping he'd share the thoughts out loud.

Thankfully, he did. "But now that we're grown up ... *ish* ..." He shrugged. "She just puts everyone in the friendzone. I think part of her just got tired of it, and another part believed in her dreams so much, it's like she put herself in a position where she didn't have anything, or anyone, to lose."

We stopped at the crest of a hill, wiping the sweat from our foreheads with our shirts.

Ben glanced over at me, his voice softening as he finished his thought. "There's no Hollywood sign in Australia, babe."

I nodded again. I did understand what he meant. Especially the part about being in a position with nothing to lose. Maggie was smart, in doing that.

My best friend in high school, Jackson, got into Julliard when we graduated. He was madly in love with his girlfriend, and he chose not to go. For her. It worked out, I mean, they got married at twenty and had two kids by twenty-four. He's happy.

But he's told me, quietly, he hated the feeling of knowing he might have lost out on a bigger, better life than the one he has.

The confusing part, though, when you're trying to figure out what you want ... is that it's also a beautiful thing to have a reason to stay. To have something, or someone, worth holding onto. It's really hard to figure out where to draw that line.

It was obvious it wasn't hard for Maggie, though.

Joining Ben and gazing ahead at her, I said, "I feel like Mags is like this ... beautiful, brave little butterfly. She just floats and darts around. I can't really picture her ever settling, you know?"

"Yeah," he said, nodding. He caught me smiling at her, which was equally satisfying as it was a little scary. Staring at me, he tilted his head. "She does come back down from the clouds … *eventually.*"

We both stood there for a moment, just watching her glow.

Ben sighed. "It's just who she is. She dreamt up a new life for herself and God bless her adorable, cotton-candy socks …" He let out a soft chuckle. "It fucking worked."

He jogged ahead to catch up with her, wrapping his arms around her from the back. It knocked her hat off, and I could hear her giggles.

I felt a little tug in my chest, watching them glow so effortlessly. I didn't let myself think that I could be the one to love Maggie all the way through … I wasn't sure enough.

They had that untouchable orbit again, and all I wanted to know at that moment was how to never leave it. I just wanted to have what they had, but I didn't know what the defining factor was.

When I caught up, I asked, "How are you both so … untouchable? If it were pouring rain right now, and we couldn't even see the damn Hollywood sign, I don't think you'd care."

"Oh, I would *definitely* care," Ben snapped.

Mags nodded in agreement and asked, "What makes you think we are so untouchable?" She took off her sunglasses and tucked them into her shirt, waiting for me to respond.

I took mine off too, meeting her eyes. "I don't know," I said, marvelling at the way the sun made her pale greens sparkle. "You both just glow."

"Aw, Chriso," Ben said, flashing a cheeky grin. "Thank you. We know."

Maggie wandered over to a patch of shrubbery, picking up sticks, and she called out, "I can tell you why!"

Ben glanced at me and nodded towards a shaded spot nearby. We made our way over and sat on the ground, wiping our sweat again.

When Maggie scurried over, she crouched down to meet my eyes. "You have to be ready." She smirked. "Are you ready?"

"Yeah. I'm ready." I nodded and sat up straight.

By the cheeky glimmer in her eyes, and the fact she was holding sticks, I expected her to say something completely ludicrous to make us laugh.

But I was very wrong. She gave me the answer.

30

A Lesson in Letting Go: Side A

Maggie

Ben and Chris had fallen behind me; I could hear their voices humming in the distance. We were close to a rest spot in the shade, and I'd already imagined the view, too impatient to stroll and see it for real.

From behind, Ben wrapped me up in a big bear hug, whispering, "I love you, Mags," into my ear.

I kissed him on the cheek. "Aww, I love you too." I wondered what had brought on his sudden urge to say it, but I didn't ask. It felt fuzzy as it was ... as a *just because* moment.

I glanced back, taking in the view of L.A. sprawled beneath us. All the buildings looked dotted, reflecting little glimmers of sunlight, kinda like a city dipped in stardust. Marvelling at the glimmers, it really was stunning ...

But the air was a little smoggy. I hoped there wasn't a fire somewhere. It was *so* hot, but I pushed away the fact that it wasn't summer anymore, because the climate crisis panic would swallow me whole if I gave it an inch.

As Chris jogged to catch up, he asked how Ben and I were so "untouchable", like we wouldn't even care if it was raining or if we couldn't catch any views. It surprised me; he looked a bit awestruck when he said it, too.

But he was very wrong. We'd definitely care, and Ben let him know. He was right about us glowing, though. Ben and I could make a perfect margarita with the shittiest limes.

We knew we could glow. I also knew a reason why.

And if I was gonna share it, I had to do it right, so I gathered a bunch of sticks to use as props.

Crouching down, I locked eyes with Chris. "You have to be ready. Are you ready?"

He sat up straight like a kid in kindy and gave me a nod. "Yeah. I'm ready."

I could tell he thought I was messing with him, but I stood up, adjusted my hat, cleared my throat ...

Then I began.

"In our youth, we have a lot of *firsts*. The time arrives for your first crush, your first kiss, first time sneaking out, first time taking drugs ..."

"Mmm," Ben chimed in, his eyes closed. "Best day."

We giggled, but I stayed on track, continuing. "You fall in love for the first time, and it's beautiful! It's sweet ... and pure ... but it also means you have your first heartbreak, too."

I handed Chris a stick, gripping one in my own hand so he could see how tightly I was holding it.

"And the pain of it kinda shocks your system. Then, for the first time, you feel guilty when you hurt someone." I handed him another stick, grabbing one for myself, too. "Maybe you feel ashamed of yourself, or disappointed in someone, or jealous over some*one* or some*thing* ..."

I kept handing us sticks, one after another, as I went on.

"It's all just part of your *coming-of-age*, as they say."

I added a wink, pausing to check that Chris was following. He gave me a little nod, so I continued, pacing a little, sticks still in hand.

"Then, you hit your twenties, and you realise ... those experiences aren't a one-time-only special. They keep coming.

"Only now" —I halted, glancing back at Chris— "it's your second heartbreak. Your second big letdown. Your third ... fourth ... fifth disappointment."

I handed him a few more sticks; both our hands were getting full.

"Before you get a chance to process any of it, you blink, and you're in your mid-twenties. And you're already carrying all of *this*." I shrugged, gesturing to the sticks in my hand.

"But you're still so *young* ... you don't know how to carry them, because no one ever showed you how. And no one ever told you that they'd start to feel so heavy.

"So"—I gripped my bundle of sticks a little tighter—"you just hold onto them. Really tight."

With steady eyes on Chris, I took a deep breath, trying to keep the words from tumbling out too fast.

"And with each conversation you find yourself in, you start to realise that the words inside them have changed.

"Because now, you're not talking to your friends about some crush or a random hookup. You're talking to them about how you're going to pay your rent. Or how you're going to tell your girlfriend of five years that you don't love her anymore.

"They're telling you how they can't get pregnant, even though it was their dream to be young parents. You're telling them that you can't fathom having to go on another first date, or how your boss makes you depressed, or that your parents are getting older, and that it's scary ... how fast time is moving."

My hand full of sticks was starting to sting, and I hoped Chris's were, too.

"It hurts, huh?" I asked.

Chris nodded; his face was fully focused, fixed in intensity.

I stepped closer. "But you've already spent all your time and money on band-aids of party drugs and stitches of sex … and it still hurts. It's a little cold. And kinda dark."

Changing my tone like I was telling a fairytale, I went on. "So, *one day*, you look at your hand, and you question it. You're like, 'This hurts, why am I holding onto this?' So, you test the waters … and you drop some."

I dropped a couple of sticks, one at a time.

"It feels a lot lighter." I smiled. "The sun comes out a little bit. Some colours come back.

"And each time you ask yourself why you're holding on so tight"—I squeezed my little bundle—"slowly and carefully … you drop a few more."

Lifting my fingers, one by one, I let the last few sticks fall.

"Suddenly, you're pushing thirty, and all this *life* doesn't stop or slow down. But you're okay."

I exhaled, smiling wider as I lifted my empty hands.

"Because you can still *feel* it"—I picked up a stick, wincing for the point—"but you don't hang on to it." Then I quickly dropped it.

Pacing again, I said, "You're just living your life with empty hands, with nothing but *yourself*. You're forced to ask, 'How do I want to respond to my life? Who am I, really?'"

Crouching down again, directly in front of Chris, I stared him deep in the eyes. "Who are you when it's just … *you?*" I added a smirk and a little tap on his nose.

I flopped onto my butt, sitting cross-legged between Chris and Ben, a hand on each of their knees.

"And that's, like, the bravest thing you can do." I shook Ben's knee. "Isn't it, Ben?"

He nodded. "Oh, big time, babe. We have to just ... *let shit go.*"

"Exactly." I giggled, and Chris shifted his eyes to my hand on his knee, so I squeezed it extra tight.

I gave him a little nudge. "Let it sink in that you can *feel* things without *owning* them. Because it's not *you* ... it's life! After a while, you recognise how brave it is to feel it all, and you kinda can't help but love yourself again."

Gazing at the glittering view, with the sun on my legs, my face in the shade, sitting between my two favourite people ... I felt so grateful. I'd always dreamed about seeing the Hollywood sign, *for real*, in person.

For so long, it felt so out of reach, that I wondered whether I'd have to keep it as a picture. Just a fragment of a fictional reality. But it was real now, and that was so wonderful to feel, as if the moment were arriving right on time.

Wrapping up my little speech, I said, "Life is much more fun when you let yourself feel it, 'cause then you actually start living it."

And with a slap on Chris's knee, I added, "*That's* when you glow."

Before Chris could react, Ben jumped up and reached his hands out for us. "We're not 'untouchable', Chris. We just ... glowed the fuck up."

I reached my hands for Ben's, letting him pull me up, but Chris didn't move. He was staring right through us; I think he was in a bit of shock. It made me giggle.

Pulling out his phone, Ben asked, "Mags, can you take some pictures of me before I get too sweaty?"

He started backing up towards the edge of the trail, nodding for me to follow. I joined him, and we continued backwards, watching Chris ... who hadn't moved.

He was still staring through us, caught somewhere between *I have no idea what you just said* ... and *wait ... that actually makes sense.*

I glanced at Ben; he looked baffled, and when he turned to face me, my reflection in his sunglasses mirrored the exact same expression.

We tilted our heads in sync, our gazes shifting back to Chris.

And Ben said, "I was gonna say I think you just broke him, but ... I think you might've just put him back together again."

31

A Lesson in Letting Go: Side B

Chris

I knew, right then, gazing at Maggie as she took photo after photo of Ben ...

I could love her all the way through.

It was me. I could do it.

And never stop.

I wasn't brave enough yet for the hard part, the part where I admitted that I *wanted* it. But I did know for sure that I could. I definitely could.

I didn't know what to say or how to react while she was talking. I couldn't think. It was just ... *feel.* But only in my chest, because I couldn't move my legs.

I braced myself, trying to stand up, and as I did, all the sticks fell from my hand. As they hit the ground ... I faced another confrontation with myself.

But this time I saw a different picture.

I didn't look like an angry coward. A scared little kid, hiding behind excuses, blaming everything on everyone else. I didn't look greedy, or needy, or desperate for approval. I didn't look the slightest bit confused, or lost ...

I looked *found*. Like a man who knew exactly where he was going, unafraid to take a step somewhere he'd never been. I looked strong. Happy. And *ready*, too.

I stepped towards Maggie, and the image of myself in my mind only became clearer. The feeling in my body came back, not slow and steady, but in a bold rush through my veins. It felt visceral, wild, a little erratic ... just like the pulse that came with being in love.

The pulse that I knew, and the one I *loved* the feeling of.

When Maggie smiled at me, I was certain. I was glowing.

Being closer to her made me the most *me* I had ever felt. The me that I wanted, the me that I actually liked. The me that I'd buried with ... *sticks, of all things.*

We made it to the top of the hike, red-faced, shirts wet with sweat that I was sure we could wring out. The Hollywood sign was right there, its letters bold against the sky, and I could see the excitement in Maggie and Ben's eyes as they took in the view. It was kinda refreshing being a tourist in your own town. Seeing L.A. through their eyes was like rediscovering a bit of its magic, which was cool.

Maggie jumped on Ben's back, so I pulled out my phone to take their picture. I called out, "Say ... gone full-feral!" They laughed; the photo was adorable.

On the way back, when we were almost at my car, Mags skipped ahead again. I seized another opportunity with Ben, knowing it would be the last one for a while. I wondered if he thought the same, because he bounced in front of me, stopping us in our tracks.

Cocking his head, he asked, "Do you miss Chelsea?"

It threw me for a loop, but he had a patient posture about him. I could tell he meant it when he asked.

Just drop the damn stick, Chris.

I replied, "No, not at all, actually." A breathy laugh escaped my chest. I felt lighter. "She brought out the worst in me. I knew, months ago. I mean, it was slow at first ... then Dom happened, and she did that podcast—"

"And you threw her shit into your pool?"

I laughed. "Yeah, yeah ... *that*. I don't know, man. I looked in her eyes, and I just saw ... myself. Like, my own reflection. And it freaked me out. I didn't like who that person was. So I just knew it was done."

Ben stepped towards me. "Yeah. The *mirror*." He nodded. "Brutal bitch, isn't it? But different people hold up different mirrors, and they have different reflections, you know?"

I smiled, nodding back because I did know. "Yeah, like with Maggie, it's the person I *want* to be."

"No, Chris." He shook his head, and with a firm hand on my shoulder, he pointed at my chest. "It's the person you *already are*. She's just shining her light all over it. So you can see it too."

He'd caught me off guard again. He was right, and I considered maybe Ben was ... always right. It definitely felt like whoever I was became easier to know with Maggie around.

He spun around to lovingly gaze at her, and in that moment, I really understood how much he loved her. We'd bonded over a shared experience, and that experience was *Maggie Marshall*.

Pivoting back to me, he said, "Also, you just said 'with' Maggie. FYI, babe—you're not *with* Maggie ... yet."

I raised a subtle brow, knowing there was no better time than now to ask the question.

I looked into his eyes, bracing myself for the answer, and quietly, I asked, "Do you think I could be?"

"No, Chriso. No," he *said* ... but he shook his head emphatically up and down. The nod was indicating that the *real* answer was actually a big *yes*.

He closed his eyes and pursed his lips, and I took it as a colossal yes when he laughed. I laughed with him and gave him another little shove.

Turns out, I didn't need a full joint to deep dive into the reason why I wanted Ben to like me. I just had to look at him, gazing at Maggie, and realise I'd had a similar look in my eyes for a long time. He loved her, and there was no way I'd ever get a chance to experience how I could love her if Ben didn't love me, too.

We started walking again, and I asked, "So how many times have you heard that speech?"

"What speech? Oh ..." He chuckled. "The *sticks* one. Only twice. Once for me, and before, for you." He turned to me and smiled. "I got rocks, though, so you got off easy."

I chuckled. "Yeah, yeah. Mags loves a prop, doesn't she."

Linking his arm through mine, he said, "It was how I knew she'd be okay, you know? Coming here. I got that moment with her a few months before she left. I just remember feeling like I'd never worry about her, because she'd let bad shit go. I mean, I still worry." He stopped us again, facing me. "But she has you. And you're, like, a semi-wanker. Not a full one."

I didn't know what that meant, but it felt nice. "Should I ask what that means?"

"Chris, *shh*." He put his fan against my lips. "Don't question it; just take it for what it is."

Keeping his arm linked in mine, he snapped open the fan, waving it over us both as we strolled to the car.

32

Horse-Sized Pill

Maggie

My cheeks were tear-soaked as I hugged Ben goodbye outside his hotel. I hated the feeling of not being able to make future plans, not knowing when we'd be able to spend time together again. It made me feel guilty and selfish, and my chest tightened just thinking about it. Having to experience it for real was a downside of dreams colliding with reality.

"See you soon, okay?" I whispered through sniffles.

I squeezed him one last time, like I was physically trying to wring out all the last bits of sunshine from his body and keep them for myself.

He got into his Uber for the airport, and I waited until the car was out of sight before I started crying again.

Strolling back to The Bennett, I tried to take it all in. The four days with Ben felt like a whirlwind. We crammed so much into such a short time, it barely felt real. I daydreamed about him living here again, in our tiny apartment with its dead plants and green cushions.

Glancing around as I strolled, it felt self-absorbed to think about, but it might've been the last time I'd get to walk anywhere like this. Especially in L.A., for a while, at least. I'd experienced a bit of fame, but only really through Chris. When I was announced for the show, it piqued interest for a day or two, but no one really knew who I was yet.

We only had one more week of shooting, then a photoshoot, a spot of press, a few weeks off, some promo rounds, and straight into filming the second lot of episodes.

Of course, everyone *could* hate the show, and we'd never do a season two, leaving me as anonymous as ever. But it didn't seem like things were shaping up that way. It felt more like my career was holding its breath, and when it finally exhaled ... I was a teeny, tiny bit worried that maybe it would knock the wind right out of me.

Halfway to The Bennett, I decided to make a detour to Bronte's.

I waited in line, and when I got to the counter to order, I took off my sunglasses and smiled at Roy.

"Maggie, my girl!" He reached out and grabbed my hand. "You don't need to tell me your order. Go sit outside; I'll have my break and join you."

I sat in my favourite spot, facing the beach in the old wooden chairs. I didn't bother grabbing cushions; I had an old tracksuit on, so I didn't mind the chairs snagging a few loose threads.

"Coffee for the lady," Roy said, sitting at my table.

"Thank you." I gave him a small smile. I hoped it was enough to mask how much I'd been crying.

"How are you feeling?" he asked. "Not long now, no?"

"I'm good," I said, nodding a little too long, like I was convincing my body I meant it. "And yes, only one week left of filming."

Roy smiled. "I saw a video of you and your co-star online. You are an amazing friend." I knew he was talking about that stupid GQ interview. I was surprised they even ran it, but I softly exhaled, thankful for what he said ...

Then I was crying again.

I couldn't help it, Roy was one of those people who spoke directly to your insides. You couldn't hide from him, no matter how hard you tried.

"Yeah, I guess," I said, wiping my eyes with my sleeves. "It doesn't really feel like it, right now." I gave my head a little shake to snap out of it and took a sip of my coffee.

"Why, Mags? Roy asked, wiggling his fingers towards me. "The world is quite literally at your fingertips." He almost sounded like a Disney narrator; it made me giggle.

Finding the words to reply was hard. "I don't know, I just ..." I paused, organising my thoughts. "I loved my life before this, Roy. I mean, it was fine. And sometimes I worry that I thought I could dream of something even better, but maybe I didn't need too, maybe it was already wonderful, you know?"

He shook his head. "*Fine* is not enough to live for, Mags. *Fine* is what people say when they're lying to themselves, or when they drink Greta's coffee from across the street."

He gave me a smirk, and I smirked right back. Roy's competitor across the street, Greta's Coffee House, had the *worst* coffee, hands down.

Roy continued, "When people drink Bronte's coffee, they don't say it's *fine*, they say it's ... *amazing*."

I gave him a little nod, but it was funny, because to me ... Roy's coffee *wasn't* amazing. At all. But he believed in it. In himself, in his business, and in his ability to execute his dream. He really believed in it.

To me, that was the amazing part. And I'd already done that part, for my dream.

It made me feel at ease to acknowledge it. I didn't know what would happen after this week, but if shit hit the fan, I could still say ... *I did it.*

I attempted to make Roy smile, even though he'd know I was lying. "That's true, it's *amazing.*" I added a big grin after sipping my coffee again.

He raised his brows and scoffed. He definitely knew I was fibbing.

Tapping my hand, he said, "You gotta start swallowing big, horse-sized pills at your age, Mags. The ones that say, *Yeah, that's right, you're a real adult now.* They're hard to swallow, it hurts, but ya' gotta do it. The decisions that you make for yourself aren't just about you anymore, so you gotta be sure."

Tilting my head, I asked, "Are they the same pills that have 'may cause permanent expectations of right decisions' written on the warning label?" I tapped my finger to my temple. "'Cause I think I've choked on those before."

"They're the ones," he huffed, winking at me.

Roy was being real; adult pills hurt to swallow. I think the warning labels are different for everyone, which made them even harder to figure out how to swallow without gagging. Feeling like I was hurting Ben by moving to L.A. had me choking on one.

It's one thing to be confident when you're only thinking about yourself, floating in a cloud like I usually did. I could be blissfully unaware of how my actions affected others. Their thoughts and their opinions ... none of it really mattered. I couldn't hear it from up there. But those adult pills were heavy enough to bring me back down, and it's something else entirely to stay confident with your feet on the ground and your ears tuned in.

Roy leaned across the table, pointing at my chest with a steady finger. "You know who you are, Mags. You're grown. Don't give it away to anyone in this business. Keep it tight to your chest. Protect it. You can't get spat out if they never swallow you in the first place."

I gave him a big, sure nod, this time. He was right. I'd protect myself.

I finished my coffee, and we sat in comfortable silence, people-watching and flicking looks at each other through secret giggles when we were being too judgy.

I gave Roy a hug goodbye and thanked him for sharing his little gold nuggets of wisdom with me. I promised him I'd hang onto them tight.

I told him I'd see him soon, another *soon* I wasn't sure of, but I felt lighter saying it.

33

Switzerland

Glancing around at the crew on our last day on set, I was trying to keep my eyes wide, taking pictures of it all in my mind so I could remember every little detail. I was about to wrap on my first show! A fluttery mix of excitement, gratitude, and anxiety stirred in my belly.

Chris and I had one more scene to shoot. It was set inside a cosy cabin at Christmas time ... snowing outside, crackling fire, and way too many pillows on the couch in front of it. Christmas lights were strung around the fireplace and kitchen. A very *romantic* vibe.

I'd never experienced that in real life; it barely snowed anywhere in Australia. Christmases were ham and salad rolls, beer, and trying to stay cool. It felt magical to play pretend.

I was in grey tracksuit pants, a matching hoodie, and fluffy pink socks. Sarah and I had a lot in common, but right now, I felt more like *me* than her. Alicia told me Chris had to wear an ugly Christmas sweater, and I couldn't wait to see it.

Someone on set shouted, "Can someone call for Chris? We're almost good!"

Chris's voice rang out from behind, "Yeah, I'm here! All good!"

He jogged up to set, adjusting the corny Christmas sweater. The fabric was bright red, splashed with cartoonish snowflakes and grinning reindeer. It was undeniably tacky, and very ugly. But it looked adorable on him.

"That sweater is ... is ... " I stuttered. I wanted to rip him off, but he looked so cute that I couldn't think of any other word.

His hair was neatly done, almost straight at the front, flopping over his forehead. He looked up at me from underneath it, still adjusting the sleeves of his sweater, and I didn't recognise the smile. It stole a little breath.

Helping me out, Chris said, "The ugliest thing you've ever seen?"

"Yeah, pretty much." I giggled, trying to catch my breath back at the same time. I figured it was just the flutters ... from earlier.

The scene had no dialogue. It was just slow dancing in the kitchen and kissing. The only acting we had to do was act like we could dance. Oh, and that we were madly in love when we kissed. It was choreographed, of course, because this was a romance show, and naturally, Sarah and Liam could slow dance perfectly on the fly.

The choreographer jumped up to set. Grabbing our shoulders, he said, "We'll do a run through, just to block it out."

Admittedly, I'd forgotten his name, but we only had one practice, so I told myself it was okay to forget.

Someone hit play on the song—it was *Best Part*, by H.E.R and Daniel Caeser, a.k.a. the prettiest love song in existence. I wasn't even sure if they'd use the song in the final cut; sometimes they'd change their mind in post-production. But right then, it felt warm, cuddly, and perfect.

As Chris put his hand out for mine, I smiled and said, "I love this song so much."

"Me too." He didn't really smile back. He looked a little nervous, which made me feel nervous, too.

I quietly hummed along to the song, smiling off into my little la-la-land while we danced. In the first part where Liam kisses Sarah, I was dipped in Chris's arms, and when he leaned me back … I almost flinched.

He was going to kiss me. Off-take.

We hadn't broken that rule one time! And why would we? Even after Chelsea, we weren't together, it would just be weird. We were at work, paid to kiss on camera. That was all.

The tip of his nose was touching mine, but he just smiled and started quietly humming along, too. I let out a quiet breath, relaxing. *Phew.*

Chest to chest with Chris as the dance was almost over, I had my eyes closed, completely immersed in my imagination. In my mind, I was in some faraway cabin in the mountains of Switzerland, and it made time slow down, so I stayed there.

Chris's hands were wrapped in my hair, warm and cosy. When I looked up at him, we were nose to nose again, right where Sarah and Liam would kiss. In that moment, I was just so happy. Happy that we'd become so close. Happy that I got to experience all of this as Sarah. And because he was my best friend, I was happy for Chris, too. That it was him who was Liam.

The moment felt whole, just as it was.

But Chris snatched it away from me. He kissed me.

And he meant it. I could feel it.

He kissed me like he'd met me in my mind, in Switzerland. Like it was just us, like we weren't Sarah and Liam, like we weren't on a set with twenty other people around watching us. Like he was just Chris, and I was just Maggie …

But he was too late. I left Switzerland in my mind the second his lips touched mine.

I stepped back, shoving him. My breathing hitched; I was on the verge of bursting into tears. My eyes darted around the room, but the lights were too bright, and I couldn't see anything. It was all just a big blur.

I shot Chris a glare. *You broke the rule.*

He opened his mouth to speak, quickly shaking his head, but hundreds of butterflies filled my mind, and the sporadic thoughts were causing chaos. I could feel the panic starting to attack.

I spun away, and Alicia leapt onto set, stepping in front of the lights so I could see her. She called out, "Maggie? Lashes, quick."

Alicia was saving me. She grabbed my hand, and I didn't look back at Chris. I honestly felt embarrassed, and I don't get embarrassed easily.

"That little *shit*," Alicia spat, slamming the door of my dressing room.

I stared at her, wide-eyed, reminding myself to breathe. *In and out, Maggie. In and out.*

Stuttering, I said, "I'm trying not to cry because the makeup you did looks so pretty."

She sighed. "Maggie ..." Then she dabbed my eye with a tissue as a tear escaped. "You are the sweetest human in the whole world." She dabbed my other eye, too. "I can fix your makeup. If you want to cry, do it now."

It was lovely of her to say that, but I was refusing to cry. I had to swallow the horse-sized adult pill, even though I was choking on it.

"I'm sorry," I said, flicking my eyes back in protest to my tear ducts. "I didn't think I'd react like that, you know? If Chris ever—"

"Stole something like that from you?" Alicia snapped, cutting me off. "He's selfish, Maggie. It was selfish. He broke the one obvious rule." She threw her hands in the air before they landed on her hips. She'd swapped her usual hot pink glasses for lime green ones, and they made her eyes look extra big and beady.

I tried to laugh at myself. *This is silly. You're being silly.* But it was futile to try and laugh about it.

Alicia was right. Chris did steal something.

He stole a moment.

We'd kissed, like, fifty times in the last two months, and only one of those wasn't on camera. It was at The Havana, and that didn't count! It was fuelled by shots, not common sense, and everyone drunkenly kisses their friends! *People do that, right?*

Regardless, if *that* moment was going to happen between us, it should have been just *ours.* A moment between Maggie and Chris. He took that from us. He was impatient, and a little selfish.

I looked at Alicia and nodded. "You're right."

She crossed her arms; her face went hard. "I just think he's spoilt, Mags. Used to getting what he wants, when he wants it. And for some dumb-arse reason, he wanted it at work. On camera."

I never really understood exactly why Alicia didn't like Chris. Right then, I figured maybe it was an accumulation of all the "spoilt behaviour" she felt she'd witnessed over time. It was the sharpness in her tone that reminded me, though ... she was close friends with Chelsea.

It had me wishing it was Cherie frowning at me, not Alicia.

I put my hand on her arm, whispering a little plea. "Alicia, please don't say anything to ..."

She shook her head. "I won't, Mags. You have my word. Honestly, at this point, I hate 'em both."

I nodded, smiling softly as a silent *thank you.*

Alicia started touching up my face, and I accidentally started crying again. "Sorry," I said, holding my fingers to the inner corners of my eyes. "I'm fine ... I just can't work out why it hurts."

Powdering my forehead, Alicia said, "It hurts because it's a moment that you wanted, Mags. I think you've just learned that. And instead of being able to take your time and figure out that you even wanted it in the first place—it was a forced hand. He played you, Mags."

Ouch. I disagreed. I didn't believe that Chris was playing me at all. He wouldn't.

Alicia was being unsurprisingly harsh, but she hadn't spent one day even *liking* Chris, let alone loving him. And I did love him. I didn't have an issue in knowing it. He was part of the life I loved and created.

I loved him because I wanted to. Not because I'd fallen for him or had a crush on him or spent all my time daydreaming about him. It was a choice. I decided that Chris was the type of person I cared deeply about and wanted to love.

I frowned at her through the mirror. "I don't know if that's true." Then, even though it felt painfully rude to do, I waved my hand, dismissing her from touching my face.

I hopped up and started walking back to set. I had to cut the reflections short and be professional. *This*, unfortunately, wasn't a TV show. It was my real life, and there were responsibilities and people other than myself I had to think about.

I didn't know what Chris was thinking. The only conclusion I could come up with was that he *wasn't* thinking. I settled on that, and when I got back on set, I didn't look at him until we were rolling.

When we were done, a few of the crew said little speeches and we all clapped and hugged and talked about the wrap party plans. Chris was hosting it at his house, so I'd finally get to see inside.

As I was headed off set, he caught my arm. "Maggie."

I spun around to face him. Looking in his eyes, I thought of what Roy said.

They can't spit you out if you don't let them swallow you in the first place.

So, smiling at Chris, I let myself glow. On purpose. I felt proud and fulfilled, and this show meant more to me, *for me*, than Chris stealing a kiss ever could.

I think he was stunned that I met his eyes with a smile, because he stuttered when he tried to speak.

"Mags, I ... um ..."

I helped him out. "You'll see me tonight, you can't wait, and it's going to be so much fun?" I flashed him a cheeky smile.

I watched his shoulders drop, his smile grow, and his eyes soften. Then he let out a big, deep exhale. It made me feel so relieved ... for both of us.

"Yes," he said, beaming. "Exactly that. Only that."

He let out another short breath, internalising all his "*desperate to say's,*" for now.

I was thankful he chose to do that.

I walked backwards, keeping my eyes on him as I headed to my dressing room. I took a mental picture of his beaming smile and locked it up, deep inside my mind. So I wouldn't forget the details.

34

Only Clockwork

Chris

Mags and I were filming our last scene, and I was slightly late to set because I was an idiot whose mind was outta space, and spilled coffee on the ugly Christmas sweater Liam wore in the scene. Standing shirtless in the bathroom, blow-drying it with a hair dryer, I was trying to snap myself back to Earth.

Liam and Sarah had kissed, like, fifty times, but for some reason ... today I couldn't separate it, and it was eating me alive.

Ever since Ben left, and I saw myself loving Maggie, I couldn't let it go. Anytime I came within five feet of her on set, my pulse would run erratic laps through my entire body, my chest would heat up, and I'd just *want* to love her. More and more.

Is that fabric burning?

"Shit," I hissed under my breath.

It felt absurd, but before I walked out, I glared at my reflection in the mirror, and muttered aggressively, "Snap out of it."

I shoved the sweater back on and ran to set.

I was trying *not* to look at Mags. I was adjusting the sweater, it was itching me everywhere, and I knew she'd look pretty, and dreamy, and she'd take me out of this world again. So, I focused on the sweater.

I took her hand to dance. Just to run through it. Like we'd done so many times; it was only clockwork. *Only clockwork, Chris.*

But when I dipped her in my arms ... I was *gone.*

Completely blasted off on a one-way rocket to the frickin' moon.

I *almost* kissed her, but she was humming along in that sweet little voice ... I smiled instead. I tried to keep my mind busy, humming along with her, but that only made it harder.

I could say it was the set, I could say it was the song, I could blame the goddamn fake fire, crackling in the fake fireplace ... but it wasn't any of that.

When the song was almost over, my hands were through her soft, chocolate hair, and I knew she was a million miles away in her dreams. Our noses were touching, and the way she looked at me ... I broke the rule.

I kissed her.

Liam didn't. *I did.* And I felt her daydream shatter to pieces *instantly.*

I only caught a glimpse of her eyes before Alicia scooped her up and flew her right off that set. The glimpse was enough. It was agonising.

The most agonising part was that kissing her at that moment was completely devoid of value. It was *only* selfish. Nothing like how I would've wanted to kiss Maggie, ever.

I thought maybe she'd think the same thing ... that it had no value. That it didn't mean anything. But I was kidding myself. I knew she'd feel betrayed.

I took something from her, and I didn't even know for sure if she wanted to give it to me. The truth was, I didn't want Maggie to *give* anything to me, at all. I just wanted to be where she was in her mind, and that moment felt like the closest I'd ever been.

I overstepped. *Fucking idiot.*

I hit my head back against the cabinets in the set kitchen and closed my eyes. I didn't move until she came back. When she did, she didn't look at me once. Not until we were rolling again as Sarah and Liam.

I glanced over at her, listening to a few of the crew say some parting words, and I was so proud of her. She was my best friend, my Sarah on this set, my Mags when we walked off it.

I didn't want to push her even further away from me, but I needed to know she wouldn't miss the wrap party. She'd just wrapped a season of her first show, she deserved it, she should be there.

I stopped her on the way to her dressing room, and when she turned to me and *smiled* ... I forgot how to speak.

She told me she'd be there, at the party. And that's all I wanted.

I was desperate to say a million other words, but I kept them burning in my chest.

They set it on fire ... and I loved the way it felt.

35

We Happen, Mags

Chris

It was almost nine-thirty, and Mags still hadn't arrived at my house for the wrap party. I wanted to text her, but I knew if I tried to pull her in, it would probably work in reverse. Even Cherie asked me where she was, seeming a little worried when I said I wasn't sure. I wasn't too worried, though. Maggie was always late when she was on her own.

She was late the night Dom invited her to The Alibi, the second time I met her. And every other time after that, unless she was with Cherie, or Dom when he was around, or Ben.

I took a couple of shots with a few of the crew, and because I'd lost count, I was feeling pretty buzzed. A few of us headed down to the pool, and when I turned my head to light a joint ... I saw her.

She was talking to Brooks, and it looked like he was gesturing at her to jump over the glass fence that lined the pool. Whatever he said worked, she burst out laughing as he pulled her up and over, setting her down poolside.

Watching her rush towards Cherie, I heard Brooks call out, "What, no thank you kiss?" He threw his hands in the air.

Maggie spun to face him, then she flipped him off.

I shook my head and chuckled, in awe of how something so crass could look so sweet and precious.

As she danced around Cherie and a few of the cast, she was lit up by the lights spilling through the porch doors. I could see her clearly. Her hair was wavy down her back, almost ethereal, like a mermaid. She had a little black dress on, tied up at her shoulders with pink ribbon.

It was a logical fact—Maggie looked hot. Like, blow-my-brains-out, rip-my-heart-up, and burned-my-skin just looking at her, hot.

There was no way I could talk to her yet. I'd be selfish again. I'd pull too hard. *Way too hard.*

I shoved the joint in Jordan's hand and jumped into the pool. A few of the guys followed suit, bombing and diving in after me.

I tried to convince Cherie to join, but she just shook her head and shouted, "Ask Maggie!" Cherie looked properly stoned, sprawled on a pool lounge. I loved to see it; she deserved it. She'd picked up every piece of mess Dom left behind.

We'd set up basketball hoops at either end of the pool, and Brooks, Jordan, and I had teamed up against three of the crew. It turned into a pretty chaotic 3-on-3 game, which was essentially just ... boys being idiots, half-drowning each other.

Brooks had tanked me in a headlock underwater, but I still heard Jordan call out, "Mags! Get in here!"

I had to know if she was getting in the pool, so I punched Brooks in the dick—softly, obviously. The guy was born to be a dad one day!

I pushed myself up, head above water, and wiped my eyes to scan for Mags. She was standing at the edge of the pool with a shot in each hand.

"Mate!" she shouted at Jordan. "I just got here! I've gotta catch up!" She downed one shot, shrugged, then downed the other. "Okay, I'm good!"

She pulled her dress off over her head, and before I could run my eyes all over her skin, she jumped into the pool. It might have been the weed because she barely made a splash, but it felt like she unleashed a tidal wave.

She swam over to the edge near Cherie and asked, "Can you pretty please pass me my beer?"

When I heard it, I swam over. "And mine too, please?" I asked. "Oh, and maybe that, too?" I pointed to the joint in Cherie's hand.

Mags giggled, and Cherie flipped us off, but she still obliged.

As Mags took her beer, she said, "Cheers, Mum!" She sounded so Australian when she said *Mum*.

Like I was correcting her, when Cherie handed over my beer, I said, "Cheers, *Mom.*"

Cherie barked at us both, "I'm not your mother!" Then she rolled her eyes. "Oh, fuck it. I may as well be."

Mags and I looked at each other like we were ten years old and had just heard our actual mother say "fuck" for the first time.

Sitting on the pool steps, I tried to play it cool, but my gaze flicked over every inch of her skin I could catch, and *damn.* Her little pink bikini, speckled with red cherries ... *god, Maggie's cute.*

Reeling myself in, I held up my beer to hers. "We did it, Sarah."

"We sure bloody did, Liam." She smiled and tapped her beer to mine, looking satisfied, but then her face dropped into a frown. "It's so cold," she said. "How are we swimming? I'm gonna go get changed, but I'll be back."

Shit. We'd spent two minutes together and she was already dipping.

She didn't come back, so I spent the entire night just trying to stay in the same room as her. I was urgently considering whether she was avoiding me, or just taking it all in ... but that caused me to urgently consider whether she liked my house or not.

I wasn't even sure if *I* liked my house, so I figured Mags probably didn't either. There wasn't really much I could do about it, except ... overthink it.

At around midnight, I lost her. I'd convinced myself she'd left, and I bolted outside to check, but she was getting into the spa with Cherie. I was losing my freakin' mind, and I think Maggie saw it written all over my face.

She called out, "Chris! Come here!"

We locked eyes, and she smiled, curling her index finger towards herself. I'd been trailing her like a puppy on the sly all night, but I think I blew my cover when I practically dove into the spa at her little invite.

I felt kind of awkward, being in the spa ... with Cherie. I joked, "Look at us, hanging in the spa, with *Mom*." I shot Cherie a cheeky grin.

"Well, that's my cue," she said, resigning immediately. *Yes. Good.* As she crawled out, she added, "Chris, I'm taking a sweater from your closet. It's freezing."

"Yeah, of course. Go ahead." Cherie could take whatever she damn well wanted if it meant she was leaving right now.

I looked at Mags and blurted out, "I thought you left!"

She frowned, seeming offended. *Shit. Why did I say that?* Must've been the booze, for sure.

Splashing me a little, she said, "Why would I leave *our* wrap party? It's not even two a.m.! That would be so rude!"

I splashed her back, and she dipped down into the spa, blowing bubbles in the water. It was the funniest, cutest thing I'd ever seen her do.

"Sorry, sorry," she mumbled, closing her eyes. "That's weird. I'm weird." She shook her head. "But you know that."

The look on her face was borderline embarrassed, and Mags never got embarrassed. It was my flag. *Maggie's nervous.*

"Don't say sorry ..." I chuckled. "For anything. Like, ever."

I could hear it in the edge of my own voice—*I was nervous too.* Just me. And Maggie ... alone in the spa.

After a moment, she switched off the jets and settled near a headrest. As the water stilled, she ran her fingers along the surface, watching the ripples fade. "So ..." She looked at me, curiously tilting her head. "What are you thinking about?"

I mirrored the tilt of her head ... a little mesmerised, for a second ... then I pressed my lips together, completely clueless on what to say.

She could have asked me why I was an idiot, why I kissed her today, why I chose the couch in my living room, for all I cared. But thinking right now?

Not that.

I ran my hand through my hair and opened my mouth, but the only sound that came out was, "Uhh ..."

Mags was intrigued. "You can't start with an *uhh.* Then I know you're making something up."

I clenched my teeth, offering a sheepish smile, and scooted over next to her. *How'd she still smell so pretty in the spa? Damn it.*

She splashed me again. "You're my best friend, just tell me! And if you don't, I'll just figure it out." Her eyes narrowed in a silent dare, and she pushed from her seat, floating in front of me.

"Honestly?" I asked, my pulse becoming erratic.

"Mmhmm," she urged softly, and I watched, hypnotised, as she dipped her hair back into the spa. I could have sworn it was in slow motion.

Spellbound and edging on breathless, I murmured, "I'm wondering how many people are still inside."

"Like, everyone ..." She giggled and smirked. "You throw a fun party."

I was drawn in, mesmerised by the way her pale greens glowed, even as she narrowed them again. They made me feel braver. Five seconds under the light in *those* eyes ... and it was game over for me.

I leaned in, floating in front of her. "I'm thinking that if I weren't such a good host who threw fun parties ..." I inched a little closer and lowered my voice. "I'd be locking that door, right now." I flicked my eyes to the door, then back to hers, holding her gaze. But she didn't flinch.

She glanced at the door, let out a quiet scoff, and pursed her lips. She was so unfazed I questioned whether she'd heard me right.

Tilting her head again, she said, "You are a bit of a rule breaker, aren't you, Chriso."

I held my breath. My heart sank.

Rock bottom at the floor of the spa.

She seemed playful about it, but I felt *so* guilty. I didn't want to be a "rule breaker". Not like this. Not in a way that would flip something that had always been easy and fun ... into something hard to reach, surrounded by eggshells.

If it weren't for the booze, and the bravery from Maggie's pale greens, I wouldn't have done it ... but my hands found her waist. And I held on, tight.

"Maggie ..." I wanted to search her eyes, but she closed them and spoke before I could.

"It's okay," she said, smiling. "I know you didn't really mean to. That's not how we'd want it ... if we wanted it."

Was she telling me she didn't want it, or that she did?

I couldn't tell, so I went on. "Maggie, I am so sorry. I'm a fucking idiot. And I feel—"

"I don't think you're an idiot," she gently cut me off, her smile reassuring. "I think you're smart, and funny, and brave. It was an idiot mistake, but it was a mistake. It's okay."

I shook my head, softly ... and stunned.

It wasn't lost on me how hard it was for Maggie to choose grace in that moment. But she chose it anyway, and she made it look effortless. She was sparkling like sunlight, rippling little beams across the surface of the spa. Just because she could.

I wasn't even sure if she realised it. But in that exact moment—I decided.

I wanted to spend a lifetime letting her know.

I loved Maggie. *So much.* And I knew I could never stop. I could love her all the way through her daydreams and back again, every single day. It would only get bigger, swelling inside my chest with every blazing beat.

And I *wanted* to love her. More than anything.

She startled me, trying to loosen my grip on her waist. I realised I was squeezing her *way* too tight.

Floating in front of me again, she said, "So, when you lock the door ... then what happens?"

It felt different, her running through my mind instead of me running through hers.

I pulled her back into me, desperately searching her eyes. "We happen, Mags. Me and you."

Nose to nose, I could feel her quick breaths against my lips, and *my god* ... it sent my mind reeling. I was *so* close to kissing her again. But I couldn't. I knew that when I did, if I ever could, I'd be sure it was only us.

Through a soft giggle, she asked, "Remember when you asked for a sleepover in your room a couple of weeks ago?"

"Yeah ..." I cringed. "Are you sure I'm not an idiot?"

She nodded. "Yes, I'm sure."

Tugging my arms around her back, she wrapped her legs around my hips and moved into my lap. Her hands slid up my chest, behind my neck, and she drew herself close to my ear.

Her voice dropped to a whisper. "Maybe I can sleep over here tonight, instead."

Oh my god. Yes. Absolutely. A million times yes.

I leaned back, holding her cheeks. "As long as it's not a maybe, then please, Maggie. Stay with me."

She sighed, smiling and pushing away from me. She hadn't run through my mind, she'd sprinted, but when she left ... I still felt steady. Like I knew nothing was out of place because she didn't touch anything, she just looked.

"Yay, sleepover!" She giggled and blew a few more bubbles. "We should go and join the party. We can hang out later."

I watched her climb out of the spa, flicking my eyes across her skin again ...

And I spent every minute of the two hours that followed wishing everyone would get the fuck out of my house.

It was pushing two a.m., and it should have been easy to kick Jordan and Brooks out. They were my closest friends, and I'd kicked them out before, for a lot less.

But this was different. It was only them, Ash, and Mags left.

There was no way Maggie would stay if they knew. Ash would tell Chelsea, and then the world would know. Ash either stayed to try me again, or she and Brooks were a thing ... I wasn't sure.

Peeking at Maggie, who was forcing her eyes open, I hated that nothing was just ours, even in my own house. I knew I couldn't even run my finger along her cheek with them here, so with a little nudge, I gave her a look that said, *It's okay, you should go.*

I walked her to the door, and she hugged me, holding on tight. She whispered in my ear, "I'm not leaving. Find me when they leave?"

My stomach did at least six backflips in a row. She had a plan, but she closed the door before I could respond.

I spun around and cut straight back to the lounge. I had to kick them out.

"You guys," I said, flicking off the speaker in the living room. "I don't want to kick you out … but …" I gave them a half-assed, sorry smile.

Jordan shot me a grin. "But Mags left, so party's over?"

"Ha. Ha." I pinched his neck. "No. I'm just tired. I just finished making a TV show."

I sounded like a douchebag; it was more than fair they all mocked me.

Eyes on Brooks, Ash said, "Let's go to mine."

Brooks jumped up at the idea. "Yep, let's do it. Jordan, let's bounce." Ash looked shattered when Brooks invited Jordan, and I kinda felt bad for her.

After they left, I checked myself out in the mirror by the front door. It felt juvenile, but necessary. I spotted Jordan's wallet on the bench, grabbed it, and ran after them. But I was too late. My gate had already closed.

I whipped my phone out, but there was nothing from Mags. I thought maybe she'd just gone home … she was tired. It was fine. Heading back up my driveway, right on the edge of surrendering the thought of her staying with me, out of the corner of my eye—

I caught a towel moving on a pool lounge.

It was Maggie. *She was staying.*

I bounded over the glass fence, dropping Jordan's wallet and banging my shoulder on the way down. It hurt, not enough to stop, but Mags was already at my side like she knew it was going to happen.

She reached out her hand, and I took it, pulling myself up. Giggling, she said, "I just did the exact same thing!" She pointed to a small graze on her shoulder.

"Damn, Mags ... I hate that this doesn't have a gate. I'm sorry." I eyed the graze. It was tiny, but I still wished I could blink and make it disappear.

I grabbed her hand, leading us back in the house. "Come inside, it's cold."

I wasn't really sure what would happen next ... all that really mattered was that she was staying.

The light wasn't going out.

36

You Just Be

Maggie

Getting ready for the wrap party, I kept thinking about what Alicia said to me on set ... how kissing Chris for the first time was a moment that I *wanted*. Mulling it over, my thoughts were kind of circling in on themselves, fluttering more sporadically than usual.

That *knowing* I lived in, the one that said, *You're happening to the world, Mags* ... I had a little feeling that maybe it was starting to unravel, and it made my head spin. The feeling appeared in my body as a tightening knot of tension in my gut. The kind that's hard to ignore.

I never wanted to put myself in a position where it felt like someone could steal that sense of knowing. I'd always held onto it tightly. The idea of it shifting into *me happening to Chris* and *Chris happening to me* ... kinda made me feel like I was fading away into someone else's dream.

Chris was, like, born to be in love, I think. Like if love were some sort of shape, it was cut exactly like Chris. He could step right into it, and it'd be a perfect fit. He just knew himself inside of it. But ... for me, it was more like an outline I'd never considered colouring in, or whether it even came in a shape that I could fit myself into.

I didn't *know* what it felt like to be in love, and I didn't know how to just be who I am inside of it. I felt like I had to surrender pieces of myself that I wasn't ready to share or give away. Like if I went too fast, I'd colour outside the lines ... and end up losing all these little pieces of myself that I knew.

Knowing Chris wanted to kiss me, for *real,* didn't equate to knowing that I wanted him to be *in love* with me. Or that I wanted to be in love with him. But thinking about it stirred up a dizzying jumble of confusing emotions, and thoughts, and words ... it felt endless! They all tangled up in each other, and it brought on a weird type of feverish haze.

I'd close my eyes and see a pattern of chaos, but I wasn't sent into a familiar spiral of panic. The way it made me dizzy felt brand *new,* exhilarating and intoxicating, and the one key word I untangled from the blurry mess of it all was ... *maybe.*

Maybe I was on the brink of discovering something I'd never experienced in any lifetime ... because, *maybe,* it was made for this one. And maybe there was a different kind of extraordinary for me to find. Not the fictional kind, or the fragmented kind, or the kind that would fade away into the edges of my daydreams.

Maybe this extraordinary would light my life up with magic, every day, *for real,* and for the rest of forever. *Imagine that, Maggie.*

On the way to the wrap party, I imagined it more and more. That's when I decided Alicia was right. Chris did steal a moment that I wanted. And I wanted that moment on my own terms, because I wanted to feel it all, properly. If *I* was going to happen *to* that moment ...

I was gonna need to steal it back.

Floating around inside Chris's house, I had quite the sneaky sticky beak. I didn't really get that far … it had a lot of walls, all the rooms were private. I thought I'd get lost if I wandered in too deep. He had a lot of art; big, abstract pieces with splashes of warm tones. Kinda like emotions thrown onto canvases. There was more personality than the outside, at least.

After a while, and maybe one, *or three*, too many shots of Chris's fancy-pants tequila, I slipped into the spa with Cherie. It was too cold to swim, so sinking into the bubbles was settling to my warm, buzzing state.

My arse cheeks hadn't even hit a seat when I saw Chris burst out the door from inside. We locked eyes, and his expression shifted from wide-eyed panic … into a deep exhale. A playful little smile bloomed across his lips, but I had a hunch he was holding back a much wider grin, catching the little dimple creasing his left cheek.

He practically dove into the spa, and I stole lots of peeks at him. I could feel the heady mix of thrill and appetite again … his bare chest, the way his hair curled, half-dry over his forehead … *good golly, Miss Maggie.*

There's gorgeous, and then there's *wet* and gorgeous. Seeing him like that sent all sorts of hot shivers up and down my spine. Stronger than the ones from the jets.

I knew exactly what he meant when he said he wanted to lock the doors to the porch. I wanted to lock them, too. But I did feel cautious about it, and peering through the roadways of his mind, I looked both ways before bolting through.

It was like I could see the image of myself getting caught, or lost inside his mind. So that's why I bolted. If I stayed any longer, I wasn't sure I'd ever leave. I needed the time, just us, to explore and find out if there was an unobscured path into his head. One I wouldn't feel so lost in.

I also didn't want to leave his arms. I mean, I was getting pretty good at swallowing horse-sized adult pills, but that didn't mean I wasn't … *just a girl*, sometimes …

So a sleepover with Chris felt necessary at that point.

At nearly two a.m., I was heavy-eyed, lounging on Chris's couch. The only people left were those I knew would tell the world if I went into his bedroom. Chris looked at me with a hint of disappointment in his gaze, trying to tell me through his eyes it wouldn't hurt him if I left. But I knew it would.

As he walked me out, I asked him to find me when the others were gone, secretly hoping there was another way to the pool lounges without jumping the fence. Realising there wasn't, I scurried down the driveway to the same spot Brooks had hauled me over when I arrived.

I jumped—and of course—I fell. Hard.

For a minute, I just lay there, flat on my back, trying not to cry …

When I heard the front door open again, I scrambled up, bolted for a lounge, and buried myself under a towel. My heart was pounding, and I could feel my blood racing from my brain to my toes.

Before I could message Chris to tell him where I was, I heard a crash against the fence followed by a loud *thud*. I knew he'd spotted me. And, just like I had, he fell over the fence! I ran straight over to him, giggling my guts out. It was hilarious!

He led us inside, and I could still feel the rush of blood coursing through my body, but I liked the way it felt. The living room was dimly lit by the lamp near the coffee table, and I left the door open an inch, so the chill in the night air would mix in with the warmth under my skin.

Chris's couch was the deep and cosy, worn-in soft leather type. I couldn't wait to sink back into it.

"So," he huffed, flopping onto the cushions. "What are you thinking about? And you're my best friend, so you may as well tell me, because I'll know if you're making it up." He gave me a wink and tapped the spot next to him.

I settled into the couch, rolling onto my back and resting my head in his lap. I lay outstretched, gazing up at him, tracing the curve of his smile with my eyes.

Before I spoke, I gave myself a little reminder ...

You're not afraid, Mags. Feel it all.

Softly, I said, "I'm thinking about how you stole a moment from us today, and that I wish I could steal it back."

I caught the drop in Chris's smile, but I didn't keep my eyes on his face.

Staring at the ceiling, a constant flow of words bubbled in my chest. The beautiful thing about being honest is that it ripples. You're brave enough to say one honest thing ... then all these other honest things echo after it.

Chris took a breath to speak, but I didn't let him. "I saw inside your mind, earlier," I said, sitting up from his lap.

He looked guarded, expressionless, like he didn't want to let me back in right now.

I continued, "I think I got a little lost. And it scared me, for a second. Like, if I stayed there, in your mind ... I'd lose myself. And I don't want that."

Chris shook his head. "I don't want that either, Mags." He sounded a little pained at my sureness.

"Chris ..." I inched myself close to him to keep my voice soft. "I love my life. Most of the time, I love myself, too. But when I look in your eyes, and you look in mine ... like *that* ... I feel like I have to give myself away. All the little pieces of me, and my mind, and who I am. Like it's the only thing I can do to make you happy."

We sat in silence for a few moments, peering into each other. I could feel him waiting, quietly, like he knew I wasn't done.

His gaze circled my face, a subtle, still smile resting on his lips.

As I mirrored his smile, he reached forward, gently easing my hair over my shoulder. His fingers softly skimmed across my cheek, lingering, tucking the other side behind my ear ... and a little breath caught in my throat.

He leaned back, his gaze catching mine again, and he held it like I was the only person who'd ever existed. His attention was full, patient, like he'd wait all night if it meant that he could hear what I was thinking.

... I took a deep, necessary breath before I continued.

"I feel like I haven't had enough time to figure out how to share who I am, or show it, or give it away to anyone. And I just ... I can't do that. I am *mine*. And I have to protect that. Especially through all of *this*."

My hand waved over leftover pieces of the wrap party scattered around the room. Meeting his eyes again, I took another breath, small and silent, shaking my head a little.

As softly as I could, I added, "I can't let myself go ... by giving it all to you."

Chris didn't look away. Not even for a second.

Shifting in close, he placed a firm hand at the back of my head, and all the blood in my body rushed to meet it. Another little breath got stuck in my throat, and without meaning to, my eyes dropped, helplessly drawn away by the overwhelm of how it felt.

His hand slipped beneath my jaw, fingertips catching my chin before it hit my chest.

Calm and slow, he lifted my face ... until we were eye to eye again.

"You don't have to do that, Maggie." He softly shook his head. "You don't have to *give* anything to me."

He moved his hands to my cheeks, smoothing his thumbs across my skin. "You just *be*. And then I love you. For *being*."

Through a glowing gaze, his palms pressed firmly in their hold on my face.

And like he anchored us both, still and steady, he added, "I meet you in your mind, and you meet me in mine."

My mouth fell open in a silent gasp. It felt like he'd whispered me a secret.

A secret that only he knew, and one that I was meant to hear, right now ... in this lifetime.

I held his hands against my cheeks, closing my eyes. I took a slow, deep breath in, careful through the exhale. Letting the moment settle deep inside my mind, every word he said immediately etched into my conscience.

I smiled, knowing that I'd never, ever forget them.

Then I locked them up, safe and sound.

Sinking back into Chris's gaze, I felt like I was looking at a map to the surefire discovery of something extraordinary. It was a promise, a very precious one. I could feel it in the way his sapphire eyes held a steady sparkle, filling my chest with a warm glow.

My smile grew, sparked by the light on my insides, and I climbed into his lap, easing him back against the arm of the couch. Trailing my hands up his chest, I held onto his cheeks, pressing my thumb on the crease of his dimple.

He wrapped his arms around my waist, smiling so wide that a little breathy giggle escaped his chest. Before it could make me giggle, too, I leaned forward ... and I kissed him.

It was soft, and easy, and natural. When his hands pressed firm up by back, pulling me in to hold me tight, kissing me harder ... it was still easy. I could feel his smile on my lips every time I took a breath.

It felt cosy, and beautiful, and it was the moment I wanted. As whole as I'd imagined.

Wrapped up in each other's minds, perfectly present in the sureness of what we were finding inside them ... I knew we both felt the same.

Just this, right now.

My hands cradled his jaw, and I whispered against his lips, "If the world was ending right now ..." I flicked my eyes towards his bedroom, then locked back in his gaze. "You know. And I know."

I smirked, just a little. Chris mirrored it, nodding.

I gave his lips a gentle kiss, then I leaned back, resting my hands in my lap. "But it's not ending. We have *time*. And I need that time. I want to feel this, slowly. All of it. I don't want to miss, or forget, any of this. And also ..." I paused, exhaling. "I don't want to forget *me*."

He took my hands, moving them back to his cheeks. "I know," he said, nodding again. "I know now. It's okay." Then he held my fingers to his lips, kissing each one and smiling in between.

He settled deeper into the couch, guiding my head to rest on his chest. With the back of his finger, he traced gentle lines up and down my cheek, tilting his head up to the ceiling. Even though I couldn't see his face, I knew his eyes and smile were still lit up, perfectly matching.

"I love you, Mags," he breathed. "You're my best friend in the whole world. And in my dreams, and outer space ... in every galaxy, in every timeline ..." He trailed off in a whispery giggle.

I smiled, feeling my cheek pressed close against his chest.

The tips of my toes tingled with the chill of the breeze drifting through the door, but I wasn't cold. His chest felt warm, sparked with a glow, just like mine. The slow strokes of his finger against my skin spread enough heat to cover my entire body, too.

I could hear his heart beating, steady and strong, and my breaths fell in sync with the rhythm, soothed by the sound.

Softly closing my eyes, I caught glimpses of our shadow through my lashes, a blurred silhouette on the wall. I traced its shape, following the gentle rise and fall of Chris's chest ... And I thought, *maybe*, I'd never need to worry about fitting into the outline.

Because maybe it just ... *was.*

We were right here, just existing ... just *being* ... colliding in a moment that felt made for this lifetime.

Extraordinary, isn't it, Maggie. The real kind.

So peaceful I could feel myself slipping to sleep, I lay down, my body melting beside him. I kept my ear pressed to his chest, listening to the rhythm, breathing in sync.

Closing my eyes again, I found my reply to what he'd said. I almost forgot to say the words, lost through my drifting.

Exhaling, I whispered, "Love you."

37

Love You, xo

Chris

When I listened to the way Maggie said, "Love you" ...

I realised something.

It was the way I'd never wanted her to say it to me.

I'd heard it hundreds of times since the day I met her. It was the way she said it to Cherie, and Ben, Alicia ... Nic. Michael Lesley after he cast her as Sarah. She even used to say it to Dom.

But I let it fill me, anyway. I didn't ask for more, because I meant what I said. She didn't have to give anything to me. It was enough, beautiful just as it was.

Ben was exactly right. *She'd come down, eventually.*

I felt her; she was *here.*

And I wasn't leaving.

After sleeping on the couch, Maggie woke me up with a kiss on my cheek. I opened my eyes, and she was holding her bag.

I shot up. "You're leaving? I'll make us coffee."

Through her soft, sweet voice, she said, "You don't have any milk, I already checked."

Damn it, Chris.

"Well, I'll drive you. It's fine, I'll grab my keys." I got up too quick; my head spun.

"Are you sure? Only if you want to."

Like I don't want to spend another hour with you, Mags.

I shook my head, smiling at her. "I definitely do. Give me, like, four minutes."

I shoved my head under a cold shower, brushed my teeth, changed my shirt, and we were out the door.

She peered out the window the whole drive, daydreaming, but I didn't try to find where she was. I just let her be, let her fly away again. I smiled, imagining how it might feel to fly with her. But it felt too distant to get a clear picture yet.

When we pulled up at The Bennett, she kissed me on the cheek again. It felt warm; I hoped it would linger.

I had to be a *little* reckless. "So, just to confirm … if the world is ending today—"

"I'll come over." She cut me off with her charming, beaming smile. Peering through the windshield, she added, "But everything looks fine, so … yeah. I think we're good."

The cheeky grin she flashed me had me clenching my teeth. I pulled her into me, wanting to smother her, but I kissed both her cheeks instead.

She hopped out of the car, her chocolate curls bouncing as they fell over her shoulders. "See you tomorrow! Love you!" Then she shut the door before I could say it back.

… I wondered if that was on purpose.

On the way home, I was running through our schedule with Cherie on the phone. We had almost a whole week of random press for *More of You,* starting tomorrow, and I got a little lost trying to figure out how I'd get through it.

Especially now I knew, for sure, that I loved Maggie. *A lot.* And I wanted to love her. *Always.* And ... I was absolutely addicted to how that felt.

... Shit.

When Mags said she wanted slow, and she wanted to feel it all, I wholeheartedly agreed. It wasn't that I didn't want that, too. I didn't want to miss a single thing.

But I'd already caught on fire. My heart had struck its match.

I couldn't stop it! I was a helpless addict for being in love! I'd been hooked on the high of the feeling since I was six years old *... this is all your fault, Josephine.*

"Chris? Did you get that?" *Oh crap, Cherie.*

"Yeah." I slapped myself on the cheek, tuning back in. "Well, no. Sorry. Say again?"

"Eight in the morning at Studio 18. Mags will be there earlier."

"Yeah, sure. Did they send through a brief? Like what's the vibe?"

"It's very ... *Romeo and Juliet* inspired. Sarah and Liam in the fourteenth century, romance-y vibe."

God damn it. I quickly muted Cherie and shouted, *"Fuck!"*

Unmuting her, I said, "Cool. Sounds good."

After we hung up, I knew that if the week was going to begin with a day of *pretending* that I was *acting* being in love with Maggie ...

I was gonna need a plan.

So, I made a mental list of a few things I knew.

One, I was in love with Maggie Marshall.

Two, if I was going to love Maggie, I had to do it differently. I couldn't be an addict about it. I had to love her from the *changed* me, not the old me.

Wait, so who am I right now?

Three, I needed to figure out how to fill the space between who I was, and who I'm going to be.

Four, I had no idea how to do that. But being near Maggie, as much as I could, was going to make that a heck of a lot easier. Because sure, I knew I was an addict. But I also knew ...

I hadn't fallen in love with an enabler.

38

Was That a Shudder?

Maggie

Chris and I had played dress-ups all day as Sarah and Liam in *Romeo and Juliet*. It was fun, but a little over the top. And my boobs were kinda spilling out in a few of the dresses, which I think Chris enjoyed ... but I could barely breathe most of the day.

After twelve straight hours on set, my body was so exhausted. I was trying to make my eyes look wide and alive, forcing them to stay open. We just had to film a quick intro bit for the teaser trailer of the show, then we were done.

Sitting side by side in director's chairs, Chris had his eyes closed, catching a quick bit of shut-eye, I guessed. He made a cute Romeo. He still had on his *romantic hero* shirt—the loose, white, flowy kind.

I was staring at him, waiting for crew to fix the sound ... I think he felt it.

He opened one eye. "Livin' the dream, Mags?"

I gave him a lazy smirk. *"Living the dream.* You?"

He straightened up and leaned in, his eyes narrowing, lips a little pursed. Then, with a quick shake of my knee and his head, he grinned. "Yep. Absolutely."

I'd be lying if I said I didn't pick up his little shake was a quick release of sexual tension. It was definitely ... *in the air.*

Chris glanced at his phone, lifting his brows. "Oh, damn. Massive storm warning tonight."

I sucked in a sharp breath and *shuddered.* I hated storms. *Big time.* Chris looked stunned, but beneath those wide eyes ... I knew he was loving it.

"Miss Maggie," he said, slowly shaking his head. "Was that a little shudder? No, don't tell me ... after all this time, I am finding out *now* that you're *scared of storms?"*

I rolled my eyes and shot him some side-eye, but I knew I was genuinely terrified of storms. There was no way I could hide it if I was with him during one.

Trying to act dismissive, I said, "Maybe just a teensy, tiny bit."

Chris raised an eyebrow, his lips twitching to hold back a laugh.

I had to give in.

"Okay, fine." I lifted my palms in surrender. "Not tiny. More like a lot."

Shaking his head slowly again, he muttered under his breath, "Oh my god. Right when I think I know you."

He leaned back, eyeing me up and down in teasing disapproval. Then he gripped the armrest of my chair and tugged it closer to his.

With his mouth at my ear, he whispered, "Would you say it makes you feel like ... *the world is ending?"*

I whipped to face him, caught his devilish smile, and started to say, "Shut the fuck—"

"Alright! You guys good?" My scolding was cut off by the crew.

Chris took a swig of water and winked at me. I felt flustered. *That little shit.*

We were able to film the intro in one take. Well, it was five, but four were us being stupid. So, it counted as one. By the time we finished, heavy rain was slapping against the studio windows … and it only got worse once we left.

It was just Chris and me in the car, heading back to The Bennett. He was going home tonight, and thinking about the storm tied my insides in sharp knots. Lightning filled the car every few seconds, so I shut my eyes, tightly gripping the edge of my seat.

Letting out a sympathy giggle, Chris poked my knee. "Maggie?"

"Yes?"

"You're *really* scared of storms, aren't you."

"Yes."

"I know, you know, storms don't make the world end. When I ask this, I want you to remember that, okay?"

A loud clap of thunder ripped through my ears, and I flinched, squeezing my eyes extra tight before I replied.

After a moment, I hummed, "Mmhmm?"

He put his hand on my shoulder. "Do you want me to stay with you?"

"No." I shook my head. "It's okay. I'm fine."

Another crack of thunder tore through the sky, and I threw my hands up to cover my ears. I swear—it shook the car!

Chris took his seatbelt off and scooted over. "Aw, Mags." He wrapped his arm behind my shoulders. "Just think of that stupid song, from *Ted.* The *Fuck You Thunder* one."

I opened my eyes, uncovering my ears to grab Chris's hand on my lap. Through short, sharp breaths, I muttered, "Yeah. *Fuck you, thunder.*"

Within seconds, the car lit up with jagged flashes of lightning, and my eyes snapped shut again. Being scared of storms was just one of those stubborn, unshakable fears. I accepted it about myself a long time ago, but when Chris hugged me a little tighter, I felt a bit sorry for myself ... for being *so* scared.

We pulled up at the hotel, and I took big, deep breaths, bracing myself to make the dash into the lobby.

"Maggie, you got this," Chris said, with a firm hand on my cheek. "You're *untouchable*, remember?" He gave me a confident nod. He was sure, and that made me brave.

I swung open the door, only to be knocked back inside by an ear-splitting boom of thunder. I accidentally squealed a little ... it was terrifying!

With my hand still on the door handle, I turned to Chris, my eyes instantly welling up before I squeezed them shut again. I felt desperate, young, and silly. My breath was panicked, I couldn't believe I'd *squealed* when I opened the door, and I hated the way it felt to feel so out of control!

I blurted out, "I changed my mind. Can you stay with me?"

He didn't respond. I opened my eyes, but he wasn't there.

I jolted at a knock on the window and realised he was outside my door. Holding up his fingers, he signalled a countdown ... *three, two, one.*

He opened the car door, I jumped in front of him, and we bolted inside.

"See?" Chris smiled, making a little circle with his hand on my back. "Easy. *Fuck you, thunder.*"

Still panting, I gave him a shaky high-five. He must have gotten out of the car before he heard me ask him to stay, though, because he took a step back towards the entrance doors.

Nodding, he said, "You're good, Mags. You got this." With a quick step forward, he kissed my cheek. "Goodnight."

In the moment his lips touched my skin, all I could see were bursts of lightning through every window of the lobby.

Before he could move as much as an inch, I grabbed his head, locking him in place between my shaky, tiny hands.

"No," I insisted. "I asked you in the car. I asked you to stay."

39

Lightning and Thunder

Chris

I felt *so* bad for Mags. The whole car ride home she was terrified. It was a new colour on her, seeing her so damn scared. She had this tearful sparkle in her eyes … it reminded me of what it felt like to watch her go dark when she panicked.

Desperate to take it away from her, I prayed to the Weather God I made up in my mind that the storm would disappear.

Come on, Weather God! I swear I won't ask for anything, ever again!

… Except for this. Every time it happens.

I ran her into The Bennett, and just seconds away from walking back out to the car, she stopped me with her tight, trembling grip on my head.

She asked me to stay, and there was no fucking way I was stepping back out that door. I couldn't leave her.

"Of course, Mags, of course," I said, loosening her fingers from my face. "I need to run out and tell Marco. I'll be five seconds."

Before I could take a step, Maggie called out to the doorman. "Excuse me, sir? Can you please let that driver know he doesn't need to wait?" She smiled sweetly, pointing to the car. "We don't need to be anywhere else so he can go. Thank you so much."

There she is. Back in control again.

She hooked her arm in mine, hurrying for the stairs.

I sighed. "Maggie, really? Stairs? Right now?"

"Chris!" she squeaked. "Look at that lightning! If we get stuck in the lift ..."

She paused. I smiled. I bit my lip, shot my brows up. We both knew what *could* happen if we got stuck in that lift.

She scrunched her eyes and nose, smiling. It was so cheeky that, without thinking, I squeezed her cheek between my thumb and finger.

Snapping out of it, I nodded. "Okay. Stairs. Got it."

Before we sat down in Maggie's suite, she shut all the blinds and switched off every power outlet on each wall, assuring me that the TV and lamp were still allowed.

We flopped onto the couch, and I suggested we eat, though I knew she wouldn't. Scrolling through the room service menu on the TV—

Cut to black. The power went out.

Mags gasped and slapped my arm. *Hard.*

As my eyes adjusted, I couldn't see her, but I heard a little teary sniffle. When lightning snuck light through the gap in the blinds, I reached across the couch and pulled her in close. With her wrapped between my legs and bundled in my arms, I sent a few extra prayers up to the Weather God.

Trying to reassure her, I said, "Last time I was here, and there was a blackout, it took them two minutes to get the power back on."

That was a lie; it actually took them a solid half an hour. But thankfully this time ... it was only five minutes.

Maggie released my grip, flopping back onto the couch with a big, sighing exhale.

Hearing the level of stress in that single breath, I had to ask. "Mags, why are you so afraid of storms?"

She hesitated. "Um ..."

Then she flashed her little *trying to think of a lie* smile. Wide-eyed, mouth half-open ...

Not this time, Maggie.

I was making her say it, so I started, "Don't say it, don't say it, don't say it ..."

She joined in, giggling and covering her face. "Don't say it, don't say it—"

She broke. "Because it makes me feel like the world is ending! There! Are you happy now?"

I was *beaming.* Elated, ecstatic, exhilarated ... it was exactly the outcome I wanted.

"Very happy," I said, crossing my arms smug and tight against my chest. "Thank you. *Finally.*"

She wrapped herself up all cosy in a blanket, and I flicked the TV back on and put on *Ted,* which felt appropriate.

Just looking at her from across the couch, the pounding beats of my heart were flamin' hot. It was intense, and I could feel the wild laps of heat coursing through my body. I loved it, obviously, but I had to throw some ice on all that, though.

I needed to cool it. Maggie was still scared, and frankly, I'd flinched a few times at the thunder myself.

And *sure,* if she left the room, walked back out here naked, and said, *Let's have sex until the storm passes* ... I knew I wouldn't say no. But there was no way in hell that was happening. I hid that idea inside a small, inconspicuous box, deep in another box, buried under another pile of boxes inside my mind ... so I didn't think she'd find it.

As the storm settled, Maggie jolted her foot against me on the couch, drifting to sleep.

I gave her a little nudge. "Mags? Do you want to go to bed?"

She dragged herself upright, nodding, so we moved into the bedroom. She went into the ensuite to change into pyjamas, which was disappointing, but understandable.

I stripped off my hoodie and shirt, thankful I was lazy and chose to wear sweats to set. Knowing the vibe of the sleepover wasn't the *naked* kind, I figured I'd keep the sweatpants on. I made sure the AC was on cool, turned it down a notch, and crawled into bed.

After a couple of minutes, Mags stepped out of the ensuite in a pale blue, oversized bed shirt ... with Care Bears plastered all over it.

I snorted, covering my mouth to stifle the laugh.

"What ..." she whined, all bashful and adorable about it.

"Nothing." I forced a straight face. "Care Bears are cool." I leaned back against the headboard, trying to sound serious. "Funshine Bear is badass."

She flipped me off, rolling her eyes with her tongue stuck out.

Are you there, God? I'm gonna need some more of that ice ...

She climbed into bed, flicked off the lamp, and as she tucked herself in, she said, "Ahh. I'm just a big, toasty ..."

"Cinnamon bun?" I tried to finish her *Simpsons* reference.

"Ha! Oh." She shook her head. "I was about to say, '*loaf of bread*'."

For a brief moment, we stared at each other through the dark. Dead-pan and masking reactions.

Breaking the silence, I said, "I mean ... I guess it works?"

Then, Maggie's cheeks puffed out, and we completely cracked, bursting into laughter. I'd never get over how *fun* every little moment felt being by her side.

Settling her giggles, she rolled over to face me. "Thank you for staying. Sorry I'm a weenie."

"Of course, Mags." A little frown formed between her brows, so I added, "Oh, I have no comment on the weenie thing. It's definitely true."

She smiled with a sleepy giggle, then she closed her eyes and whispered, "Goodnight, sweet dreams."

It was so sudden; I didn't know how to respond. I knew how I *could* respond, but I also knew I shouldn't just take her by surprise and kiss her again. I figured it'd be better to ask.

"Mags?" I whispered. "Maggie, can I kiss—"

And ... she was kissing me.

It knocked the wind out of me; she held such a tight grip on my face. I wrapped my arm around her back and pulled her on top of me. *Fast.*

I lifted us up against the headboard, and as I felt her hips sink onto mine, I was hopelessly desperate not to lose my mind. My fingers slid straight through her hair, and I held it tightly in firm fists.

The electric energy from her palms pressed against my chest had me charging up. I felt her fingers weave into my hair, and I was captivated.

She was pure magic to kiss.

I gently tugged her hair to tilt her head, deeply enjoying the small sound of a caught breath, and started trailing my lips up her neck. She smiled, and her perfect, angel giggle whispered in my ear.

Don't you dare giggle right now, Maggie.

I moved my hands to her cheeks, pressing soft kisses to her jaw. She giggled again.

Mags, don't.

Running my hands down her chest, the tips of my fingers grazed the curve of her waist ... and I felt her little body completely tense up.

Are you ticklish, Maggie Marshall?

I slipped my hands beneath her shirt, lightly brushing my fingers over her waist again, exploring the idea ...

She flinched, jolting back a little. *Big yes. Definitely ticklish.*

Her reaction was instinctive and, inevitably, I was thrilled. It sent my mind wandering through all the possibilities of her other ... *instinctive reactions.*

Clutching her hips, all I wanted to do was touch her. Everywhere. Urgently. Desperate to learn the feel of every inch of her skin, in a way that was anything but slow.

I shifted my hands back to her face.

Cool it, Chris.

I pressed my thumbs along her lips.

Slow the hell down.

Gazing at her, taking her all in, I grinned ...

And she tried to push the corners of my mouth down.

Fuck.

I took a sharp breath in. *We have the same turn-on.*

I knew she caught my gasp, because she eased off me, lying at my side.

I slid down beside her, wrapping my arm around her waist, pulling her in as close as I could. With her body melting against mine, I took a deep breath, holding on to the nape of her neck.

I smiled, she smiled back ... and I covered her exquisite face in a hundred little kisses. Smothering her cheeks, forehead, jaw, and nose. Every few breaths, I returned to her lips, mostly kissing her teeth because she giggled so much.

Pulling back just enough to meet her eyes, I said, "I think I could kiss you forever. Like, for real."

She tilted her head and smirked. "How much would you bet?"

Pretending to consider it, I mirrored her head tilt, then whispered the answer in her ear. "Literally everything." And because I'd just learned that Maggie was ticklish, I had to throw in a tickle on her waist.

Squirming and laughing, she spoke through the cutest little squeak. "I don't like that you know this about me!"

"I love it." I surrendered my hands. Raising my brows, I added, "New superpower ... unlocked."

Eventually, the heat in the room settled, lingering warmth in a cosy, snoozy kind of way. Our eyes were locked, unhurried in exploring details, our bodies lying in soft stillness. The only sounds became our slowing, sleepy breaths and the light drizzle of rain left over from the storm.

With Maggie tracing slow, soft patterns across my chest, my hand rested steady in the centre of her back, holding her close. We stayed there, for a while ... until I caught her eyelids fluttering, fighting to stay open.

Quietly, I asked, "Are you sleepy, Mags?"

"Yeah." She yawned. "I really am." She yawned again.

As if I hadn't already melted enough, she snuggled herself into me as close as she could, tucking her head into my chest. It felt like she'd found her little spot.

"Okay, storm warrior." I gently moved her hair from her face, trailing it softly down her back. "Sweet dreams."

She giggled one last sleepy giggle, her voice a slurred, dreamy mumble. "Goodnight. Thank you for staying."

Curling the ends of her hair around my fingers, over and over, taking my time ... I felt kind of overwhelmed that I got to be here, touching it like that. I stared up at the ceiling for at least an hour, listening to her breathing slow and deepen.

I wondered what she dreamed about; every now and then, she'd make these little faces, as if she were reacting to whatever she could see in her dreams.

I could hardly imagine what it would feel like to do this every night, to have it be normal. I couldn't picture it ever not feeling so rare and precious, kind of like ... *catching a butterfly.*

I thought about what I told Ben, about Maggie being like a butterfly. Thinking it through logically, a butterfly really only lands on something that feels steady. Something that feels still. And safe.

I meant it when I said I couldn't picture Maggie ever settling. But when I pictured the version of myself she helped me see, it made me feel like I could be a sure place for her to land. She could rest ... I'd keep her safe ...

I liked that idea. It was a lovely idea to hold on to.

I knew it would live inside me for a while, getting to kiss her like that. To have her in my arms and watch her dream. Being near Maggie made me feel like I knew things, and knew them for sure.

And I just *knew* I'd need to hang onto this feeling. Tight.

So, I replayed it in my mind, over and over, until I fell asleep ... hoping it'd preserve the memory.

I was right about needing to hang on to the feeling. Especially the kiss.

It was the last one I'd get for a *very* long time.

And when I tell you it lasted inside me, it did ...

But after a while, it started to fade away. And it started to hurt. I didn't know for sure if I would ever get another one.

Every time we spoke, I'd tell myself, *She'll come down, eventually* ... because I knew.

There'd be a time when she'd land again, and when she did—
I'd be ready.
I'd be still. Steady. Safe.
I'd meet her in her mind, and she'd meet me in mine.

Chris's Epilogue

Chris

On December 19, I called Maggie for her birthday. She made a dark joke about hoping to make it through without joining the *27 Club*, and I imagined her cheeky face when she said it.

I hadn't seen her in six weeks, basically since we wrapped work for season one.

She was in London, shooting an indie film she was cast in. It was all so last minute … like I blinked, and she was on a plane.

She was so excited about it. She talked about it for two whole hours when she told me she got it. I was mesmerised, though, watching her talk about it. I say watching because, after the first hour, my *listening* had turned into … *observing*.

Thankfully, she was coming back in two days, and I couldn't wait to see her again.

To *feel* her again.

I hadn't completely forgotten how it felt to be near her. But I could feel the distance. I was hanging on to our last kiss for dear life, sure it would fade away soon.

Or, if I'm being honest, as an addict of being in love …

I'd say I'd been experiencing some rather *unhinged withdrawals.* I even made a few phone calls to Cupid about it. I wish I wasn't being serious about that.

As was the current custom, on the phone with her, I internalised all the things I wanted to say. Then, I made a bit more small talk just to keep listening to the sound of her voice.

She talked about how pretty the lights were at night in London, and glancing at the script for season two of *More of You* sitting on my coffee table … I felt extremely impatient.

When we were about to hang up, she said, "Goodnight! Love you!"

Then she hung up before I could say it back. She did that *every. Single. Time.*

I never wanted Maggie to feel like she had to lose any part of herself to me, or anyone, or anything. Ever. But I could tell, by the way she'd hang up on me … she still felt like she was going to.

Her flight to L.A. ended up getting cancelled because of some crazy storm near London airport, and I didn't sleep. At all. I just couldn't stop thinking about how scared she would have been.

I'd also have to wait another day before I saw her. And I'd have to meet her at our first table read for season two.

She'd be heading straight there from the airport … which wasn't really the reunion I'd imagined in my mind.

Driving to the table read, I was excited, obviously. But I was also running through the plan I'd made for when the time came to see Maggie again. I felt pretty solid about it, thought I had it all under control.

Turns out I was completely clueless, though. Because that plan was about to implode into a thousand tiny pieces.

I glanced to my right, and—

Oh my god. I could see her; she was waiting for me.

Standing inside the entrance of the lobby, peering through the glass doors.

There she was. *Maggie Marshall.*

A sparkling ray of sunshine. Chocolate hair below her waist in loose curls, pale greens brighter than ever.

I did what I could only call the worst reverse park of my entire life, but I left it and bolted through the side door. I didn't want to meet her at the entrance; I was worried there'd be snoops near the front.

I ran towards the lobby, halting when I saw her. She was still peering through the glass, probably wondering where I went after she spotted my car.

Sounding shocked she was in front of me, I called out from behind her. "Maggie!"

She spun around, and *that smile. That frickin' smile.* It was beaming the second she saw me. I waved at her to get the hell into my arms—immediately.

As she ran towards me, she yelped a little, "Yay!"

I braced myself for the feeling. *The rush.* The inhale of her glow, and the exhale that would follow it.

I was *so* ready.

Steady, gaze fixed on hers, feet rooted in the ground ... I counted down.

Three, two ... one.

She jumped into my arms, and I couldn't let go.

I was hugging her so tight, she squeaked, "I missed you so much!"

Lifted in my arms, she leaned back to see my face. But I couldn't speak. I just hugged her tighter.

"We should go in!" she said. "We're late, 'cause I know I was late, and you were here after me!"

I mumbled into her neck, "One more minute."

She giggled, and all at once I felt everything I'd missed for the last six weeks and four days ...

And I changed my mind.

"Actually," I said, hiking her up a little higher. "I just won't let go."

I pulled her legs around my hips and carried her like that, bundled in my arms, all the way to the table read office.

She giggled the whole time, and I was absolutely *soaked* in her light.

Acknowledgements

To my family, thank you for your evergreen support.

To my nephew, Jack, I hope you think
I'm cool when you're older.

To Kev and Les of Busybird Publishing, your passion for
storytelling is infectious and extraordinary. I am forever
thankful for your belief in this project. And in me.

And, to Emily.
This is for us, my girl. Because what if ...?
Let's find out. Love you.

Abbey Gebethner is an incredible
tattoo artist in Newcastle, Australia.

She drew this line art of Chriso and Mags.

Find her on Instagram: @birdytattoos

About the Author

Lily grew up on the east coast of Australia, where she still lives and creates. Most passionate about the experience a human has in the journey back to themselves, Lily is a full-time word searcher—fixated on finding the true words that encapsulate life in real-time, for herself and her peers.

Her primary dream through her work is to help someone with the language of that journey. The words on her pages are snippets of real moments, real observations, real experiences and there's a reason they feel so relatable to the reader ... they are in the pages, too.

Meet Me In My Mind is Lily's first novel.

Continue to meet Lily in her mind, and subscribe to her newsletter.

Visit
www.writtenbylilychristie.com to drop your email on the list.

Go on, have a lurk across socials. Find Lily here:

@writtenbylilychristie

Lily Christie

Psst. Hey. Hey, you.

I knew early on that there was more to Chriso, Mags, and Ben.

Consider this an introduction. We'll meet back in their minds soon.

Real soon.

Lil x